COLD BLOODED
LOVE

Girish Dutt Shukla is a computer engineer by education and a digital marketer by profession. Before pursuing his passion for writing, he worked as a software engineer for two years. In June 2015, he left the job and started dabbling in writing and marketing. In his seven-year stint as a marketing professional, he has helped both established brands and startups to grow digitally with his writing skills and marketing acumen.

Girish is also a regular contributor to a variety of websites, magazines and newspapers, including *The Pioneer*, *The Daily Guardian*, *ThoughtCatalog*, *SelfGrowth*, *Elephant Journal*, *Theravive*, *BestLifeOnline* and *HumanWindow*, among many others. Through his writings, he has been promoting psychology and mental health. He has a proclivity for perceiving psyche and behaviour and hopes to study the subject further in the future.

Maroon in a Sky of Blue, his debut novel, was published in 2020. Amitabh Bachchan expressed his appreciation of the novel through a personal letter written to the author.

Connect with the author at
https://www.instagram.com/girishduttshukla/
https://www.facebook.com/authorgirishduttshukla
https://twitter.com/GirishDttShukla
https://www.linkedin.com/in/girish-dutt-shukla/

'Fast-paced and riveting, Girish Dutt Shukla's psychological thriller is simply unputdownable.'

—K. Hari Kumar
Author and Screenwriter

COLD BLOODED LOVE

Girish Dutt Shukla

RUPA

Published by
Rupa Publications India Pvt. Ltd 2023
7/16, Ansari Road, Daryaganj
New Delhi 110002

Sales centres:
Allahabad Bengaluru Chennai
Hyderabad Jaipur Kathmandu
Kolkata Mumbai

P-ISBN: 978-93-5702-006-0
E-ISBN: 978-93-5702-002-2

First impression 2023

10 9 8 7 6 5 4 3 2 1

The moral right of the author has been asserted.

*To all the couples who fight and
make mountains of a molehill.*

Prologue

A happy family. What is it that makes a happy family? Is it the people or the connections between them that make it a happy one? The big extended family that stays together and comes together for all the celebrations and intimate moments, yet they never have a real, hard conversation. Or is it the couple and their kids, possibly with a pet, who are there for each other at all times? I have tried to find an answer to this fundamental question but have always struggled to conjure up something satisfactory, probably because I have never had a happy family.

As I steal a glance at the family picture kept on my side table, I am reminded of my ex-husband Om. I dial his number only to be informed by the operator that his phone is in a no-network area. Of course, he is likely to be on a trek in some dangerous terrain. Despite my objections and repeated requests, nothing stops him from these adventures. It is almost always an insanity. The fact that we are separated makes it so much harder for me to have any influence over him, or his decision-making. Mired in my thoughts, I open a bottle of red wine, ready for another adventure, *my* kind of adventure. I turn on the television and settle into watching a repeat telecast of my favourite show. In it, Albert, the protagonist, meets Hank, the antagonist, for the first time and it results in an altercation. I know this will happen because I have seen the episode multiple times. However, the way the scene builds up is beautiful. Just as the layers come off an onion, the evil intentions of Hank are revealed to Albert. I pause the show and get up to refill my glass. I promise myself that this will be the last glass of the evening and that I will now watch the show. The moment the characters begin to hit each other with beer bottles, I hear a strange sound. I have a feeling that it has something to do with the road outside my house. It was loud and for a moment, I wonder whether something had crashed into a pole or a house. 'Is it an accident? Maybe…' I thought.

I scamper off the sofa and move towards the window. Throwing it open, I peek outside to find out what has happened. Everything seems normal at first sight. I can't spot anyone or figure out where the sound came from. Everything is still and silent. Most people are minding their own business on the street. It seems like I am the only one to be alarmed by the sound. I can see no one else standing by the window, screening the neighbourhood. I am pretty sure that I heard a loud crash. 'Or did I get it all wrong? Was it more like something heavy, perhaps a big rock, dropping on somebody's head?' I am not sure now. I keep looking around in the hope that I will chance upon something abnormal, but much to my disappointment, things appear perfectly normal.

I return to my sofa and call Om. His number is still not reachable. As I am putting my mobile away, a calendar notification pops up on the screen and leaves me dumbfounded. It reads:

OM IS NOT WITH YOU ANY MORE!

I toss the eggs into the frying pan and let the water boil until I hear the kettle whistle. I check my watch and the calendar. It is 1 p.m. on a Thursday afternoon. Like most days, I got drunk last night and slept through the morning. I pick up the newspaper that has been neatly slid under the front door. I bring my measly breakfast to the sofa and start reading the news to get my daily dose of gloom and cynicism.

My eyes fall upon something that excites me. The headline reads, 'The best things to do when you're out of a job'. The article doesn't offer any great insight or things that I could apply to my life. Having been unemployed for a few months, I still did manage to get a fair amount of freelance design work that pays well. The fortune that I have been left with is, at the very least, enough to sustain a couple of lifetimes. I finish my breakfast and pop my pills with nothing to do for the rest of the day.

I fall back on the sofa and let my eyes dance around the house. A deafening silence and a dreamy stillness engulfs me. Boredom and monotony. My thoughts drift off, allowing me to savour these inconspicuous moments that have no significance attached to them. My mind goes in a hundred different directions before being overpowered by a dominant impression. Newer paths are squashed before they get a chance to form. The same old worry plays all over again.

The moment of sullen quietude is broken by the ringing of my mobile phone. It is Osheen—a friend who has stuck around since college despite everything. Although now she is far away, it still feels like she is closer than all the others who are near me.

I answer the phone. 'Hi! Long time. How are you?'

Osheen says, 'I'm good. How have you been?'

I say, 'You know, I'm all right. What's been happening with you? I saw your vacation pictures from France. They were stunning. You always look so pretty.'

She stifles a laugh. 'Oh! Thank you. Yes, it was a much-needed break after all the gruelling work I had been subjected to in the last one year or so. How are you dealing with the new house and the neighbours?'

'I feel like the house is too big for me. I curse my real estate agent every day for convincing me to buy the property. It's a beautiful house...it's just immense.' I purposely ignore the question about the neighbours as there is nothing to rave about. I have hardly had any interactions with them. Just the passing smile and a gentle nod every time I bump into them on the street. However, I knew Osheen would press me about it.

'And the neighbours? How are they?' Osheen asks.

'They are great. They hardly ever bother me. They are always lurking in their houses and cross my way every now and then only to nod and smile, never uttering a word.'

I knew Osheen would not be pleased to know that I haven't taken any initiative to be more social and approachable. Moving to Delhi from Mumbai, leaving all my friends behind, was probably the hardest decision I had had to take in years. It's been six months since then, and my social circle has dwindled. I have absolutely no one to talk to or share a good laugh with. I look around and find myself trapped within the swanky and ritzy decor of the house. There's nobody whom I can rely on for support and that scares me. I am lonely, probably isolated, and I haven't done enough to change that.

She sneers. 'Are you serious? How many times do we need to have this conversation that for you to move on you will have to form new connections and friends. Everyone needs a support system and you probably need it the most at this time. How difficult is it to step out and knock on your neighbour's door, Ziva! How hard is it to join an art group and socialize with people who share your passion for design!'

She waits for me to answer. I am sure that her eyes have narrowed, nostrils flared and deep lines have appeared on her forehead as she spoke, like they always do. *Gosh! I miss her so much.*

I take a deep breath and manage to give a half-hearted response. 'I will try. I promise.'

'You say this every time I call you and scold you about it. I think I will have to come down to Delhi and chide you in person.'

I smile. 'I would love that.'

'I would love it even more if you make friends in Delhi and I meet them as well when I visit.'

I have never been an introvert, someone who would shy away from going out, from meeting new people. However, the trauma of separation from Om has changed me. I have become a distorted version of myself, all my striking and likeable traits shrouded somewhere within me. Once my emotions were as vivid and varying as my dreams—sometimes subtle, and on other occasions, harsh. Now, I find myself stuck in this damaging labyrinth with no way out. My face, which always gleamed with a gentle smile, now wears thick lines of sorrow. Worn down by this new disposition, I had slowly started losing clients in Mumbai and developed sour relationships with people whom I had been close to. Even though every Sunday my friends visited me with a bottle of wine and a new book on design, nothing seemed to brighten my mood. My thoughts circled back and forth to Om and his new dwelling. The distance that separated us was too much to bridge and the possibility of us getting back together was exiguous.

I light a cigarette and the smoke twists in an artistic fashion, forming curls before vanishing in the air with its stink of sweat and last night's wine. I save a calendar event to call the cleaners over the weekend. However, for the time being, some air freshener and my forbearance will have to do.

Switching on the laptop, I open LinkedIn to find freelance design gigs to earn extra money and have something to keep me occupied. At least this way I'd be able to distract myself from the endless stream of thoughts bombarding my mind. To my disappointment, there were no freelance projects. Everyone wanted to employ a full-time graphic designer.

FUCK IT!

Time flows like cement when you have nothing to do.

I check my watch for the thousandth time. Only five minutes have passed since the last time I checked it. However, sitting in this huge house all by myself, with my feelings bordering on exasperation, it almost feels like an hour has passed. The chances of me getting a relevant design job seemed slim and waiting for it was pointless too. Maybe, I should pay heed to what Osheen said and go out there. With this firm resolve in my head, I take my diary and pen and head to the nearest coffee shop for the first time in months.

The air is thick with the aroma of freshly brewed coffee, a stark contrast to the stench in my house. I drink in the scent of the coffee shop while waiting in a queue for my turn. I order a hazelnut cappuccino and a croissant, and proceed towards the table that just got empty. A wave of nostalgia hits me as I remember how often I frequented coffee shops to take my caffeine and rekindle my creative streak. I grab my pen and start drawing the scene in front of me intuitively—the barista steaming the coffee, people standing in a queue, the cashier printing the bill, and the server holding the tray. I take a bite of the snack and a swig of the coffee, and I go back to my drawing. The café is buzzing with endearing chatter and earnest silence. It blends in beautifully with the soft music in the background. With no particular thought, I start to sway. The pen keeps moving in a near-flawless motion as I complete the depiction in front of me. I had almost forgotten the sheer joy that drawing brought me. *This is a necessary reminder.* It provides me a shelter through my storm, and weaves a blanket of warmth and affection to keep me protected even on my darkest days.

As I sip more of my coffee, I am transported to my last day in Mumbai. All of my friends had gathered in my apartment for a grand farewell. What was going on inside me was hard to describe, but it was bloody painful. Having to leave all these wonderful people, people whom I had spent more than a decade with, felt damaging.

My usual steady gaze got replaced by a blank look, as my focus shifted away from the people surrounding me and settled on the centre table. From the corner of my eye, I could catch a glimpse of my house. I wanted to take in the environment one last time. Once I had done that, I got up and went about giving bear hugs to each one of them. I held them tight, for as long as I possibly could. I had a whole farewell speech planned, but the constriction in my throat was making it hard for me to breathe. Yet somehow I had managed to say, 'I love you all so much, and god knows how much I'll miss you.'

Overwhelmed by a feeling of comfort and contentment, I walk back to my home where no one waits for me. *I should probably buy a dog again.* The good news is that the coffee shop is only about 500 metres from the house and I can make a habit of going there for my daily dose of caffeine and creativity. It could be something to look forward to, I think, as I map out a plan in my head to reach out to people through LinkedIn and share my design portfolio. For the rest of the time, wine and Netflix could offer the perfect respite.

As I enter through the gate of my society, I find a couple of mammoth trucks almost blocking the main entrance of my house. Brown cardboard boxes with white parcel labels of varying shapes and sizes leave a scratch on the metallic surface of the trucks. There were around eight to ten people gathered—packers and movers who were carefully unloading the boxes and moving them in through the black door. Someone must be shifting into the empty house opposite mine. My initial instinct was to hide in the safe haven of my abode.

However, bolstered by the courage I've gathered from

today's outing, I decide to meet my new neighbours and ask if they need any help. They could probably rest in my living room until everything is placed inside the house.

I can vouch for the fact that moving to a new place is never easy, and the day of transferring one's belongings is possibly the hardest. All familiarity is gone and locked away in cardboard boxes, only to be opened in cold and frigid spaces. Memories keep striking you callously till you empty your heart to form new ones.

I check my pants, tuck my top in, and move around the trucks to find a young couple barking orders at the labourers.

The lass shouts, 'Be careful with that one. It's fragile.'

Her beau stands with his hands in the jeans pocket, looking intently at the workers and stealing a glance at his wife every now and then. They are probably in their late twenties or early thirties, which would mean that they have not been married for too long. They lock eyes with each other and their hearts, future dreams, joys and sorrows are exchanged, all over again, all shared within the small space that separates them. They have found a home in each other and are shifting to this new physical home. It would probably be a smooth journey.

I put on a smile and walk towards them. They look at me, smile back and the young woman takes a step in my direction. I take my right hand out for a handshake.

To my utter surprise, she moves my hand out of the way and gives me a tight, affectionate hug.

She says, 'How are you, Ziva? Long time!'

That day, just like any other day, my father came home late and drunk. Alcohol was his coping mechanism, one that had expunged all joy from his life. Even though he and my mom had married for love, all that remained now was a marriage devoid of any feeling. She was shattered, every facet of her personality denigrated and shunned.

To the people outside, they might have seemed like a happy couple, and yet my mother hid the bruises, the purple ribs and the blackened skin on her legs. With each breath she drew in that house, her pain only increased.

But that day, things changed.

The clock read 11.30 p.m.

My mother, a caring wife, asked my father, 'Do you want to eat?'

He looked at her as if she had asked the stupidest question ever, and then struck her. It came out of nowhere and for no reason whatsoever. Even though it was just his hand and not any other object, the blow was quite strong. It was enough to throw her back, as though she had been hit by a large piece of meat. It stunned her, but she kept standing. She had endured a lot more in the past.

He announced, 'I don't want to eat the shitty food you prepare. I want to drink. Fetch the bottle I bought on Sunday.'

Whimpering, she said, 'You drank all of it yesterday. Don't you remember?'

A sullen quiet filled the space between them before he got up and grabbed her by the neck, his hands tightening around her throat. 'You never miss an opportunity to bring me down just because I can't control my urges!'

His grip grew stronger around my mother's neck.

She struggled to open her mouth. 'Please stop—', was all she could muster before better sense prevailed over my father and he let her go. This was a cycle—he comes home, he beats her, and she cries. Then, rinse and repeat.

She was hoping that he was done for the night, but the sad truth was that he had only got started, he had just begun warming up. He relished beating her, his fists leaving marks on her skin. With every hit, a cold zing of delight ran through his veins, a buzz that wasn't second to that of alcohol.

She asked again, 'Should I serve dinner?'

He didn't answer but got up from the chair. He took out his belt and thrashed her with it in an unceasing motion. The blows landed on her ribs, back, hands and legs. My mother never tried to defend herself. She knew if she tolerated the pain, it would get over sooner. She lay on the floor, her ribs fractured, blood seeping from her skin. There would be no doctor to tend to her injuries. She'd just pop a few painkillers and go on as if nothing had ever happened. Just as water rushed into a sinking ship, the house reverberated with the cries of my mother and I could no longer pretend that I was asleep. I left my bedroom and got hold of the empty whisky bottle I had stored in my drawer for many months. The day had come for it to be used. I tiptoed and entered the drawing room where the fracas was unfolding.

I saw the battered and bruised face of my mother. Then my eyes fell on my father who was holding my mother by the hair while she continued to scream and writhe in pain. I dashed towards my father and smacked him on the head with the glass bottle—all in one stroke. At the moment, the consequences didn't matter. All that mattered was ending my mother's pain and preventing any such incidents in the future. The glass smashed into a hundred glittering fragments while I continued to hit him with the glass chunk that was still intact in my hand.

He let go of my mother and collapsed on the floor. Blood was oozing out of his head, rather quickly. Within moments, all life had been sucked out of his being and he lay there, fallen and slain.

My mother couldn't believe what she had just witnessed. She rushed towards me. 'What have you done?'

I loosened my grip on the glass chunk, and as it hit the ground, I could hear a distinct clink. 'At least now I will be able to sleep peacefully at night.'

2

I take a long hard look at the face in front of me, trying to remember where I have seen her before. Nothing! I am not revered for having the sharpest memory but I would have recalled whether I had seen someone before. I take a step towards her to get a closer look. However, that too is in vain. I close my eyes momentarily, more in embarrassment than in recollection.

She shakes her head in disapproval. 'You don't remember me?'

I am taken aback by the accusatory tone and flinch. I have nothing to offer in my defence. I think of running back to my house, hiding within the four walls of my living room and sipping some delicious wine. *Why did I even come here?*

In the end, I manage to open my mouth and say, 'I feel terrible, but I don't. However, you could always blame it on the grey streaks of hair.'

A wave of surprise sweeps her face as she laughs. 'Don't! Don't say that. You haven't aged a day and look as lovely as ever.'

I blush. 'You're being generous. However, I am sorry I can't quite place where we have met before.'

She smiles. 'Dr Ziva, I am one of the many students who attended your design conference in Bangalore and one of the few lucky ones who had lunch with you after the conference was over. I am Ovya Malhotra.'

A sudden realization hit me as memories of the conference swarmed over me like a hurricane. That had been a two-day conference where eminent people from the design industry had gathered to talk about what lay ahead and what innovations and technologies were being adopted by existing designers to stay in the game. I had given a thirty-minute talk, which was followed by a fifteen-minute question-and-answer round. Overenthusiastic students, much like Ovya, had taken full advantage of the latter and asked questions and follow-up questions until the time ran out. After that, I went out for lunch with a few students where I got to interact and connect with each one of them on a more personal level. This was indeed one of the rare occasions where I had actually gone out for lunch with the students. Most times, I just preferred to go back home or engage with the other speakers. The memory of the day came back to me. *Yes, I remembered Ovya now.*

I laugh. 'Yes, I do recollect the conference and how your questions never ended... But it was such a fun session and lunch. How are you? Are you moving in here?'

'Oh yes, those were the days. You could get away with not knowing the answers. Yeah, we are moving from Bangalore to Delhi. That is my husband, Aadit.'

The husband looks at me and gives me a slight smile. I raise my hand in acknowledgement.

She continues, 'He is a sales professional, while I freelance as a brand designer.'

I say, 'Always good to have neighbours who share the same passion for a profession.'

Aadit shouts, 'Ovya come here. Need your help with something.'

I realized that I had been interrupting the moving-in and it was time for me to head back home and laud my efforts at doing uncharacteristic things.

I say, 'You carry on. I will definitely see you around and through the window.'

She titters back, 'You bet.'

Ovya is soft, as mesmerizing as a waking dream. She is easy to talk to and fun to be around. There's a rare beauty in remembering a single meeting and the conversation you have had. I remembered her as someone who seeks connections and finds joy when looking at things from someone else's perspective. Her big round eyes twinkle with curiosity. Her crimson cheeks are accentuated by prominent dimples whenever her pretty face brightens with a smile. She is gifted with an enchanting beauty that makes those plastic models look as fake as they are. She is marked by realness and robustness. Nothing can touch such a belle.

I, on the other hand, had left my youth like a forgotten purse at a restaurant table. The day I separated from Om, I realized it was gone, never to come back. For the most part, I simply shrugged it off and moved on. However, at other times, it bothered me. I had lost the confidence of a grown woman and now I never took the initiative of meeting a prospective boyfriend or husband. My face, which had once been as fresh as the morning dew, now looked like a melange of dried petals and spices. My hair, once pitch black with waves, has now thinned, and for the most part, streaks of silver cover it. The brown eyes, which were warm until a couple of years ago, are now hardened by the unfounded loss of joy and idiosyncrasies. My voice of quiet confidence and calmness has now dissolved into a puddle of fuzzy and foggy phrases. Though I am one year short of forty, whenever I close my eyes, it feels as if I have seen it all.

I call Osheen. 'Hey! When is it that you said that you were coming to Delhi?'

Osheen laughs. 'As soon as you make friends in Delhi so that I don't have to watch your sorry face all day long.'

'I think you should start packing.'

She speaks with an air of doubt in her voice. 'Care to elaborate?'

I grab a packet of chips from the kitchen, tear it open and start munching on them before continuing. 'The house opposite mine, which had been empty for more than six months, has now been occupied by a young couple, and as it turns out, by a girl who attended my talk in Bangalore a few years ago. Her name is Ovya and her husband is Aadit.'

'You are telling me that you had a conversation with someone other than me?'

I pour some wine and take a sip. 'A conversation that was fully initiated by me. Even though I have barely spoken to her, I have a feeling that we can become friends.'

There is a momentary silence before she says, 'That's amazing. Just don't forget your old friends as you make new ones.'

'I know *you* are not going to stop troubling me.'

I realized that if I truly wanted to move on, I couldn't afford to become stagnant. I needed to flow like a river, even if that meant going through hell. After time unmeasured, I had given myself a chance to truly move on after that debacle of a marriage with Om. I couldn't fail. My psychiatrist, Dr Lekha Rajan, had suggested this move. This way, I could leave the demons of my marriage behind in Mumbai. A part of the treatment also involved practising meditation to make me calmer. The other parts involved taking pills to keep my stress hormones in check. I never did the former and would often forget the latter, and this paved the way for episodes of anxiety, agitation and extreme restlessness.

When I don't feel anxious, I feel odd. As if something is amiss. Anxiety for me has become some kind of background noise. It's like an alarm system of sorts, always ready to sound even when there is no impending danger. Being confined and sitting still would amplify the electrical storm in my head. However, I never really had enough courage to move around either. My anxiety sits below my straight face, hides behind my smile and is the reason for my tears. It is always there, and I am frozen in a panic that has nowhere to go.

It is 1993 and Diwali. The lights adorn the front door and balcony as if they would keep the darkness that is already rampant in our modest house at bay. My mother and father are grinning from ear to ear. I don't catch the joke—if at all there was one. Tension and uncertainty run wild and unchecked in our house usually, only taking a recess when we have to project our false joy and peace to the world outside. I await instructions from my mother on how to make a rangoli just outside our main door. Packets of colours and diyas lie unopened on the floor waiting to be used. Mother turns the light on, the walls dazzle. I almost explode, itching to get going. Mother sits down and guides me as we come up with a simple yet elegant rangoli design. Looking back at this memory of making a rangoli with my mother feels strange—somehow I feel like time is crawling. An image of the two of us working on the decorations gets conjured, and it feels like we spend hours together, longer than I remember. If my memory serves right, we were done with it pretty quickly. The bedecked house looks picture-perfect. It is rather uncanny how small incidents stay in our mind when the more important ones do not. However, I am glad they do. Otherwise, I'd just be flooded with bad memories of my parents arguing and fighting, like cats in a sack. This memory reminds me of how my parents tried to love—at least faked it—despite their many faults and differences.

Until the inevitable happened.

Unfettered light streams through the large window as I delete posts from a few Facebook groups. About a month back, I had posted that I was looking for a tenant to occupy the basement room. I wanted to have someone around. It would have given me the opportunity to interact with someone on a regular basis and make me feel somewhat secure. The huge house I live in tends to get scary and unnerving, especially during the nights. I had also thought about hiring a full-time house help to take care of the daily chores. However, I was unable to find anyone reasonable for either position, leaving me to endure these disconcerting and forlorn walls on my own. Although now that my neighbours have moved in, I hope things will change for the better.

Their living room must be chock-full of brown cardboard boxes. There are more on the roof, it seems, and more are being added as the labourers unload from the truck. Going by the multiple rounds taken by the shifting crew so far, it looks like they have a lot of things. Given their belongings, it will probably take them a month or even more to set their house. I can imagine the dust swirling in the afternoon light as the walls devoid of any painting or artefacts await their new pattern and design. The furniture that once stood pompously in a different setting will now stamp its grandeur on the new house. Similarly, all odds and sods will find a place in due course of time. It's the people who have trouble moving to a new dwelling place in a completely new city. I still struggle with my house as familiarity hasn't set in. Often, I switch on the fan when my intention is to turn on the light and vice versa. Frequently, I find myself in the kitchen when I have to go to the study. Despite having been here for more than six months, it feels as if the house hasn't accepted me yet. I hope theirs is better, more homely and welcoming. Sometimes during the night I look out from the window and find my new neighbours wrapping their arms around each other in a moment of complete serenity. Ovya lets her head rest on Aadit's chest. They stand close to each other and all my thoughts stop, as if their love has brought in a semblance of some into my own life. I bring my binoculars and focus to get a closer look. He squeezes her hand as if he needed to check she was really there with him. My heart fills with a thousand emotions of warmth and affection. It is as if my body has merged with my soul after a long time. She moves closer to Aadit and runs her hand over his bare chest. I wonder what they must be talking and thinking about.

It was our third marriage anniversary. Om and I decided not to step out to celebrate. Instead, we stayed in to gloat over our new home and the effort it took us to put everything in its place and to adorn the walls with accessories and intricate artwork. Our previous home had been filled with music, love and the warmth of family and friends. Soon enough, this residence too would be filled in a similar fashion.

I ordered food online while Om found something interesting to watch on television. Ours was a partnership formed in laughter, frivolity and serious consideration. Forged in fire, our alliance was stronger than ever. There had been the usual hiccups—squabbles and arguments— that, I feel, are central to any relationship. However, like it is often said, with time, these hiccups only strengthened our marriage. For most of my life, I had been led by emotion whereas Om had always relied on reason. While I pondered over small details, Om buried himself in the things that he loved—his work and golf. Every step I took had to visibly take me closer to him, whereas he could walk in the opposite direction if that meant a bigger and better future. We were always on the same page yet we happened to be reading different lines. That's just how we were as people—I was always the idealist and he always the pragmatist.

I turned off the lights and lit a few scented candles, placing one of them on the table and one in each corner of the room. In the flickering yellow light, the furniture was discernible. Om was as handsome as ever. The muted colours of the room set the perfect atmosphere for us to bask in the glow of each other's company. I reached out, interlaced my fingers with his and a half-smile quickly turned into a beam of satisfaction. Everything seemed to be perfect and in harmony—our new jobs, our new house and most importantly, our marriage.

Om squeezed my fingers, placed his hand on my shoulder and started caressing it softly. At that moment, I felt like I was God's favourite child and that no hardship could ever come my way.

He said, 'You know, I have been thinking...' He paused before continuing, 'I have been thinking that maybe we should take a break.'

I jumped at the suggestion in excitement. 'Yes, that would be nice. Where do you want to go? How does Australia sound?'

He stopped rubbing my shoulder and sprang off the sofa. 'What? No, I didn't mean it like that. I think we should take a break from each other...'

3

When you're an island, you are surrounded by water on all sides. Similarly, when you are alone, a sense of loneliness and nostalgia settles all around you. I am used to irregular routines that in some way keep the monotony at bay. When I wake up in the morning, there isn't much to look forward to; similarly, when I go to sleep at night, there isn't much to look back at. Days just keep changing without me ever having to take account of them. The only way I know that the month has changed is when I receive different bills for the house. It's as if I am stuck in a loop—without a stop and pause button. It is not as if I have something better to do. I am just blessed with this innate capacity. Over time, I have honed my ability to not tamper with this state of being. I can go on being sad for days without ever making an effort to find an excuse to move towards joy, and if, by some miracle, I find a tiny reason for being happy, I quickly fall back into my downcast condition.

Today, however, is one of those rare occasions when a wave of enthusiasm has washed over me. I actually woke up before my alarms went off. As I switched them off, I checked the date—8th of March. I remember it is International Women's Day. It seems apt that a woman like me has found her zest on such an important day.

Cometh the hour, cometh the ~~man~~*, woman!*

In the past too, I have felt moments like these, when the light has just been so brilliant that it has forced me to heal and let go of my sense of pessimism and cynicism. I have had the opportunity to beckon all my strength and senses so that I can take small steps that are more potent than the greatest strides. However, every time I have done that, there has been a wind strong enough to sway me off my path and knock me down. Like a timid suitor, I don't have it in me to get back up and keep moving forward.

Not breaking my tradition, I order two slices of opera cake. This upbeat mood needs to be rewarded. I settle on my sofa and open LinkedIn again to look for freelance and part-time opportunities. This time, I add 'part-time' on the search bar, expecting that nothing would pop up on the screen. To my surprise, two start-ups need a part-time graphic designer to come up with branding solutions for them. I quickly go through the requirements and begin to apply. However, when I look at their budgets for the work, I laugh—my laughter stopping and starting like a leak from a tap. I rub my eyes and study their requirements and budgets again before cracking up.

I can feel a heaviness growing in my chest and my face muscles tighten. I had read on the internet that the economy was floundering but was the damage this widespread? I had no idea.

I reach out to my old partner and friend by email.

Hey Sasha,

I hope you're having a great week! I've been keeping up with you on LinkedIn and I feel so proud of you for doing such incredible work for all your clients.

I'm getting in touch to let you know that I'm currently searching for freelance/part-time opportunities in Delhi, preferably south and central Delhi. With my background in graphic design, my ideal projects involve anyone looking for a branding consultant.

Since we used to work closely and I know you're so well connected, I'd love it if you could let me know of any opportunities that you think I'd be a good fit for. I've attached my résumé to this email, just in case that helps.

Of course, I'm always willing to return the favour whenever you need my help.

Thanks so much, Sasha. I have so many fond memories of our time together at Generators and I hope things are even better for you since then.

Best,
Ziva

Almost immediately, I receive a response from Sasha.

Dear Ziva,

Such a nice surprise to hear from you. I hope you're well.

Of course, I will keep an eye out for any such opportunities. Do let me know when you plan to come to Mumbai. Would love to meet and catch up with you.

Good luck!

Best,
Sasha

Sasha and I had always shared a warm and collegial working relationship. During the five years that I worked with her, there was always an air of genuine respect for each other. We were a team. We complemented each other, like the beige walls and melamine desks in our boring office. The morning would grow old, the coffee would get cold and the ticking clock would stop, yet our penchant for great work, for our clients, kept us going. The only thing we ever craved was the subtle flavour of hazelnut in our cappuccinos and to be served in cups with festive colours and to have our names inscribed on them. The only thing we kept getting (without any complaints) was quality work and that kept us going.

One day, we had to go to a client's office in Juhu for a meeting and we decided to take a cab—probably the second-worst decision we ever took at work. The first was agreeing to go to the client's office. The fact that it was one of the biggest projects that we would have worked on probably influenced our decision. Ambitions are desires that grow with every success. At times, we tend to turn a blind eye to our limitations and take outrageous steps. Going to a meeting in a cab on a day when it had already been predicted that it would rain was our fault. We were stuck in the cab for what seemed like a lifetime. We could never reach the client's office, the meeting was postponed for the next week, and when we eventually met, they told us that they didn't like our work as much, which was just an excuse since they had already hired a rival agency for the job. However, during the time that I had been stuck in the cab with Sasha, I learnt more about her than I had ever in the past working odd gruelling hours, or over shared lunches and dinners, or having gone out to de-stress for a quick drink or unimaginative team activities. Sasha said, 'Whenever you can't decide, always listen to your gut. Always remember, a bad decision is always better than no decision at all.'

That day, upon the rain-wet windows of the cab, I had imagined clear blue skies enveloped by fuzzy and ominous clouds. Brilliant white sunlight tried to break through the cumulus and shine upon us. With the purpose of taking my career to the next level, I always found time to be fascinated by the simplest of objects. Similarly, for the people in my life, I held immense love for the simplest of gestures and actions. I had a way of seeing people without their need to reveal these things. Alas, somewhere down the road, my speculations have interfered with my sense of wisdom, making me lose out on professional goals and interpersonal relationships.

After forever and a day, I step into the kitchen to cook for myself—*pasta it'll be.* I play the song 'My Immortal' by Evanescence and start humming unconsciously. I take out the flour from the cupboard and fetch the eggs from the refrigerator. I dip the cup into the sack of whole wheat and crack the eggs open and mix the two in a bowl. As I whisk the combination, the consistency doesn't seem right. I add two more eggs, a little flour, a tablespoon of olive oil and some water to combat the dryness. I whisk again and voilà—mission accomplished. The dough is a satisfying ball of hard work that now has to pass through the pasta machine, which Om and I received as a wedding gift. The machine has rarely been used and is as good as new. I feed the dough into it and it passes through rollers, making it grow longer and thinner. I turn the dial to make it a little thicker and longer. The grainy texture is now silky soft. I heat the pan and add the freshly made pasta into it with white sauce, vegetables and olive oil. I let it simmer for a while. In the meantime, my Opera

cake arrives. As the whiff of pasta sauce fills the air, a
sudden feeling of delight overwhelms me as I perch on
the dining table and indulge my senses.

I step outside into my little and neglected garden. As
a child growing up, I loved tending to the garden of our
house with my mother. The green leaves, the delicate petals
and the golden fruits were a playground for dancing birds
and darting squirrels. It was as if the subtle moments of
verdure were a song that made them scurry and peck. The
garden had enough music for anyone who tried to listen.

My present greenhouse, however, has been ignored
for far too long. I remember that I had called a gardener
a few months ago, but he had never showed up. Making
a note to call him again, I pull a chair from the patio to
rest outside. I wonder what Ovya and Aadit are doing.
Would she have finished unpacking? *Probably not.* They
had enough stuff to start a small community. It would
take them weeks, if not months, to arrange everything
in the house. How strange it is that after all these years
and a single solitary interaction, I have met her again.

My line of thought is broken by the iridescent glow of
butterfly wings. If ever there was magic in the sky, it had
to be a flapping butterfly. It flutters up and down, beating
the persistent breeze. It alights upon one of the few
dahlias left and folds its wings neatly in a single harmonic
motion. As delicate as moonlight and as beautiful as
painted silk, the butterfly holds my attention but a silvery
voice that sounds familiar shifts my focus. I turn and find
Ovya standing outside my main gate.

'Hey! I have got you something.'

I too jumped from the sofa and shouted as loud as my vocal cords permitted. 'What? What did you just say?' There was pain in my shouts. The anger was just hiding the pain. I was more hurt than angry at the absurd suggestion. How could he say that we should take a break? Was he out of his mind?

Om took a step back and in his calm voice said, 'It is best for the two of us.'

I retorted back saying, 'Since when have you started making decisions for the both of us without discussing it first?'

Om didn't show any signs of vexation. With a sage-like composure, a voice as warm as spring and a heartbeat as steady as a clock, he said, 'I know this might be hard for you but it isn't easy for me either. After what happened last year, things haven't been the same. You do know that, don't you?'

This was his way of doing things. He simply stated things in a matter-of-fact way. Whenever something was wrong—the food wasn't nice, the clothes weren't ironed properly, the traffic was bad, the boss didn't give him the appraisal, the doctor rescheduled the appointment and a countless number of things—he would simply say these things. Om didn't react as much, he responded after absorbing. He mitigated situations more than aggravating them. He was always the gentle breeze whereas I was the unruly storm.

I started pulling my hair and was hoping that by taking deep breaths I would be able to gather myself. I was struggling to find the right words. I opened my mouth twice but didn't say anything. Finally, I gathered all the courage in my bones and said, 'After all this time?

After all the things I have sacrificed for you, I get this?'

He took a pause, measured his words, and said, 'This has been coming for a while. I know that. You know that...'

I scoffed, cutting him mid-sentence, and said, 'No, I didn't know anything. I have never known what has been simmering in your shit head.'

'Look, I don't want to go all over this again. I think it's best if we take a break for the next two months and think deeply about our marriage, our relationship and decide after that.'

Our anniversary cake was on the table. My first instinct was to take the knife and drive it right into Om's chest and slice him up like an apple. My eyes were bloodshot, and tears were gushing out in an interminable stream. Fires of fury smouldered in my body as my hands and legs began to shake. I held the knife and savaged the cake with it. I put out the candles and threw the wine bottle on the floor. The bottle hit the ground and shattered into a thousand splintering fragments. The day that had begun with a lull had ended with the breaking of a wine bottle, yet this time, his words had pierced right through me. Om had sentenced me to this invisible prison without even listening to my side of the story.

4

I let Ovya in. She was wearing a smile on her lovely face. Her smile is the prettiest thing I have seen in a while, it extended the twinkle in her eyes and the dimples in her cheeks. I simper and guide her inside.

Stepping in, she says, 'The weather's rather pleasant today.'

I shake my head in affirmation. 'Yeah. It's been a delight all day. Do you fancy sitting in whatever is left of the garden?'

She says, 'Yeah. That would be nice.'

I pull a chair from the patio for myself while she settles herself on the other chair.

'How's the moving in?' I ask.

She lets out a deep breath and sighs. 'You know, it's going to take a while before we settle. Changing cities and houses is overwhelming, isn't it?'

Immediately, I am reminded of the ordeal I went through when I moved to Delhi. 'Tell me about it. It is a disaster.'

Ovya stands up impulsively and says, 'Oh, before I forget, here's something I got for you.'

I tilt my head to the side and say, 'What is it?'

'It's a showpiece made of sandalwood—a speciality of Bengaluru.'

I hold the gift that has been neatly wrapped in a white packing paper. I spread my fingers and feel the weight of it. It is quite heavy. My skin tingles and the muscles stiffen as I realize the sheer thought and effort that would have gone into buying this. I had seen idols, deities, showpieces and figurines made of pure sandalwood in the city in the past. The soft, aromatic wood had been delicately carved to create elegant and sumptuous masterpieces. I assume the piece in my hand would be similar.

I keep it on the table and say, 'Thank you. I didn't expect this.'

She licks her lower lip and quips, 'I guess you'll have to get used to the unexpected with me living opposite your house now.'

My breath catches in my chest as a wave of fear and paranoia washes over me. Surely, she means it in a harmless way. Moreover, she doesn't seem like the kind who would ruin things or people just for her hedonism. Instead, she appears to be a free-spirited, self-aware and empowered woman who is unafraid to explore and express her feelings. The problem with the newfound cynic in me is that I can't ever really see a person beyond what is reflected in their eyes.

I shake my head and manage to say, 'I'll try and be careful.'

Though my house is in one of the busiest neighbourhoods in the city, for some reason it always feels as though I am being forced to live in the most remote and desolate part of Delhi. Now with Ovya, my new neighbour, dropping by every now and then, things might change. I know I had never taken the initiative, or made efforts to be friends with my neighbours. Just a smile doesn't cut it. It's odd because I feel that I am a good person and will make a good friend as well. I know I have made deliberate choices all my life despite always being able to predict the ramifications. I am slow to love and quick to judge. There was a time when I would walk the extra mile for strangers, and now, taking a single step seems arduous. I have been living alone for a couple of years and even though it is terrible most of the time, a sense of relief always accompanies me for I am discharged of all my responsibilities towards others. It's always better to be authentic and alone than change yourself to fit in, I think.

The mailbox is just outside the main door, obscured by the clump of trees bordering the side road. Beaten, rusted and dust-laden, it is one of the blots in my rather grand house. Just like the bright old man on the street, it stands and endures the sun, the winds and the rain, waiting to share the messages inside. I put my hand inside and find an envelope. Pulling it out, I head straight back. The envelope is as light as a feather, which means inside it is only paper. In my six months of living in this house, I haven't once received a letter from anyone. Not even the banks or the internet service providers have ever dared to contact me.

I quickly dash towards the kitchen looking for a knife to cut open the envelope, with precision. I always fear that if I use my hands to tear an envelope, I'd surely destroy whatever is inside.

Could this be from Om?

Somehow, the wound that Om has left begins to fester again. Indignation, which has been following me like a shadow, overpowers me. Pain, just like a faithful companion, squeezes me. I find myself drenched in tears and sweat. I take the paper out. It has been neatly folded.

My breathing rapid and shallow, my pulse pounding in my temples and my heart racing under my fingertips, I unravel the paper. It definitely isn't from Om. I check the envelope again to see who sent it. There is no address. In fact, it is a spotless, immaculate white envelope with not even a smidgen of ink on it.

I read the paper.

DEAR ZIVA, PLEASE BEWARE OF AADIT. HE IS NOT WHO HE SEEMS TO BE.

At night, I take my oversized binoculars out and watch the married couple through my window. The semblance of a happy family has always intrigued me. In addition, I just want to observe Aadit and form an opinion on the research that I do from my house. I am certain that they won't be able to spot me hiding behind the curtain, trying to get a view of what they are up to. I stay out of sight using my pitch-black curtains as the perfect camouflage in my dark drawing room. Ten minutes into my little adventure and there's no concrete activity on the other side. *Watching a documentary on Netflix would have been far more interesting.*

'Five minutes more and after that, I'll retreat to my sofa, wine in hand and Netflix on the TV screen,' I tell myself, almost convinced of the purpose of all this snooping around. Some people watch the world go by through their front windows and find contentment in that. But here I was. Unsure of my intention of holding an unabashed and unwavering gaze at my recently moved-in neighbours. A sense of curiosity lingered through the lens. There were no signs of the wife and the husband. *Maybe they slept early?* I stay at my position and adjust the binoculars in my hand. I decide to count till twenty backwards, telling myself that if they don't appear, I'll retreat to my sofa.

20, 19, 18... 3, 2... and there they are!

∽

After one month of separation, Om realized that it was impossible for him to live without me. I too had my own realization when Om said that he wanted us to take a break. We were made for each other. That's the only thing I was sure about. Who on earth is happy all the time while living with another person? There would be times when husband and wife can't stand each other and I guess that's what happened to Om a month ago.

He was so infuriated by my habit of excessive drinking. He had asked me to get help a couple of times but I wouldn't have any of it. I had to consider it when he left the house and rented a flat in another part of Mumbai. I still didn't meet a therapist or a doctor for my habit, but just out of sheer will, I had kept my proclivity for wine under control. However, I wondered. 'For how long?'

5

Last night was a painting in velvet and black, which blended into a constellation of stars. It was this softness that steadied the rhythm of my heart as I kept my eyes fixed on my neighbour's house. Ovya appeared first, followed by Aadit. Ovya had a fluffy towel wrapped around her hair. It was possible that she had just come out of the shower. Arranging and rearranging different items in the house does make you dirty. She was wearing a nightdress, while Aadit was in pyjamas. Nothing seemed out of place. They looked like the quintessential young couple who were focused on their professional goals, but in a way those goals didn't impinge on their married life. Although no one else but me is as aware and experienced in knowing that there's always more to things than what meets the eye. Still, I am not sure that Aadit has a dark side.

What was I looking for and why did the letter say that Aadit isn't who he seems to be?

Just like the other night, they sit on the sofa and turn on the television. The sounds emanating from the television were just a way to fill the room as they were engrossed in their own conversation, though their eyes did not waver from the screen. I am not sure what they were watching. Maybe they loved watching old classics, just like me. A mild smile surfaced, one that only I could see. At that moment, I saw them as mirror images of Om and myself from a decade ago, back when our love was still innocent and innocuous.

Suddenly, Ovya got up from the sofa as if the fire alarm had gone off. Aadit, who had been lying comfortably all this while, straightened his back and caught hold of his wife's hand. He kept a firm grip on her hand as she tried to release it. As he pulled her closer, she fell on her side, on the couch. The two held a steady gaze. He kissed her gently—the way they do it in the movies. Then, as if a match was struck, he leaned on her and smooched with the sweetness of passion, and that ignited a fire in Ovya. She reciprocated and brought her lips around Aadit, letting the tongue show its deft movements. It was a real kiss—a promise that bound them together the day they would have met for the first time. I saw the primal desire that lives in each one of us manifest in the moment, marked by a million thoughts of love. I, thus, became aware that Ovya and Aadit were, indeed, connected by an invisible cord. They were just a normal couple, and there was nothing to indicate that Aadit was anything other than who he appears to be.

I wonder who sent me that peculiar note and what the intention behind it was. How many people even know that Ovya and Aadit have shifted to the house opposite me? I haven't yet spoken to him properly, apart from the solitary 'Hi' and the smile that followed the day he shifted with his wife. Could it be a prank? But, who would want to trick me like this? I barely spoke to anyone. I look at the note again. It is Gotham font size 16. I might not have designed anything credible in the last few years, but I still know my fonts.

My eyes are fixed on the note. It had made me think about ten different things at once, but I had not one clear, coherent thought. The couple had spun a web around me with their erratic mannerisms. My head spins as my innate desire to know everything overwhelms me. One moment I'm absorbed in the note and the very next moment my eyes search outside for a possible explanation. There are always more questions than answers. I strain my ears for the voice within me in the hope to find clues. Maybe there is no need for me to obsess over the note. It could be just a bad joke. I glance upwards, my mouth pursed but slightly open. The sound of my mobile ringing breaks my rumination.

It is Osheen. She speaks brightly. 'I sense you have forgotten your old friends just because a certain neighbour has moved to the house opposite yours.'

I almost laugh. 'I sense your intuition has failed you again.'

In a calm voice, she reiterates something she has been maintaining over the last few years. 'My intuition is as accurate as the predictions by your favourite app—Daily Horoscope.'

Osheen stresses on the last two words to mock me as I did have a habit until last year of checking the app before starting the day. I believed whatever shit the app spewed with all my heart and spirit. Mostly flawed, all my actions for the day were governed by the fallacious beliefs imparted by it. The only resolution for this year was that I'd uninstall the malicious trickster and go about my days in ways that felt right. The result is that I have found a great fondness for letting my whims and desires run wild and for not doing things that need to be done.

I always neglect my priorities. I still haven't enrolled and paid for the online course that was supposed to keep me abreast of contemporary design methods and techniques. I still haven't taken an appointment with the dentist for a check-up, and that reminds me—a visit to my gynaecologist is long overdue.

Both of us are aware of how wrong she is to assume that her clairvoyance is spot on. 'Whatever happened to those canonical instincts every time you venture out to meet people of the opposite gender,' I say jeeringly.

She gasps. 'That is monstrously rude of you.'

I, of course, have no right to say anything of the kind to her. I am amongst the rare 1 per cent falling under the category of failed marriages in India, while Osheen has never been married. She has had a string of relationships, yet not one has lasted more than a year. Osheen has a strong disposition that makes her incredibly stunning to talk to. Her chiselled features and twine-thinness is a testament of her love for working out. She is snow white, but with a burnished complexion and curvy eyebrows that look down on a set of enticing brown eyes. Her dainty ears frame a button nose. Her calamine pink lips cover a set of dazzling white teeth. Her midnight black hair tumbles over her shoulders. Her presence in a room lingers long after she leaves.

I say, 'Of course, I know that.'

She chuckles. 'You're so evil. How are you doing? Any luck with any freelance opportunities?'

'Have been feeling much better since the last couple of days. No luck as of yet, but I'm hopeful something will happen. I reached out to Sasha as well.'

She says, 'I'm so glad to hear that. That was smart.

With all her connections, Sasha will surely be able to help you.'

I nod as if Osheen is sitting right in front of me. 'I miss you.'

'I thought with Ovya around you, rather opposite you, you don't miss anyone any more.'

I fall on the couch, roll my eyes, and say, 'Not yet... but she did come over and brought me a present. I'd be lying if I told you I don't like her. She seems nice but...'

'But you need more time to judge conclusively,' she completes my sentence.

'Of course, I need more time. Like I always say, there are three layers to each of us. What we pretend, what we present and what we preserve. Can't know anyone properly without knowing all of them.'

∽

Osheen and I were meeting after school for the first time. We had decided to catch up at Backyard Drinks. I was overflowing with excitement as I stepped into the pub, my eyes searching for my best friend. At first, I couldn't spot her, but then I noticed a raised arm beckoning me to join the table at the far right. I scurried along.

Osheen got up from her seat and squeezed me tightly. I reciprocated with the same fervour and warmth. As we hugged each other, both of us couldn't stop saying—'It's so good to see you' and 'How have you been? I missed you so much!'

After a little while, we finally let go of the embrace and sat opposite each other.

Osheen's eyes widened as she said, 'Ziva! You look

so pretty. Have you been working out recently?'

I said, 'Oh, thank you! I just go for a morning run, that is all. As usual, you look amazing and I absolutely love those earrings.'

She tapped her earrings and said, 'Thank you. This is actually a gift from...' She blushed and I almost shouted in delight. 'Are these from Lakshya?'

She smiled and nodded her head. I gushed while taking a sip of my martini. 'Wow! He has great taste.'

She suddenly frowned the way she did before saying something serious, and then plunged into uncontrollable laughter. 'You bet he does. After all, he is dating Osheen Wadhwa.'

We leaned back on our chairs and laughed uproariously, as if we were the only people present in the pub. Thankfully, the music masked the harsh sounds of our laughter.

'I think you too should dive into the dating pool,' Osheen suggested.

I shook my head in disappointment. 'I think my perpetual scowl keeps boys away. Anyway, when it has to happen, it'll happen organically.'

She took a slice of the pizza and said, 'The only way it'll happen is when you let go of that scowl.'

Out of the blue, a man moved towards our table with leopard-like grace. He was towering, probably taller than six feet. He had a peppered stubble and hair as thick as wool. His almond-shaped eyes twinkled with every step. His aquiline nose was complemented by defined cheekbones that ended in a concrete jaw. Handsome in an understated way, he had the shoulders of a Spartan warrior that testified to his strength. An earthy fragrance swirled around him as he addressed me with a deep voice and smiled.

'My name is Om and I'm new to Mumbai. I was wondering if I could talk to you for some time as you are the first person who's made this city feel like home.'

Surprisingly, my cheeks turned rosy and I stole a glance at Osheen in an attempt to look for a prompt as to how I should respond. She didn't give away anything. She was busy admiring his presence.

I took a few moments, tilted my head and cleared my voice before saying, 'Wait till you stay a little longer and aren't a visitor any more. Mumbai will feel home in no time.'

6

I walk to the little porch adjoining the backyard and stand there gazing out. For the first time in this house, I am developing a habit of looking out, observing, listening and contemplating my surroundings. I have received two more notes since all of this began. One read:

DON'T BE AFRAID TO SEEK THE TRUTH.

The subsequent note, the third one to arrive, was a little more alarming. It said:

I KNOW YOU ARE SUSPICIOUS. KEEP AN EYE ON AADIT. IF NOT FOR ANYONE, DO IT FOR OVYA.

The sense of familiarity that the anonymous writer had hinted at in the last note unsettled me. 'Am I being watched?' I thought. Is this a reaction to my new neighbours moving in or is it a response to those upsetting notes being slid to my mailbox? Perhaps, it is a combination of the two that is making me more watchful. But this cannot go on forever. I need to relax and let the residents of the community carry on with their activities, just as they used to, without keeping a track of everything. I can't decide if I need a cup of coffee or a glass of wine to loosen the edge.

To appease my restlessness, I settle with coffee sangria, a recipe that Om taught me before we got married, when we were happier and possibly more genuine. Come to think of it, the best relationships are unconfined by a stamp of togetherness. They are at their finest when people are not the same and complement each other by bringing out the qualities that are lacking in the other. But they become intolerable the moment the partners try changing themselves.

My doorbell buzzes. There is still some time for the month to end and for people to come and collect the rent for the different services I have subscribed to and hardly use. I have always pondered over getting rid of the newspaper as I hardly ever read it, yet there's something about holding the curled and crisp paper and placing it on the table.

It is Ovya at the door.

She smiles and lights up the entire space. I can't help but smile back.

She says, 'Won't you let me in?'

My cheeks and forehead burn as I find myself stuttering, 'Of course. Please come in.'

I feel an emotional pull towards sluggishness. Inertia is what I crave the most. Having visitors doesn't help that yearning one bit. Every moment, it feels as if my brain is in overdrive and wants to press the brakes. A weariness settles all around me. I need to go back to taking my pills. At least, they keep me active and give me enough strength to go on through the day.

She walks in with definite aplomb, as if every step of hers has purpose. It is a freestyle motion that announces that she is happy with where she is in life. With eyes fixed on my wilted garden, she says, 'That needs help.'

I nod in agreement. 'I have been meaning to get around to fixing it. It's just that I haven't been able to find enough motivation to actually do it. Rest assured, it's on my to-do list.'

Ovya's eyes brighten as she says, 'You know, I would be happy to help...if that's okay with you.'

I realize that whenever Ovya speaks, there is a gentleness in her eyes and her facial expressions are relaxed. She is always calm and composed, but possesses an underlying playfulness that surfaces every now and then, as if to underline that she is still a child at heart. I thank her. 'That is so nice of you, but I wouldn't want to trouble you, especially not now with all the shifting still to be done.' I point at her garage that has boxes piled.

She says, 'But I insist. I want to help you.'

I grin in agreement. 'Okay, okay. I will let you know. Do you want to just stand here or will you come inside?'

I usher Ovya in and seat her on the couch while I sit opposite her.

Her eyes dart around the living room, pausing over the minimal interiors and decor. She nods her head in approval. 'You have immaculate taste. I love the way you have decorated your living room.'

I say, 'You are too kind.' She waits for me to continue. 'I guess that has to do with the genes of my mother. She liked to keep the house a certain way.'

She asks, 'Where is she now?'

I answer dispassionately, 'She passed away a few years ago.' I do not want her to ask about my parents and I change the subject by asking her about Delhi and if she has been to any markets.

She sighs as if going around and visiting places in Delhi is the last thing on her mind. 'I am exhausted with all the shifting. I haven't even had the time to check the local markets. Aadit has been buying groceries all this while. Once we settle in and get used to the new house and the neighbourhood, we shall start exploring Delhi and other places. There is enough time for that.'

I smile. We have a false notion that we have enough time to do things, but time soon begins to dissolve into itself, as shapeless as sand, leaving us with no way to hold on to it. I listen intently to her, then get up from my chair in a flash. With a tingling in my stomach, I cover my face with my hands and say, 'How stupid of me to not offer you anything? I have prepared some coffee sangria. Would you fancy some?'

She hesitates. 'Coffee sangria? What is that?'

I announce with confidence, 'If you like coffee, you'll love it.'

Luckily, I had prepared two glasses. I fetch them along with crackers and chips.

Ovya takes a sip of the drink. Her doubts clear as soon as the fruity and zesty concoction hits her palette. She almost jumps in elation and says, 'This is the most fantastic coffee I have ever had, and mind you, I consider myself somewhat of a coffee connoisseur. What goes into it?'

I say proudly, 'Thank you. My husband taught me the recipe. It was his speciality.'

She says, 'Where is he now? I would love to meet him.'

I look away through the window and into the distant horizon. I respond with a lump in my throat. 'Oh, we are separated.'

My conversations with Om were always inundated with smiles and laughter. Those exchanges formed the basis of our communication. We didn't need words to convey our feelings. We kept them concealed, unspoken, forbidden. Our emotions were as conspicuous as stars on a clear night; we were as honest as a mirror. Emotions flowed like water when our talk filled the air, closing the gap that separated us.

When the time for our parting arrived, there was a consistent gloom that we both felt.

My relationship with Om was a fresh start free of all the demons from the past. Despite having seen only pain and suffering, which had always come tumbling down whenever I tried to get close to another boy—this was to be a blank slate. I had been open about my past with Om and so had he and that had given us such freedom to look into each other's souls without any malice. We felt at home in each other's company and wished to stay that way forever.

It was this honesty that allowed us to get so close so quickly. It had only been a couple of months since we started dating, and I had left my flat and moved into Om's home. The way he was and his stoic but loving spirit brought a sense of stability in me, one that I had craved for years. The idea that he could be himself and I could be myself without filters or pretence was powerful. It was enough for both of us.

7

The silence that echoes in my house is liberated every time Ovya visits. Her delicate, citrusy perfume lingers even after hours of her leaving. I read somewhere that once you have mastered the art of living alone, it is easy to allow people into your life. Only my heart kept beating in this house over the past six months, but today it was different. I had brought Ovya into my house—the first person who had transgressed the boundaries of my residence. I have mixed feelings about it: relief blended with apprehension. Relief because finally I have someone who would probably fill the lacuna I experience amid these unforgiving walls. Apprehension, because I'm not sure if I should let someone I barely know breach the protective layers I have formed around me all this time. It isn't as if the people living around are all despicable human beings. In fact, it is my inadequacy that has not permitted me from forming any connections with them. When I had first moved to the locality, Mrs Mehra and her husband were kind enough to visit and invite me over for dinner. However, that didn't go as planned.

Mrs Mehra, with a certain loftiness to her voice, had said at dinner, 'We have been living here for the last twenty-five years and yet we haven't met anyone as mysterious as you.'

I took a spoonful of chole and said with a shake of the head. 'Mysterious? Who? Me? I think you mean introverted.'

She said, 'No, dear. I mean mysterious. You hardly step out of your home and keep indoors doing god knows what. I am certain that you don't even know the names of all your neighbours.'

That was true. I didn't.

I put the spoon on the plate and stopped eating. My voice was low, rumbling, but louder than I had intended. 'I step out to do my chores. Other than that, I don't feel the need to gossip or cause scandal, the way most people do.'

That day was my last invitation to Mrs Mehra's abode or anyone else's. I still maintain a pleasant demeanour whenever I come across the Mehras, or anyone else for that matter. I keep asking myself whether I should invite them for a meal as an act of apology and clear the air.

When I had moved to Delhi from Mumbai, I had believed the change of air would provide respite from the pain that ran deep in my veins after Om and I had parted ways. Despite the welcoming door that leads into a wide hallway, I always feel out of place. The floor is an old-fangled parquet with a mix of deep cheerful beige and the walls are sea-green—straight out of a painting. Delicate picture frame mouldings and gilded mirrors offer a variation on the rather austere walls. The vibrant curtains add a brilliant splash of colour, texture and dimension. Vintage accessories, such as neoclassical-style columns, marble busts and porcelain urns lend patina and character to the decor. The architect who designed the house and the interior designer who decorated it had thought through every detail. In contrast, my decision to move into it was spontaneous and reckless. At times, I wanted to run back to Mumbai and my old house despite wanted to run back to Mumbai and my old house despite the nightmares that were inside.

However, every time such a thought occurred, and I shared the same with Dr Lekha, she asked me to be strong and face the challenges that lay ahead. Little did she know that there doesn't exist a pill or exercise that can make me forget my marriage and the pain it left when it ended. This is what makes me apprehensive and vulnerable when people surround me. I have become wary of companionship and I probably will need a lot more than mere meditation to rewire that part of my mind. If I could learn how to thrive in peril the way I used to when I was a child, I'd definitely be more inclined to loving, which I could then use to heal my heart. A captive of my married life, a happier life, my porcelain skin has now become ashen, almost anaemic. My coral hair is now swamped by streaks of white. My brilliant black eyes that sparkled every time they blinked are now sterile, almost lifeless. The prominent wrinkles under them are a testament that I have aged fairly young. The dainty nose leads the way for cheeks that are recessed and sunken. My lips are still full and pillowy, as if they want to be kissed instantly. I hardly ever smile to reveal the shiny, halo-white teeth. Yet of late, I have beamed more than I have in the last few years. I feel a strange comfort in realizing this, but the solace disappears as soon as my eyes fall on the strange notes I have received so far.

I get my laptop to look for Aadit on the internet. All the reasons not to do this trap me in a spiral of indecisiveness. I look at myself in the mirror and get up to look through the window to see if I can catch anything suspicious. Aadit is moving stuff and placing it on different shelves. Ovya is right there, guiding him. I keep focusing and scrutinizing every move he makes but there is nothing fishy. I return to my seat and decisively search for him online. I feel the soft panic growing in me and beads of cold sweat glistening on my forehead.

I hit the enter key.

The links to his LinkedIn and Facebook profiles appear. I go through the former first. He is a sales head at Tangience. He has described his work experience verbosely, using plenty of technical jargon. I glance through without fully comprehending it. I open one more tab and search for his Facebook profile. I scroll through the results until I find his profile. Aadit Malhotra. Thankfully, his bio isn't filled with his work credentials. The profile photo is a vacation picture from France with Ovya. I comb through the other pictures. They are primarily close-ups of Aadit with Ovya; a few are from their wedding and a few, I guess, are from the time when they were dating each other. Then I come across a picture of Aadit with a girl that isn't Ovya. Who could she possibly be? His sister, a friend? An ex?

I get hold of my phone from under the cushion and search for Aadit on Instagram to find more pictures. However, his Instagram profile is private and I can't possibly send him a follow request.

All the adrenaline building inside me fizzles. I retire on the couch and close my eyes.

It was our first anniversary of being together. Om settled beside me. I smiled. 'I have new makeup on.'

He squinted my way and went back to his mobile, appearing decisively unimpressed. 'Babe, I don't see any difference. You look the same to me.'

I punched him lightly and said, 'So I have wasted all this time trying to look different?'

He remained immersed in the screen and spoke without even looking at me. 'You do know I'm a man whose senses are not easily appealed to.'

'You are just the epitome of boring.' I looked at him but he didn't meet my eye. I smiled wider, took a sip of the coffee sangria he had prepared and waited for him to retort. However, he did not say anything. To keep the conversation going, I spoke again. 'Where are we going tonight?'

Finally, he let go of the mobile phone and said, 'How about Backyard Drinks, the place where you were bowled over by my charm?'

I nodded. 'Yes, the place where you were bowled over by my beauty?'

He pulled me closer and kissed me on the cheek. He took my hand as we stood up and asked me to close my eyes. I didn't know what was happening since Om was hardly ever secretive about anything. I shut my eyes and waited for a few moments before I heard his voice.

Om said in his deep, gruff voice. 'It isn't about Mumbai feeling like home. Instead, anywhere I live with you will always be home. Will you marry me?'

I opened my eyes and saw Om kneeling on his left knee, holding a ring near my hand. For a moment, I froze as I couldn't believe my eyes. I stood still for a while, then I moved my hand and let him slide the ring in my finger. I hugged him tightly and kept saying 'Yes' as tears flowed in an uninterrupted stream.

8

I wake up with crushing pain on the right side of my head. The migraine is back with a fury. I remember the last time such throbbing pains were unleashed on my skull. I can't sit, lie down or relax. I pace about aimlessly through the house as if it will help mitigate the pain. My eyes water and my nose starts running. I am helpless, almost a prisoner surrounded by this impenetrable cage of agony. I try to scream but as soon as I open my mouth, the beating inside my head intensifies. I am blinded by colourful spots and darkness. Nausea swamps me and I vomit. An uneasy quiet and stillness ensues. The pounding in the head grows and I wonder why my skull doesn't crack open. I stagger back to the kitchen, a hand clamped on my forehead and the other on the walls that help me traverse. I open the medicine drawer and pop a pill in the hope that the misery in my head will subside. But I know it has to run its course before it starts to get better.

Perhaps, I need to start following the treatment prescribed by Dr Lekha Rajan. Those pills did help with the migraines as well.

I call my dentist to reschedule the appointment for next week. The splintering headache won't allow me to venture out of the house. I play soft music and close my eyes. My father too struggled with migraines. His suffering filled me with compassion for him, even though we had a strained relationship. His thin grey hair, his tiny feet wobbling on the stairs—the threat of an accidental fall, of being thrown out of balance, hovering like a dark cloud over his head—him pressing his hand against his head firmly while cursing all the time, him crying, and rubbing the snot on the banister… It reminded me of his temper and vulnerability. Growing up, I feared that I too would have a similar fate since most migraines are hereditary.

However, my mum always comforted me. 'You are not your father. You don't have his temper. You won't get a migraine.'

I believed her, but not entirety. Probably that's why I inherited this infliction. Your beliefs manifest your reality, don't they? I am not sure what I believe about Ovya and Aadit. Are they the perfect young couple I think they are, or are they marred by deep, dark secrets?

In the evening, the loud thumping of the migraine comes down to a rhythmic whisper. It is something that I can endure quite easily. I step out to get a whiff of fresh air. In that welcome amber glow, the sun sinks lower. The sky is dyed a brilliant, orange hue. I close my eyes and take a deep breath. My mind becomes a perfect empty canvas. I open my eyes and watch the fading sunlight and colours subdued by the night. I open my arms and let the soothing breeze wash away whatever remained of the migraine. I let the music of crickets slowly absorb and consume me; my eyes drift towards the never-ending horizon.

A sharp, impatient honk breaks my reverie.

Who the hell honks like that?

I dart outside my door and screech, 'What is your problem, asshole?'

However, by the time I reach the black car, it speeds away with a squeal of its tyres. I continue standing at my position, waiting to confront the unruly car in case it returns. I wait for a short while and grow a tad surprised that none of the prying residents are out. Surely, they couldn't have missed the honking.

Through sheer instinct and habit, I push my hands inside the mailbox. I find another envelope.

I rush inside with it and notice that this too does not have a return address. Just like the previous ones. My thoughts swirl into a whirlwind. I feel alarm as I carefully tear open the envelope and find another note inside it. It reads:

KEEP WATCHING. YOU'll UNCOVER AADIT's SECRETS SOON.

My hands tremble and I drop the note on the floor. I'm taken aback by what is written. 'Is somebody keeping an eye on me? How can anyone know that I delight in watching my new neighbours through the window?' I scamper towards the windows and pull the curtains in an attempt to hide my dwelling and myself. I check the door and ensure that it is properly bolted by unlocking and locking it again. I rush towards my bedroom and shut the windows there. My heart thumps loudly, adrenaline pumping—as if my heart is trying to escape but can't find a way. My eyes are wide open and I have stopped blinking. Fear floods my system. Sweat trickles down my back and my clothes get soaked. What began as beads of sweat on the forehead now flow freely, just like condensation on a windowpane. Sweat drips from my chin.

When my nerves settle, I wonder who could be

sending me such notes and what they want me to find out about Aadit. 'What secrets of Aadit's do I have to uncover? Should I tell Ovya about it?' However, these cryptic messages wouldn't make any sense to her either. I probably need to dig further and find facts before I approach her. Yes, I would have to find out. Even if it is all a joke, I need to be certain. I raise my eyebrows as I devise a plan.

Despite all the fear and anxiety, at night, I watch them again through the window in the hope that I might detect something unusual that would give away Aadit's secrets, if he is hiding something. My inquisitive nature surfaces as I focus the binoculars on Aadit rather than on Ovya. Just like every day, they are relaxing on the couch, popcorn between them, watching something on the television. I can't make out what they're watching but it appears to be a movie. I look harder but it is difficult to identify anything out of the ordinary. Aadit is moving his long index finger gently on Ovya—starting at the shoulders, traversing the skin along the entire length of the arm, until he reaches the wrist. She looks gorgeous in a black tank top and white yoga pants. She takes Aadit's hand into hers and plants a soft kiss on it before returning her gaze to the movie. He too shifts his attention back to the movie. Out of the blue, my doorbell rings, catching me by surprise. My feet wobble and I lose my balance, dropping the binoculars on the floor with a loud thud. I quickly kneel down, feeling a bit thrown off by the fear of discovery. 'What if they find out and catch me peering in?' I crawl, slowly and softly, conscious of not making the slightest of sound. It is pin-drop silence. The doorbell rings again.

Who could come at this ungodly hour?

I whisper, 'Coming, coming.'

I open the door carefully and find the most unexpected visitor.

∽

Om and I got married in a private ceremony with a handful of close friends and family members present. The notion of big crowds to celebrate the occasion had churned both of our stomachs. Despite the small gathering, the rituals took forever to be completed. When we were finally done with it, Om and I reached our new home.

The corners of my mouth turned upwards and warmth spread through my chest. A sense of lightness possessed my body and I could feel a bounce in my step. Tears of joy appeared in my eyes as I tapped my fingers lightly on the table.

'I don't remember the last time I was this happy,' I said.

Om slumped into the bed and said, 'And I don't remember the last time I was this exhausted.'

I frowned at him and chided him. 'Not today, please. You can't be tired today.'

He stretched his arms, yawned a couple of times and said groggily, 'Let me nap for an hour and then we'll have the most spectacular sex we've ever had.'

I retorted, 'I don't think so.'

Trying to get out of bed, I moved away from Om, but he arched his back slightly. He grabbed my hand and pulled me towards him. He spoke softly, in that self-assuring tone. 'Today is the last day that you should be so irked.' He ran his fingers slowly over me, starting at the forehead, covering the nose, until he reached my crimson lips. His finger danced over my lips, covering the upper lip followed by the lower one.

My heart skipped a beat.

I played with his hair and he pulled me closer. Our bodies started to melt into each other. His hands were strong and yet gentle at the same time. He placed his lips on mine. Our breaths quickened. With each stroke of our lips and the occasional fluttering of our tongues, we quivered against each other.

It seemed like ages when we finally broke our kiss.

9

It is the watchman at the door. I don't quite remember his name. *Rajesh, Rakesh, Ramesh...? Err. I don't remember and I hardly care. Why the hell is he here at this hour?* Anger boils deep in me, as hot as lava. My eyes turn bloodshot red.

I fume. 'Is there a problem? Why were you ringing the doorbell?'

He takes a step back and fumbles. 'Actually, ma'am, you forgot your glass. It was kept at your main entrance...'

I nod and accept the glass from him.

I fumble, 'I am sorry. I'll be more careful.'

A flash of annoyance overpowers me and with it comes a bad idea. Isn't that always the case? The two always seem to travel together. At that moment, I try to gather all my wisdom and try to walk away from this awful plan. It'll be better in the long run, I tell myself, yet my persuasion doesn't work. I find myself scurrying to find my car keys. I look for them in the drawers, the closets and under the bed in vain. Then, I hurry towards the living room and search for them under the rug, the couch, in the cupboard and everywhere else until my eyes fall on the key holder where the car keys are neatly hung. I grab them and they jangle in my hand. I pour myself a glass of wine, return to the couch with a firm resolve to follow Aadit as he goes out tomorrow.

I call up Osheen in the morning. Her cheerful voice is, as always, music to my ears.

She says, 'It took some time for you to return my calls.'

I snicker. 'What can I say, I have been busy.'

'Busy doing what? Befriending your new neighbours?'

I say, 'Who is feeding you this information? Who is your source?'

She considers my question for a short while and says, 'I can't tell you that.'

I get up from the bed and speak softly, as if someone could hear me. 'You know... I want to tell you something.'

She mimics me and replies in a whisper. 'What is it?'

'I have been getting strange notes in my mailbox for a couple of weeks now, ever since Ovya and Aadit shifted to the house opposite mine.'

She gasps, and her tone becomes a touch serious. 'What do they say? Tell me.'

I rush through my words the way broadcasters do when reading an investment disclaimer, 'The first note said that Aadit isn't who he seems to be. The latest one, the fourth to arrive in my mailbox, said that I should "keep watching", and that I will "uncover Aadit's secrets soon". I haven't even properly spoken to him yet. I wonder why such notes are being dropped in the mailbox and if there is any truth in them. Or is someone just trying to play a cruel prank on me. What do you think?'

She takes a pause as if considering the gravity of the situation, the way she always does. 'Before I answer, I want to ask, have you been watching them?'

'Once in a while. It's harmless, Osheen.' I break into a sheepish grin.

Osheen chastises me. 'You shouldn't do that, Ziva. You shouldn't.' I can feel Osheen throwing her arms out, frowning and shaking her head in disapproval.

'I know, I know. But what should I do now?'

'For starters, you should stop looking through your window and ignore any such notes and with time, they'll stop coming,' she says, confidently. After the call, I prepare a measly breakfast and get ready. I also look for Tangience and note the address on my phone. I check the time. It is 10 a.m. Aadit might leave any time for work. I know today is his first day at work. He updated his status on LinkedIn. I take my car keys and lock the door and dash towards my black Honda City. I turn on the ignition and drive just outside the main gate of the residential complex and wait for his blue Toyota Camry under the shade of the massive mango tree.

I put on the radio and hear more ads playing than music. As I shuffle between stations, Aadit's car arrives. He stops at the corner paan shop but doesn't come out of his vehicle. I see the shopkeeper hand him a packet of cigarettes and take the money from him. I'd never observed him smoking in the balcony of the house… but then again, I only ever saw Aadit and Ovya at night. A big smile encircles the shopkeeper's face. *Maybe they shared a joke.*

The engine of his Camry roars back to life as he weaves his car into the main road effortlessly. I wait for him to be sufficiently ahead before I start my car so that there is no way for him to catch me in the rear-view mirror. I thread my car in between a few other cars and two-wheelers, almost seamlessly, like the shuffling of a deck of cards.

The traffic snakes up every time the traffic light hits red.

It is the only anomaly on an otherwise smooth and

fast-moving traffic. I keep an eye on his car through the vehicles and I keep up with him but make sure that I don't get too close. I check my maps. I am sure he is headed to the office and the chances of finding anything suspicious are remarkably slim. Despite that, I continue my investigation since my curiosity needs to be silenced.

Just then, he slows his car down in front of the grandest building on the street. A girl—one whom I believe I have seen somewhere before—opens the door of the car and sits on the passenger seat. She gives him a little hug. He hugs back awkwardly before driving off. I keep up with them. His office is now only a kilometre away and that's where I think he is going. I steal a glance at the towers on the right side and find the name Tangience etched in capital letters on one of the buildings. At the intersection, he brings his car to a halt and the girl steps out of the car and walks away. I can't quite grasp the expression on her face but it appears as if she is disgruntled. He waves but she does not look at him and walks away. Aadit takes a U-turn and pulls into the underground parking of the building. His car disappears into the darkness. I too turn back and drive away, back towards my empty, lonely house. As the car swings into relatively deserted roads, I relish the boisterous winds that twirl my hair and whistle past my eyes.

Come nightfall, I begin the ritual that I can't seem to abandon. I pour myself a glass of wine and collapse on the couch. I go over the events of the day and almost pat myself on the back for being daring enough to follow Aadit. *Was it audacious or plain stupid?* I tell myself that's a question that can be pondered over later. At the moment, I just need to focus and remember who that girl is. I'm pretty sure I have seen her somewhere before. It's odd because I saw Aadit only a few weeks ago. I take a sip of the drink and close my eyes to recollect where I could have seen her. I glance at my neighbour's window and then quickly turn away. I take a large gulp of the elixir in my hand and close my eyes again. Suddenly, like a flash of lightning, I recall where I had seen her. I latch on to my laptop and open Aadit's Facebook profile. I go through his pictures until I arrive at the one I am looking for.

There she is and there is Aadit.

My head is blank. Normally, I would have come up with varied notions and explanations for something like this but today there is nothing.

∽

It's Sunday. Om and I had decided on Thursday that we would clean today. We woke up a tad late, which meant it wasn't such a great start at the task in hand.

I said, looking at the mess in the kitchen, 'Om, we need to clean this today, no matter what. I get a migraine every time I look at the house.'

He took a bite of the toast and nodded. 'Of course, I'm at your service all day, and all night as well. If you know what I mean.'

He winked at me and I couldn't help but smile.

I joined him in the kitchen and said, 'You'll get what you want after we are done cleaning.' Then I bit him on the ear.

He leapt from his seat and started picking up objects lying on the floor and placing them on the designated shelves. Ten minutes into the activity, he got a call from his office. They required him to get on a Skype call with clients from the United Kingdom in the next half an hour. He agreed reluctantly. He said, 'Babe, I need to get on a quick call with a client. It won't take more than an hour. Please.'

I shook my head in disdain. 'You do whatever you have to. I'll manage.'

He made an apologetic face, shrugged his shoulders, and extended his arms as if he didn't have an option. *He had an option. He had the option to say 'No'. He could have just told them that he was busy.* One hour can easily turn into two or three hours or even more. Once Om started working, he always lost track of time and I was sure today would be no different. After three hours, Om returned and sat down next to me.

'I'm so sorry. I had no idea it would take this long. I'm sorry, love. We still have time to do the cleaning.'

I kept silent. Tension grew in my shaking limbs as I suppressed the anger building up inside me. The thick silence became a deluge as I feared I would say something that shouldn't be said. Bereft of any winds that made the trees outside rustle and whisper, the quietness made the atmosphere eerie. This anger had been building up for a while now, spotting every opportunity and then capitalizing on it to find an escape.

I put a leash on my anger and didn't set it free that day.

One day, I would snap. All that rage building up would come out and spread as fast as wildfire, destroying everything in its way.

10

Growing up has been a trial by fire, nothing short of an ordeal. I have always asked: *Why? Why did it happen to me?* But I have never received any convincing answers. I never flinched when trying to find possible explanations. The truth is out there somewhere, never revealing itself to me. I never expected the truth to be comfortable. In fact, I knew it'd be hard and terrifying and I'd have to be steadfast in order to face it completely. There are still plenty of clarifications and elucidations to be had and only one person could give that to me—my mother who left me a few years ago. All that remains are unanswered questions.

Part of maturing was forgiving and moving on because unresolved situations give rise to hostility. It never helps. Accepting the flaws and failings of everyone I held dear led to inescapable distress since they weren't adept at controlling their opposing urges. I tried to make a cocoon of sorts, which has a place for love and compassion not only for others but also myself. It has been my lifeboat, allowing me to ride the unruly waters. Looking back, a feeling of pride fills me as I have changed and adapted to keep growing, irrespective of the surroundings.

The pains and lessons were all a part of growing up—imperative and indispensable.

The cool and steady breeze provides a much-needed respite from the oppressive and suffocating heat in Delhi.

The soft sunlight streams through the clouds. I open all the windows of the house in a bid to welcome the pleasant weather. The remaining dahlias tilt their blooming faces towards the sky. The idea of removing weed, shrubs and creepers seemed like a good idea today. I proceed towards Ovya's house and ring the bell. She comes out in a pink robe and with a towel draped around her head.

Her face is red. 'Wow! I didn't expect you. Please come in. I'll be ready in two.'

A desire to run away grows, which I strongly expunge through sheer will. With half a smile I say, 'Oh, no. Please carry on. The weather is lovely today and I thought I'll ask you if you want to help me clean up the abomination of the garden I have.'

The bright smile returns to her face and she says, 'Of course, I'd love to help you. Just give me an hour and I'll see you at your house.'

'Perfect.'

I fetch the trimmer, mower and pruner. I bring the pipe and connect it to the waterline. I also bring the pots and the few seeds that I bought yesterday and place them on the floor. I change into black yoga pants and a blue tank top and wait somewhat eagerly for the assignment at hand.

The doorbell rings and I know it has to be Ovya. I hurry towards the main door and greet her with a friendly embrace. She is dressed for the occasion in black pyjama pants and a beige top.

With a bright smile on her face, Ovya says, 'Hi! I have got gloves on and am super ready to engage in some horticulture.'

'Can't wait. Let's get started, shall we?'

She nods and we begin work.

We mow and trim the grass, which hasn't seen any maintenance for a long time. It takes us more than an hour to do it. Despite the cool temperature, we are now sweating like a porous pitcher. Taking it easy, we take a water break and flump on the chairs.

She gasps for air and says, 'This isn't as easy as I thought.'

Taking a big gulp of water I chuckle. 'I know, right?'

We rest for a short while before we mulch, edge and weed the garden, removing all the undesired undergrowth. We prune and trim the bushes, the shrubs and the plants. We collect all the waste in the dustbins.

She bends over and says, 'I am starting to enjoy it.'

I look at her and wink slightly. 'I'm sure you are.'

We plant the seeds and place the pots in different positions. Thereafter, we water them and I promise Ovya that I will be more regular in nurturing the new plants and maintaining the garden. Ovya and I catch our breaths and exult in a hard afternoon's work. We continue sitting in our chairs, marvelling at the new, refined look of the oasis of green, which is now speckled by a variety of colours.

A drop of rain kisses my hand. Another drop traces my neck and collapses on my stomach. The clouds gather and the air anticipates the looming downpour. My soul stirs as I can't wait for the rainwater to enrich the brown soil and polish the leaves and flowers.

Ovya breaks my musings. 'I think it's going to rain.'

I look at her and smile. 'Isn't that lovely? As if the gods approve of the good work we have done today.'

She looks up at the sky and says, 'I think I should go back.'

'Don't be silly...let's go inside. You can clean up in the bathroom while I'll make us something. I am famished. I am sure you are too.'

She says, 'That isn't necessary. I don't want to give you trouble.'

'Please. I insist.'

She drops her handbag in the living room and goes to the bathroom while I clean up and fry the mashed potato croquettes to chomp on. I had already prepared more coffee sangria and it is being cooled in the refrigerator.

Ovya steps out and follows me into the kitchen. 'That looks good. What is it?'

I say, 'Nothing fancy. Just potato croquettes. Why don't you settle on the couch and I'll bring everything there?'

'Can I help you in any way?'

Taking out the croquettes on a plate, I say, 'Trust me. I got this. I'll join you in five.'

I take out the coffee sangrias and place it along with the croquettes on a tray and bring it to the living room where Ovya is doing something on her mobile.

I catch her eye as I place everything on the table and announce: 'A paltry reward for the grind.'

She looks up. 'This sangria is worth every effort.' One bite of the snack and a sip of the drink and Ovya says, 'This is incredibly delicious. You're a great cook, Ziva.'

I shake my head, 'You're too kind. Tell me how you and Aadit are finding the neighbourhood.'

She leans back on the couch and says, 'Apart from you, I haven't really met anyone. A certain Mrs Mehra did invite us for dinner and I guess it was nice. There are not a lot of people our age here, are there?'

I take a brief pause and say, 'I'm the last person you want to ask about the residents. I hardly know anyone properly but I think there are likely to be people our age here. We are not living in an RWA that is exclusively for the senior citizens, are we?'

She roars with laughter and says, 'Aadit is just like you. He doesn't like to be social. He is just the opposite of me in that regard. I love meeting new people.'

I smile. 'I'm sure we'll like each other.'

She says, 'It seems we got married only yesterday. Life is so much simpler when he's around.'

I think about Om. How he always managed to help us get through whatever life threw at us with a rare kind of ferocity and clemency. How he always made me laugh, no matter how stressed I was. *God! I miss him.*

I fetch the bottle of red wine and pour some into our glasses. Ovya protests but I don't listen to her and say, 'I only drink wine with people I like. It's a holy experience for me.'

She takes a sip of the drink, rocks back on the couch and says, 'This is good. We ought to share more such experiences.'

My phone beeps. I look at it and say, 'It's Osheen, a dear friend from Mumbai. She is open to meeting new people like you, looks ten years younger than her age and gets excited about almost everything. Full of life—just like you.'

'Where is she?'

'Oh, she isn't here. I will try and get you to meet her soon.'

'I'd love that.'

I lean in and ask, 'How did you meet Aadit?'

She looks into the distance as if recalling the first time she met him, and then she shifts her gaze on to me. 'Oh, he was a speaker at our college. He gave a lecture on how to marry skills with marketing to get sales. I guess I took the session way too seriously.'

I narrow my eyes and say, 'You seem to have a fixation on all your speakers?'

She bursts into a peal of sweet, joyful laughter. 'Only him and you.'

Seeing her laugh makes me happy like a lark. We drain our glasses and I fill them instantly.

I take a large swig and say, 'You know, seeing Aadit and you reminds me of the time when Om and I were still together.'

Ovya gets up and clamps her hands on my shoulders. 'Don't worry. You can always count on me and Aadit. If you ever need anything, we're here. Why don't you join us for dinner on Saturday?'

I wonder if I can count on Aadit. The person sending me notes definitely doesn't think he can be trusted. Feeling conflicted, I consider whether I should tell her about the cryptic and peculiar notes that I have been getting in my mailbox. I decide against it. There's nothing to suggest that Aadit can't be trusted. Moreover, she might believe that I am planting seeds of doubt about her beloved husband and that might ruin whatever little companionship I share with Ovya. I can't risk that.

∽

We were seated in our favourite pub, Backyard Drinks, celebrating Om's promotion. We picked up our glasses of whisky, raised them in the air, clanked them against each other and said, 'Here's to more such nights.'

Om leaned back and said, 'You know, I have been thinking about what you said the other day. I think you're right.'

I emptied my glass, asked the waiter to refill it and stuttered, 'What did I say?'

Om leaned forward, kissed my hand and said, 'That we should have a baby. It's been five years since we have been married. I think now is the right time. What do you think?'

I almost sprang up in my chair and whooped, 'You're not kidding me?'

He looked me straight in the eye. He gleamed with the same passion that he had on the day we met for the first time. 'No,' said Om with great emphasis. 'It also means that we'll have a lot more sex and honestly, I can't wait.'

11

The night sky is the most pristine art form, pulsating with raw energy, a treat for the eyes and food for the soul. I feel alive, as if the vibration has hit my nerves and whispered in my ears. Despite my life being utterly devoid of love, I feel affection. The stars shine like rice grains spilled over an endless canvas of black. To me, the night arrives when the curtain gets pulled back. I go out and see through the window to explore the beauty beyond. It also offers me an opportunity to shift my attention to Ovya's house and see what she and her husband are up to.

I get my binoculars and peek through them. The fear of someone watching me, or getting another note from my 'anonymous well-wisher' is quashed by my growing curiosity, which has only heightened over the course of the few weeks that I have been observing them. A tingle of excitement runs through my skin as Ovya and Aadit appear in the living room together. Just like always. *They are inseparable.*

Watching television together and munching is almost a daily ritual for them, and today is no different. They are glued to the flickering screen of their TV set. I wonder what they are watching. All of a sudden, Aadit put the popcorn on the table and got up. This is the first time that they don't finish their leisure activity. The television keeps playing in the background and Aadit keeps standing. He looks flushed, irritated. His face has gone red. He is giving an impetuous look. Anger is draining from his eyes as he rubs his temple belligerently. Ovya too gets up and points to something on the table. Aadit keeps standing. He doesn't make any movement or speak anything. He is still. Ovya doesn't like this. She seems furious. She burns with feral intensity. This is a bitter, burning rage. Words flow from her mouth. Aadit remains unmoved, his eyes suggesting that he doesn't have an answer to whatever they are arguing about. A small laugh escapes his lips as if he is saying, 'You are unbelievable.' She retorts calmly, almost with an air of finality to her words. Aadit walks out of the house and lights a cigarette outside. She crumples into the chair, her lovely eyes now a teary mess, whereas he smokes, as if inhaling the stench of their argument.

In that instant, I realize that the concept of a perfect family is a farce. We tend to endure each other's differences and revel in the similarities, that's all.

∽

Lying down on my bed, I could hear the first familiar rumbles of the day from the kitchen. This had become an undesirable part of my life. But, there was absolutely nothing I could do to change it. My father's thunderous shouts shook the entire house, which always seemed like it would collapse under the pressure of all the commotion. It was challenged by my mother's shrill screams.

I used to hide under the bed in a failed effort to shut the noise. The only thing I could do was wait, wait for the storm to blow over and then the sacred silence would descend. It would come after my father had muffled my mother's voice by hitting her brutally and repeatedly.

∽

It has been two days since Ovya and I worked on the garden, and it already appears as if the toil will result in colours, scents and beauty of the most immaculate kind. I take a deep breath and appreciate the sight in front of me for a moment before returning inside. It is 1.11 p.m. According to the angel number—111—I'm attracting everything I have been focusing on. My gaze shifts to the bottle of red and I fill my glass with it. *I can't defy the divine messenger.* I put on a random episode of my favourite show and recline on the couch.

I wonder why I love this show so much. Is it because pixels and emotions are the primary way to communicate with our minds? The parables, metaphors and symbols of each dialogue carry a specific meaning for me, and the different expressions and idiosyncratic movements of each character are laced with familiarity. Or is it because these shows and movies are healing? They are reflections of us and we are reflections of them. This could be the reason why we are so drawn to the stories of the unknown. We get invested in the tales of actors navigating towards their goals. Perhaps, that is why I keep going back to this one particular show.

I reach my favourite part and the phone rings. It is Osheen.

I answer. 'Hey babe, what's up?'

She says, 'My serotonin levels rise after hearing your voice.'

I cackle, pausing the show. 'Why don't you compile a book of witty responses?'

'Naah. My wit is reserved for a blessed few. What are you doing?'

I say, 'Bringing my social life score from being extra negative to a little less negative.'

She teases, 'That is a mighty difficult task and you've been at it for quite some time, haven't you?'

'It took Edison a thousand attempts to invent the light bulb.'

She quips, 'Apparently, someone else in the UK had already invented it. The bloke just took all the credit.'

I set down the glass and refill it. 'It doesn't matter who invented the fucking light bulb. The only person that matters is the one who discovered the art of making wine from grapes.'

She guesses. 'Are you drinking at this hour?'

'I didn't know that there was a government advisory regarding when to drink and when not to.'

Just like Om, she cajoles me, 'Excessive drinking is bad for you.'

I slur, 'Excessive is a *relative* term. Something that might be excessive for you might just be normal for me.'

'Why are you acting like a little bitch?' And then she laughs, just like always, and says, 'Don't tempt me into activating my mean mode.'

I laugh back, shiver and say in a stuttering tone, 'Oh, I'm so scared.'

'That reminds me, have you still been getting those notes in your mailbox?'

'Oh, I haven't checked. Let me just do that.'

I walk to the mailbox while still on the call. Osheen

tells me about this new guy she met through Bumble and advises me that I should try the app as well. 'You never know where you may find your future partner,' she says. I slide my hand inside the mailbox and there it is—another note. All my wit and meanness evaporate into thin air. I fetch the scissors from the kitchen and cut it open. Upon reading it, my hands tremble and my legs give way. I fall like a pack of cards, dropping the phone on the floor. The house reverberates with the sound of Osheen shouting. 'Ziva? Are you there? Is there another note? Please answer.'

But my eyes are transfixed on the note as the words inscribed send a shiver down my spine. I think my heart will explode. My eyes widen with fear as I read the note one more time.

HOPE YOU HAVE A LOVELY DINNER. YOU'll SEE WHO THE REAL AADIT IS.

∽

Whenever I fumed at Om for something he did and something he promised but didn't do, he had a lovely way of making it up to me. He would serenade me, play different songs and make me laugh and cry at the same time.

Om picked up his guitar and started playing the song 'She Will Be Loved' by Maroon 5. At first, I didn't look towards him; however, as he picked up the tempo, I stole a glance at him and my face broke into a slight smile. As he kept seeking my attention, with his singing, occasional smiles, and a rather dramatic opening and closing of the eyes, for effect, I guess, I used to stand there, shaking

my head from left to right. It was all a part of his grand
gesture and when the performance was over, he came
closer to me and put his arms around my shoulders and
said, 'Next time onwards, I'll have to start charging.'

I chuckled. 'Next time, don't let a situation arise that
would require your serenading me.'

He smiled. 'But I love singing to you.'

I smiled back. 'And I love hearing you sing.'

12

I do a quick scan of the house in the hope that I'd find a spy camera and microphone lurking in some corner, recording everything that happens here. There was no other explanation for the letter. How else could somebody have access to such information? My breathing is jagged and harsh. Saliva thickens in my throat, which almost makes me throw up. Heat gets released from my body as motes of sweat trickle.

I start to rearrange sections of the living room, pushing furniture aside, eyes darting wildly with every passing second, looking for the eye of the photographic equipment and the speaker. I begin to call out 'Where are you?' repeatedly, getting louder every time I speak. I yell again, louder, my voice almost cracking as I rummage under the couch and the central table. A sea of objects and artefacts stare right back at me.

I crumble on the floor and whisper to myself. 'Calm down, calm down.' I keep sitting on the floor for some time before I get up again.

I go through each fraction of the massive wooden panel, pasting a red clip on the ones I have examined. I gaze through the living room. 'It looks like a house where there has been a break in,' I said to myself. All of a sudden, I remember what Om always said whenever I misplaced anything. 'We often find things we're looking for when we tidy up.'

So, I start cleaning up the disarray with detailed meticulousness. I start sifting through the objects on the couch, the table and the cabinets, and then move on to sorting the artefacts and decorations in the room. My eyes are constantly on the lookout for a gleam of silver that might be reflected from the camera. After a few hours of extensive searching, all I could find are a few old coins, hair clips and plenty of dirt.

The simmering tension rises and permeates my entire body. Frustration captures me like a sharp cry that is impossible to ignore. I think I might blow up and shatter into pieces. I take a deep breath. The flow of wine calls for me but I push against the idea. I keep sitting on the floor. I want to shout, throw a tantrum and beat my hands on the mirror until I crack it. I want to let it all out. I want to bemoan my failure at not being able to find a simple camera with a mic. I desperately want to vent but I maintain my composure.

However, the fear in my chest remains, waiting to take over with ferocity. For all I know, its only intention is to protect me but I try to convince myself that there isn't any danger. I move forward, bit by bit, from fear towards anxiety and depression. *I am in no position to handle this.*

I open the windows and let the air in. I can hear the chirping of the birds at a distance. I should probably prepare something nutritious to eat or take a nap. Research claims these things help with stress.

I don't do either, instead I choose to focus all my attention on an old photograph of my mother and me. She is draped in a red saree, smiling with her eyes, leaning down and pulling my cheeks while I just stand with a sullen face and empty expression. Before the picture was taken, I had cried and howled for a long time since I couldn't find my favourite doll. I remember how my mother was so good at finding things. She always knew the exact spots to search and find what was missing in a matter of minutes. The same thing happened that day as well. This was before my father's teacups were replaced by glasses of whisky. This was before the affection in his heart had been replaced by hatred. This was before the joy and love had been replaced by constant arguments and fights.

I survey the entire living room again to determine if I left any place unexamined, but I haven't. I think of calling the cleaners but then I decide against it. I make a note on my phone to call them tomorrow so that they can look through every corner scrupulously.

I shroud my plump form with a black evening gown speckled with golden trinkets. Although the invitation didn't demand special attire, I still slip into the dress that I bought in Rome a few years ago. I would have probably preferred to wear something casual, but I'd rather err on the side of elegance than simplicity. I apply foundation to hide the few pimples and give myself a more uniform and smooth appearance. I put on glittering eye shadow and touch the eyelids with a kohl eyeliner. After that, I apply mascara and finish the exercise with a pink velvet matte lipstick. I get up and look at myself in the mirror. I turn around and look at myself again. I walk the length of my bedroom and return to the mirror to admire the good work I have managed to do.

Brimming with nervous anticipation, I feel a surge of excitement, even some giddiness. I remind myself that I have to get through the entire evening in one piece.

A tingling feeling spreads through my entire body as if it is the most natural thing in the world. I regain my composure and say, 'You can do this without embarrassing yourself. Just stay calm.' Ovya had asked me to be there by 8 p.m. I check the watch. It is 8.15 p.m. I decide to leave in another fifteen minutes.

∽

It was unusually quiet and empty today at Hotel Malibu—our getaway for the weekend. All our attempts to make a baby had failed while doing the act in the house and Om thought that it would be a good idea to change the setting. I thought that there was no harm in trying in a different place. It had been quite a long time since we had come to this property. It was one of our preferred locations to spend a leisurely weekend.

We had a light dinner and got inside our room.

Om imitated a bark and said, 'What bones do I get to devour today?'

I shook my head and said, 'None, if you continue to be cheesy.'

'This is just an innocent question from someone who's famished.'

I break into a smile and gesture for him to join me in bed.

Despite being married for half a decade, an instinctive, unsatisfied desire always lived in us. I leaned in and kissed him softly at first. He kissed me back and took me into his arms. After that, he brushed his lips against mine slowly, and then with greater urgency and passion. The sensation transported me back to our first kiss, before all my thoughts were blacked out. I pulled him closer to me until the little indignation I felt every now and then dripped out of the pores of my skin.

He pulled my blouse and tugged my bra straps and caressed my breasts. There was a newness to how he fondled and licked them while his hands traced my thighs little by little. He then moved his lips slowly down my stomach, covering my warm and delicate skin. My breathing quickened and my body quivered at his movements. He removed my underwear and held it between his teeth and tossed it away. He kissed me around the pubic bone for a moment and inserted his stiff penis in my vagina. It felt both hot and cold at the same time. A strange carnal pleasure enveloped me as his scent, taste and touch overpowered me. I squeezed him further and further inside of me.

All of a sudden, I felt tiny fireworks going off all over my body as if it was a confirmation that we were ready to take our marriage to the next level.

13

I check myself one final time in the mirror. I lock the door and march towards their house. The inky darkness of the night dims the feeble light of the moon. My head buzzes with possibilities. I hear the hum of excitement and nervousness again. I press the doorbell and wait for it to be opened.

It is Ovya who opens the door and her arms squeeze me tighter than the first time she embraced me. I breathe slowly, letting my body melt into my new friend's embrace as the last bit of tension fades away. At this moment, the love we share will fill any void. We look at one another as if we both had decided that today's evening will mark the beginning of a great friendship.

Ovya is wearing a casual peach cotton shirt and black jeans. She is dressed, but not as extravagantly as I am. She looks lovely as ever. She says, 'Come in. Aadit and I have been expecting you.'

Aadit is standing just behind his wife. He shakes my hand. The handshake is firm, eye contact is maintained, and we smile back at each other. This is the first time I am seeing him in such close proximity. He sports a spade-shaped smooth beard that encircles his face. His orb-like round eyes are soft and glimmer with interest. His slightly long and straight nose is turned upwards. His prominent cheekbones carve down towards a rigid jaw. His genuine and cheerful smile frames his handsome face. A woody scent fills the entire room.

'Hi! We are meeting for the first time, aren't we'?' he says.

I say, 'Properly, yes, for the first time.'

Ovya guides me to the couch and brings a glass of wine each for us and whisky for Aadit. She sits beside me while Aadit makes himself comfortable on the sofa opposite us. He is wearing a white shirt, sleeves folded, revealing the veins popping out from his forearms. I could totally imagine him working out in the gym with weights as heavy as my worries. He is sporting a pair of blue jeans. He looks good, but I can't decipher if he puts as much effort into his legs too. I let my eyes shift to the expanse of the living room. All the boxes are gone and it seems like they have finally managed to furnish and decorate the space.

Ovya says, noticing, 'It broke our backs just to get everything in order.'

I shuffle on the seat to sit more comfortably. 'Trust me, I know the pain.'

She stretches her hands as if remembering all the work she had had to do. 'Oh yes! Aadit, did I tell you that Ziva moved to the locality six months ago? All by herself.'

He looks at me and raises his eyebrows. 'You did?'

I nod slowly. 'I didn't really have a choice.'

Ovya gets up and goes to the kitchen, leaving Aadit and me in the room. We look at each other momentarily before his eyes shift towards the kitchen to look at Ovya. The way he looks at her exhibits the joys and sorrows they share with each other. It is as if all of him, heart and soul, is present there and then, with his wife, Ovya.

He seems to cherish every moment that he shares with her. I can almost hear the sound of their laughter, their spontaneity and their soft whispers. I can almost see their late-night adventures, early morning breakfasts and the lazy evenings together, where all they can do is doze off next to each other. Aadit is handsome and these steady breaths and gentlemanly demeanour complement Ovya nicely.

He says, 'What do you do?'

'Nothing at the moment,' I say. 'But I am a graphic designer.'

He covers his face with his hands. 'Oh yes. Ovya told me that you'd taken a session on design when she was in college.'

'I know what you do.'

His eyes widen and he twists his mouth. 'How?'

'How do you think? Ovya told me,' I reply with a smile.

'Yes, she is our connecting string. She has always been like that, bringing people together. She is lovely, isn't she?'

'As lovely as a newborn's smile.'

Ovya walks in with a tray filled with cheese straws, chips, guacamole and Caprese bites. She places the tray on the table and says, 'This should hopefully get the evening started. Ziva, I know you're shy but you'd let me know if you need anything?'

I take a bite. 'This is delicious. Could I get a refill?'

Aadit takes my glass, his fingers touch mine. He fills it and hands it back to me. He refills his whisky too.

She says, 'It's just so nice to sit together, the three of us. It's intimate.'

I am taken back to a time in Mumbai when I was

surrounded by Osheen, Sasha and a few other people whom I was meeting for the first time. They were either Osheen's friends or Sasha's. The gathering was quite awkward because, like me, a bunch of people didn't know each other and were meeting for the first time. I had learned about a new technique that could make people open up in a matter of minutes. The trick was saying something about the person you were seeing for the first time by making an assumption. By the time the night ended, everyone got to know so much about everyone. It wouldn't have been possible without the game and alcohol added to the mix.

I think of doing something similar here.

I say, 'I'm going to ask both of you a question each. Try and answer as honestly as you can.'

They both look intently at me. 'If you could choose just three people to have around for the rest of your life, who would they be?'

Ovya shrugs. 'How can you choose just three people for the rest of your life? That's absurd, isn't it?'

Aadit closes his eyes for a second, looks at Ovya and says, 'For me, choosing one person won't be difficult.' He pauses. 'But choosing the other two is a mighty difficult choice.'

Ovya pinches his arm slightly and asks, 'Who would you choose, Ziva?'

I say, 'Osheen, my best friend since school, Dr Aashna, she is my dentist, I have had dental problems all my life and she is brilliant, and you, Ovya. How else would I trim my garden?'

We break into a puddle of laughter.

Ovya then says, 'Now, it's my turn to ask a question.

The next word you say will become a superpower. What word would you say and why?'

Aadit lifts his head slightly. 'Memory. I'd want to have an incredible memory so that I don't forget any moment and get to live it with the same ferocity in my head.'

I cross my arms. 'Love, so that I always feel loved at all times.' I look at them and smile.

Ovya squeezes my shoulder. 'Wisdom, so that I can look at people and decipher what's on their mind.'

Aadit refills everyone's glasses. He says, 'Is it my turn now? Okay. If you could go back in time to when you were a child, would the childhood version of you be proud of the person you have become and why?'

Ovya takes a sip and looks up. 'Absolutely, because the value of honesty I was raised with is still intact. Honesty towards work, family, friends and everything else.'

I say, 'I'll be candid. I would not want to go back to being a child. Growing up was terrible. Keeping that in mind, I think the childhood version of me would probably go on an ego trip considering what I have been able to do.'

Then Aadit says, 'I always had a tendency of making bad choices in my youth. I managed to steer my life in the right direction a few years ago. The child version of me would be pleased with where I am.'

It seems like the three of us are getting along well. All of us are in the zone, asking countless questions about each other and knowing each other a tad better in the process. Ovya takes a quick look at her phone and says, 'Oh, look at the time! We should eat.' Then, the three of us head towards the dining room. On the long oak table are dishes of mushroom soup, Thai red curry with rice and verde flatbread. A sensation of fullness hits me as I look at the spread of delicacies on the table. I tell Ovya that she is a sensational cook and should consider opening a restaurant. We begin the feast and pair it with waterfalls of wine. Aadit sticks to whisky. By now, we have lost count of the number of glasses we have finished and there is a sense of propinquity to that. Being this open, this vulnerable, is hard for me, especially as Aadit is present as well. But I let go of my inhibitions and that allows him to open up as well after his initial reservedness. I wanted to be confident and not let my insecurities take a jibe at me so that I know and uncover him as much as I can in this meeting.

As I take the last helping of the flatbread and start to clean up, Ovya says, 'There's something else as well.'

She leaves for the kitchen and comes back with a carrot cake and each of us get a generous helping of the dessert.

I say, 'I'm so full. This is such a feast. I wonder how long it took you to prepare everything.'

She says with her mouth full. 'Not long, trust me.'

After finishing our meal, we recline on the couch. I check my watch. It is almost midnight.

I say, 'I think I should get going.'

They both say in unison, 'Stay a bit longer. Let's drink some more.'

'It is hard to reject the couple.'

We sit with our glasses full again. Ovya says, 'Can we ask each other one final round of questions?'

Aadit leans forward. 'I'll go first. If you could get away with murder, whom would you kill and why?'

My mouth opens and I put my hands over my mouth.

I freeze and stare with my eyes wide open.

'That's a strange question, but I like it. I would probably kill my husband's girlfriend. He cheated on me with her. I would have no regrets either,' I say immediately.

Ovya narrows her eyes and glances sideways. 'I don't have it in me to kill anyone. I would probably try to change people rather than kill them.'

Aadit raises his eyebrows. 'Instead of killing people, I would rather have them not being born. There's a whole bunch of them. My ex-boss tops the list.'

Ovya looks down and away before asking her question. 'If you could know the total and absolute truth to one question, what question would you ask?'

I answer, 'What should I do with the rest of my life?'

Aadit considers the question, starts to say something, retracts, then says, 'I wouldn't want to ask anything because if I do, I would probably stifle my curiosity and my need to find meaning in life.'

Ovya slurs, 'I'd want to know if a part of Aadit still fancies and loves his ex.'

∽

A sheen of sweat covered Om's face after another session of passionate sex. The way it featured on the contour of his muscles reminded me of how brawny he looked. I adjusted the pillow and sat on the bed gently.

'Have you ever killed anyone?' I asked him.

He keeps lying on the bed and then he breaks into a half-closed smile. 'Many times with my looks. Have you?'

I nodded slowly. 'In fact, I have and I'd like to do it again.'

He snickered. 'Whom have you killed?'

I kissed his chest. 'I don't remember their names but there are people I have mur-der-ed.'

'Is that why you keep a gun?'

I nodded. 'Yes, you never know when you might have to use it.'

'Have you used the gun before?'

'When the day is right, I would.'

'Are you a serial killer?'

'I am not sure. How do you define a serial killer?'

'I am no expert but perhaps if you kill two people or more, you can be considered one. Am I in bed with someone dangerous?'

'As long as you behave yourself, you're in no danger.'

'Am I behaving myself?'

I winked and made eye contact. 'Yes. I have decided not to kill you today.'

14

Aadit raises his inflamed eyes, his fingers curl tightly around his whisky glass and he grits his teeth in an effort to remain silent and maintain his poise. His form exudes anger like acid—slow, burning and caustic. With suppressed rage, he looks at me and breaks into a half-smile before diverting all his attention to Ovya.

'What is that supposed to mean, love?'

She finishes her glass of wine. 'You heard me.'

He glares, hands still tight around the glass. I fear he might break it by the sheer pressure he is exerting. He whispers, 'I have told you there is nothing between Saachi and me. It was over the day I married you. Hell, I don't even want to meet her. I love you and that is absolute and final.'

She taps her fingers and sighs. Then she shifts her attention to me, as though to elicit some support. I have nothing to offer apart from the mysterious notes that keep coming to my mailbox, but I keep it to myself. That has the potential to aggravate the situation further. Helplessness creeps over me like freezing water numbing my senses. At this moment, my mind shuts down all thoughts except one: *Get out of here.* My feet become heavier as if they are set in concrete, and I find it awfully hard to move. All I can do is pray that things fall into place and Ovya calms down and doesn't challenge Aadit's defence.

Ovya pauses before erupting into loud, raucous laughter. She slaps her knees and pours herself another glass of wine. Her body writhes as she cackles. She is in a state of mercurial intoxication, releasing herself of the frustrating sense of self-consciousness. She plunges into hysterics, unable to control herself. She makes convulsive body movements. She tries to control the laughter by keeping a still face but fails terribly; and in a matter of seconds, she slips into another bout. Tears spill from her eyes as Aadit and I exchange looks and stare at her, not knowing what is happening. His mouth is pursed but slightly open, while I sit in anticipation, waiting for Ovya to explain and she does.

'I was kidding. Look how serious you have become.' She pulls at Aadit's cheeks as he breathes a sigh of relief. She eyes me and gives me a bear hug. However, something tells me that she is serious about the accusation.

I'm back home. It is late and I'm exhausted. I don't bother removing the makeup. I slip into my nightgown and collapse on the bed. Tiredness sweeps my chest; my breaths and thoughts drag in slow motion. The outside is eerily quiet. I change my position in bed as I am unable to find that perfect spot. It is one of those nights, where darkness, the comfort of the bed, and my lassitude aren't enough to let me sleep. My mind chimes and lights up with thoughts of Ovya and Aadit. They are certainly not the happy family I thought they were. There's something awfully wrong. Could it be because Aadit cheated on her with his ex? But he did say that it was over the day he married Ovya. Even though she acted cool after her little skit, I still think that it wasn't an act and she believed every word of what she said. After all, there might be some truth to the claims made in those notes that keep appearing in my mailbox every now and then. More importantly, who could be sending them to me? Someone who knows Aadit?

And just like that, 2 a.m. morphs into 3 a.m. Time trickles by, and the only way I realize it is by observing the changing numerals on the wall clock. I try to empty my mind and push away the thoughts. Yet, the more I try, the more these ideas come flooding in. I close my eyes again and they burn from being open for too long. I open them again and rest them on the silhouettes left by the street light. My mind goes to the medicine cabinet where I still have some sleeping pills. I don't want them. I shouldn't take them after all the drinking I have done tonight.

I turn my attention to the last time I went out for dinner to a friend's house. It was in Mumbai and I was meeting Osheen. We had been drinking till the wee hours of the morning and I had felt happy, albeit momentarily, after a long time. This night, however, has been a touch spoiled. A vortex of swift, uncharted and incessant thoughts lead nowhere and spin me around like an untamed beast.

In the morning, I wake up late with an excruciating migraine. I prepare black coffee and take aspirin with it. As soon as I sit on the chair and open the newspaper, my phone reminds me that I have to call the cleaners today. I make the call and the company tells me that they will be in the house in an hour. I had gotten some deep cleaning done through them in the past and was mighty pleased with my previous experience. They arrive at my residence in less than an hour. I tell them to make the entire house spick and span and, in the process, try and find a hidden camera with a mic as well.

They start with the living room and dust and clean electrical appliances, windows, doors, side and centre tables, display shelves and walls. It is followed by dusting and vacuuming of mattresses, sofas, carpets and rugs. Next comes the cleaning of curtains and cobweb removal. Afterwards, they mop and clean the floor and other surfaces using chemicals and all kinds of equipment and finally, they tidy up and polish glass walls, artefacts and other objects. They carry out the same exercise with modifications throughout the house, making it lighter and brighter. It transforms into an area that welcomes peace of mind and serenity but it still has the camera, for despite all the brilliance of the cleaning team, they were unable to locate anything close to a snooping device.

∽

I had imagined my baby born out of Om, and my sheer need to love someone who was our own, as a constant confirmation of our never-ending love. The child would be protected in a mesh of emotions that would nurture, guide and care. In the process, Om and I would become the best version of ourselves, and let go of all our petty offences, slight transgressions and minor faults. All babies want at their age is to be loved infinitely. That's the only thing their intuition ever searches for. I saw babies in search of affection from their parents. I would never let go of the precious bundle of joy and do everything in my power to safeguard my baby.

Om was driving us to the doctor, neither of us was

saying anything to each other. All the reasons not to do this came flooding in. The soft panic grew in me like a tumour.

He looked at me and I knew he understood that I was distressed. He put his hand on mine. 'Trust me, it'll be okay.'

I too put my hand on his. 'You think so?'

'I know so.'

15

I dread teeth-cleaning sessions but I can't postpone it any further. Further delays would only lead to graver problems. The prodding, the rumbling and the occasional pain prevent disaster. Though I had gotten it done a few times in the past, the apprehension of going through it again almost makes me puke. But I call Dr Aashna and fix up an appointment for the evening.

I start scrolling on my phone and discern it is a bundle of memories. It holds all the pictures, the messages, the music, the games and the apps. These applications can narrate a story about who I am and the few relationships I share with different people. The messages I type and the voice notes I have recorded but never sent and the silences that are simply waiting to break—all of it has something to say about me. A phone probably remembers more than I ever can.

I feel like I am losing myself to a spiral of thoughts, the same ones going round and round and making me anxious. With every rotation, the thoughts become wilder with no destination in mind. It's pointless.

But today, I worry about Ovya. I have developed a liking for her. I look at the pictures we took the other day at dinner. She is smiling but it isn't the lovely, spontaneous smile I associate with her. The lips are curved into an awkward and disfigured shape but it does not reach the eyes or cheeks. It's a fake smile hiding all the pain and misery. I can see the reluctance to be moulded so easily. Is it possible that Aadit cheated on her after their marriage or does Ovya let her suspicion and cynicism take control of the relationship they share?

The woman I first met months ago was fragile yet blessed with a rare boldness. Her face always nestled in a genuine, enchanting smile that made her all the more beautiful and delicate. There was a grace to her movements that exuded candour, which made it easy for me to connect with her. Watching her and the husband through the window was a pleasant experience for it gave me the belief that two people of the opposite sex can live under the safe roof and be happy. The concept of a happy family might, after all, just be a fantasy. 'They lived happily after' doesn't exist. It didn't exist for mum and dad. It didn't happen for Om and myself. It doesn't take place for Osheen and now it is Ovya and Aadit. I know all of this could just be an exaggeration based on my past experiences with people, but I am certain things aren't as rosy as they may seem.

I leave for Dr Aashna's clinic and drive away all the brooding thoughts of the upcoming dental treatment. Upon reaching her clinic, I notice that it has gone under renovation. The overall structure of the clinic remains the same. Minor changes have been made to the furniture; the green walls have been turned off-white, the paintings on the wall have been replaced by to-do lists for healthy gum and teeth, and the *Vogue* and *Filmfare* magazines swapped by *Health* and *Experience Life*. In addition, the gruff face of the previous receptionist has been changed. There is now a brighter and more pleasant face. The new girl tells me that there is a patient inside and I'm slated to go in next.

After waiting for about fifteen minutes, I go in. Dr Aashna greets me with a smile as wide as the ocean.

'How are you doing, Ziva?'

I tremble as I look at the instruments, many of which will poke and nudge the insides of my mouth in the next few minutes. 'Somewhere between bad and worse.'

She says, 'The good news is that the procedure won't take as much time as you have spent dreading it. Now open your mouth.'

She uses a small mirror to check the gums and teeth for any underlying issues and concerns. This is how she always proceeds before getting on with the cleaning and flossing.

'Everything seems good. Let's go ahead, shall we?'

I nod as I want to get it over with quickly.

Using the mirror to guide her, she starts working with a scaler to remove the tartar and plaque that has formed around the gum line and between the teeth. As she does that, a scraping sound is produced making the process a tad uneasy. But I don't feel any pain.

She murmurs, 'You're doing good. Keep still.'

Next, she employs a high-powered electric brush to deep clean and get rid of any tartar left behind. This part is particularly scary because of the grinding noise it generates. The toothpaste she uses has a gritty consistency that gently scrubs the teeth and tastes like mint. After that, she expertly flosses. I am terrible at flossing and getting it done by her means she'd be able to remove any leftover plaque and toothpaste.

She says, 'You can rinse now.'

I do as asked to clear away any debris.

She announces, 'One final step. What is your favourite flavour?'

'Any flavour will do as long as you let me go.'

She places a minty foamy gel into a mouthpiece that fits over my teeth neatly. I keep it on for a minute or so before she removes it. Afterwards, she paints a fluoride varnish on to the teeth with a small brush. She then proceeds to write something on the prescription. 'It wasn't as bad as you thought, was it?'

I shake my head and whisper, 'No.'

'Ziva, you need to floss regularly. I have written a couple of medicines; they are mainly multivitamins. Take them for a week and we'll meet next in six months, but of course, if you have a problem, you know what to do.'

I step out of the treatment room.

Suddenly, I turn as white as snow. My eyes and mouth open, and I stutter for a moment at the sight right in front of me. My nostrils flare, the blood drains from my face and I stand still like a statue with an unblinking stare. Every part of my being is suspended and my brain is temporarily incapacitated, unable to comprehend and decide what to make of this strange encounter with the two people in front of me.

∽

One time, when I was young, and just like every time my father and mother were fighting, only this time, my mum didn't back down. Instead, she fought tooth and nail, answering every abuse being hurled at her with a brutality I hadn't seen before. She took dad by surprise as he rarely had any valid arguments up his sleeve. Next, he went on to do the only thing he was good at—he hit her. However, my mum wasn't taking any of it and his punch was met with the resistance of a storage box. He winced in pain and called her a bitch, and strangely, my mother broke into the faintest of smiles while my father was lying on the floor, writhing in agony and hurt. I could only observe the scene unfolding from a distance in stunned silence, unable to move my legs while my finger jumped rhythmically.

ço

That's how I feel now. I seem to have forgotten how to breathe, unable to speak and hide my shock. I am rendered paralysed as Aadit walks towards me with the same girl I had seen on Facebook, and the other day— the one who was with him in the car.

ço

Om and I waited outside. Dr Lavanya Parekh was one of the city's top gynaecologists, who also happened to be a friend of one of Om's colleagues from the office. Despite trying for more than ten months, we hadn't made any progress. So we wanted to go for a medical check-up and see if everything was fine. The floors of the waiting hall were granite black while the walls were spotless white. The air had a whiff of perfume with an undertone of bleach. The seats were plush and comfortable. The garish flowers and plants kept in every corner added to the character of the place. The centre table had a booklet containing dos and don'ts during pregnancy. The calendar hung on the wall had a picture of an infant, a being I couldn't wait to hold in my arms.

Om kept telling me that everything would be fine and if there was a problem, there would be a solution as well. My legs were shaking as I had a hundred different thoughts about what could be wrong—specifically with me.

The receptionist told us that the doctor was ready to see us. Dr Lavanya was likely in her fifties and she had a dominating presence. Her eyes fixed on us from behind gun metal spectacles. With a hawkish nose and lips that parted only when she spoke, she reminded me of a design teacher from college.

She began, 'How can I help you?'

Om looked at me. 'We've been trying to have a baby for almost a year now but have failed in all our attempts. I don't know what is wrong but we were hoping you could probably enlighten and guide us.'

She said, 'I get it. Don't worry. Stress can often be the reason why things don't work out. Just relax. I'm going to ask you both a few questions. Kindly answer them as honestly as you can.'

Accordingly, she asked her questions one by one—if we had any chronic illnesses, use of caffeine, alcohol, drugs and cigarettes, exposure to chemicals or radiation, sexual habits and how often we had sex, whether I had been pregnant before, frequency of periods over the last year, any changes in blood flow or blood clots, methods of birth control used and so on. She noted the responses.

'Since it appears that there are no pre-existing conditions, we'll have to get a few tests done for both of you in order to move ahead. I have jotted them down on the prescription and would suggest you get them done so that we can decide our future course of action. Sound good?'

On the way back in the car, Om again reiterated that everything would be fine. However, I was worried. Gloom-ridden thoughts looped around in my head until there was no room for anything else.

16

Aadit walks warily up to me, his feet are moving but he does not seem to cover any real distance. Though we are only a few feet apart, the time it takes for him to reach me seems like eternity. His friend too is a tad nervy, pressing at her jaw softly with her hands. I know that she is the one who's come to meet the doctor.

He wipes the sweat from his forehead, drops his gaze and bites his lips. 'Oh, Ziva! What a pleasant surprise. This is my friend Saachi.'

He glances at her. 'Saachi, meet Ziva, our wonderful neighbour.'

She shakes my hand. 'Hi, Ziva! Pleased to meet you. I'm sorry I'm unable to display adequate joy in meeting you. It's just that my wisdom tooth hurts like a knife in the gut.'

I say, 'Hi Saachi! The feeling's mutual. I have just gotten out of a cleaning session. It's odd that I am still feeling a tad uneasy.' I eye Aadit and then shift my gaze back to Saachi. 'The good news, however, is that you're in a clinic where they care about you.'

I stare at Aadit one more time. 'You two have a good evening. I'm going to head back.'

Saachi says, 'Of course. Meet soon.'

Back home, I think about what I witnessed at Dr Aashna's clinic. Aadit brought his ex to the dentist to get her wisdom tooth checked. This is the second time in less than ten days that I had seen the two together. It is clear to me that something is amiss and Ovya's suspicions and conjectures are well founded. Or was I thinking too far ahead of myself? 'Maybe, they are just friends...and he is just helping her out...because they are good friends.' People break up and share a cordial relationship all the time.

I hold a mirror in my hand. It is one of those small cheap kinds about the size of a ping-pong ball. It is easily available in any local store, thickly rimmed in pink plastic that ends up in the dustbin within days of its purchase. The shiny surface of the mirror is covered with a red lipstick smear and thick greasy fingerprints. Despite the marks, I can still see myself. It is as hard as pine knots to really know someone. Uncover what they hide behind their face and unearth all the hidden secrets. Aadit seems like a great guy, a devoted husband. Ovya is unpretentious, lovely and charming. The two make a wonderful pair and I love watching them together. However, being Ovya's friend, is it my moral responsibility to tell Ovya what I saw or should I just let it slide and forget about it? I can't decide. Frowning slightly, I glide my hands over the mirror, leaving a sweat trail on the pane of glass. Drinking wine would probably help me think better and make a decision. I pour some in a glass and return to the couch.

The doorbell rings. Surely, it can't be the watchman again at this hour. I open the door and Aadit is standing in front of me. He looks tired, as if he has aged since the evening. He needs sleep, a good night's sleep and then another one.

He comes in and slumps on the couch. I get him water.

He holds the glass in his hand and looks at it before taking a sip. 'You know, it is not what it looks like.'

He is barely audible. I wait for him to continue but he doesn't say anything.

I say, 'Sorry, I am not sure if I quite understand.'

He fumbles. 'There's nothing going on between Saachi and me. She needed help and I couldn't say no to her. She's just a friend, nothing more. I promise.'

I furrow my brows. 'Why are you telling me this?'

'Ovya is a sensitive soul. There's no one in this planet I love more than her. But she has these episodes where she starts doubting everything about our relationship. It's as if the dark clouds of doubt obscure her vision and make her unable to see complex things. It just takes a little incident for things to go wrong. The other day, when she asked about Saachi, she was serious and the laughter that followed I guess was just a way to shift attention to something else. I have known her for eight years now, she wasn't kidding.'

I tighten my lips. 'What do you want me to do?'

He took out his phone and showed me a picture of Saachi with a man that wasn't him. 'This is Saachi's late husband, Arin. She married him a month after Ovya and I tied the knot. He died of pancreatic cancer last year. Saachi has never been the same person since. She might seem like a bubble of joy but there's intolerable pain behind the grin. I help her every now and then, whenever I can.'

I say, 'I'm sorry. I could have never imagined.'

He shakes his head. 'Could you please do me a favour and not tell Ovya about what you saw at the dentist? I know she'll freak out and there will be an argument, then bickering and quarrels. I could totally avoid a clash with my wife. Please.'

I sit down next to him, place my hands on his, and say, 'I haven't met you since that amazing dinner at your house.'

In my bed, I have twin arguments running through my head. One pertains to Ovya and the other to Aadit. They run parallel to each other, but soon are twisting and getting entangled with each other. Aadit does seem sincere in his devotion to Ovya. However, she might have good reason to doubt him. No one knows better than me how easy it is to be swayed by half-truths and make bad decisions. It's like watching the news where they show only one side of the story, never revealing all the details about the incident. So Ovya does not trust Aadit, and his claims about his relationship with Saachi. However, why would she do that without any reason? She doesn't seem the kind to pick a fight for the sake of it.

I feel sorry for Saachi. She lost her husband due to cancer while I lost mine because he wouldn't look at things the way I did. However, Om, with his clarity and discerning capabilities, would have known how to find a way out of the situation. He'd know what to do.

I know I have promised that I can't really talk about it with Ovya and I won't. Yet, I can't stop thinking about it.

∞

The day I have been dreading since last month finally arrived. While Om couldn't wait to meet Dr Lavanya Parekh, I was on pins and needles. I had zero inclination to meet her again. She had analysed the test results and would inform us what the problem might be. Om was supportive and tried his best to calm me down by suggesting that if there were any problems, there would be plenty of solutions as well. I wanted to believe him but something within kept shouting that it isn't as simple as he made it out to be.

Our appointment was scheduled for 7 p.m. and as soon as the clock struck, we were called in. We handed all the test results to her.

She studied them carefully and made notes on the prescription, not saying anything and building up unnecessary suspense. At last, she said, 'Om, your reports are fine. The sperm analysis has no problem whatsoever and the other reports too are good.'

Om squeezed my hand. 'What about my wife?'

She leaned back on the chair. 'We have a problem there.'

My worst fears were being confirmed as I waited for her to continue.

'In Ziva, I am afraid ovulation isn't taking place. While there are extremely targeted solutions, you'd have to make a lot of lifestyle changes such as eating healthy, exercising and abstaining from alcohol and smoking. My assistant will give you a chart of the things you should do and shouldn't do to turn things around and at the same time, we can begin treatment as well. I know this is hard to hear, but the good news is there are ways we can change this.'

On the way back, I couldn't stop crying. The walls that had been holding me up all this while had collapsed, piece by piece. My lips trembled and my shoulders heaved with the magnitude of what Dr Lavanya had said. *Ovulation isn't taking place.* My face was covered in tears and my hands clenched into shaking fists as Om kept on saying that we'd come out of it. That was the moment when we knew we wouldn't.

Heavy sobs left my throat and I buried my face in my knees, as though hiding would take me away from this affliction.

17

I dial Osheen's number. She picks up. 'Hello, my love. Finally, you have decided to call me after all this time and after so many missed calls.'

I stir the sugar in the coffee. 'You called me twice. Since when is twice cited as many times? Having said that, I have been busy and I'm sorry.'

'Busy snooping on your neighbours?'

I grit my teeth. 'Much to your joy, I have been trying to reduce that. No, I had gone to dinner at their house and after that, I went to the dentist for my customary cleaning session.'

'How was dinner?'

'It was wonderful. Had a great time indulging in everything Ovya had prepared. She is a wonderful cook. Along with that, we asked each other a bunch of questions and learned quite a bit about each other.'

She says, 'Anything you want to share that might interest me?'

I nod quickly, as if she is there sitting in front of me. 'I am stuck in this conundrum and can't decide what to do.'

Her voice becomes serious. 'What is it, Ziva?'

'Ovya suspects that Aadit might be cheating on her with his ex, Saachi. Hell, I have seen Saachi with him on a couple of occasions. Once he gave her a lift and the next time at the dentist when I had gone for my cleaning.'

'Did you see anything that might confirm Ovya's suspicions?'

'No, not really. Aadit came to my house yesterday and he told me that Ovya has this habit of doubting him every now and then. There are these days when she doesn't believe him. He also told me about Saachi and how her husband passed away due to cancer and that he's only helping her.'

'What do you think?' she says.

'I don't know. I don't think Ovya is cynical and neither do I believe that Aadit is lying.'

'It's simple. You do nothing. Let the husband and wife sort their personal matters. You focus on you. Any luck with any opportunity?'

It isn't as simple as Osheen makes it out to be. Being troubled is nothing new to me, but in the past, all the consequences were confined to myself. This time, however, it affects people I care about. I wander outside with my coffee, lost and muddled. The sight of the budding flowers and cultivated garden doesn't pacify me. Anxious and fidgety, I bite my nails—a habit I have acquired from my mum. She used to start biting her nails as soon as the clock struck 8 p.m. because my father would start his drinking then and more often than not, things went out of control thereafter.

Ovya and I have been meeting each other every day. In the beginning, the conversations were primarily around each other's likes and dislikes. However, of late our exchanges have moved to discussing Aadit, her wedding and their ongoing issues.

I observe a butterfly flap its tiny wings on a dahlia. I go close to the flower and snap my fingers and the butterfly rushes past, only to return a few seconds later. I snap my fingers again and it leaves in a hurry. But it is adamant. It returns and perches on the same dahlia again. Aren't humans similar? We return to the same place and people over and over again. Is this what Ovya and Aadit were doing? Aadit was bound to Saachi because she needed his help while Ovya was going back to her tendency of being suspicious. Both of them have their reasons. It's just how they were.

I step outside and check the mailbox. There it is. Another note. I am not surprised. I feel almost relieved at having received another one. I hold the envelope with the same dimensions, the same white colour and the same thickness, containing another cryptic statement to vex me one more time.

Like always, I cut it open with a pair of scissors and spread the note on the table. It reads:

AADIT IS A GREAT ACTOR, ISN'T HE? DON'T LET HIS ACT OF INNOCENCE FOOL YOU.

I dart into my bedroom and bring all the previous notes that had been sent, open them and place them next to each other. I hover over the notes, shudder at the eerie similarity before drawing back. All the notes are in Gotham font, size 12, double spaced. The content was placed exactly in the middle in each one of them. Amidst all that was written on every note, I somehow find this symmetry too important to ignore. The note is being sent by someone who is particular about maintaining consistency and careful about never divulging any extra details. He or she wants me to find out the truth for myself. I must navigate through these clues I am being handed and arrive at a conclusion regarding their veracity. They have left no space for ambiguity. But isn't truth based on perspective? When two perspectives are separated, one person's truth becomes another person's lie. Om always said that whenever we would get into a fierce fight. His zen-like poise and presence overpowered my rowdy and unruly conduct every time. *Oh God, I hate him but I still miss him.*

The cup falls from my hand, it shatters as it hits the ground, creating a small pool of coffee. The breaking doesn't upset or irritate me, but it evokes an emotion of comfort. A tiny shard pierces the sole of my right foot but I don't wince in pain. It is as if I am passing through a tunnel that is dark and yet I possess sight. The darkness has the clarity of a moonlit night. My wound heals in an instant, bringing lucidity to my mind.

At last, I know what I need to do.

The doorbell rings. I hastily keep the envelopes and the notes inside. The doorbell rings a second and third time. I hurry and open the door. It is Ovya.

I have always loved watching rains and storms, but here is Ovya, crying. Her sobs have the force of a gale. She doesn't sob quietly; instead, every modicum of her being wails in unison, robbing my house of its silence. Her crying only stops when she needs to draw a breath. I let her collapse into my chest and caress her hair in a repetitive motion. Her sobs remind me of the pain I endured when Om left me. When her irrepressible bawls turn into a whimper, I feel the grief pouring from her eyes.

I can't bear to listen to her crying any longer.

I decided not to go to the office.

Om asked, 'Are you all right, love?'

I nodded. 'Just feeling a tad weak. You go on, I'll see you in the evening.'

He kissed me on the head. 'I'll come back early.'

Throughout the day, I kept drinking wine and vodka in alternation, and when Om returned home, I was utterly, hopelessly inebriated. I staggered my way back to the chair, struggling to keep my balance. My legs didn't listen to my brain and didn't work as I wanted them to. The rosiness of my cheeks and eyes gave away how much I had drunk. Om never asked and neither did he get angry.

He simply said, 'You can't do this. You can't drink. Dr Lavanya asked you to abstain from alcohol.' He threw his bag on the couch and did not stop shaking his head.

I tried to get up but slumped onto the floor, hitting my head on the table.

I slurred, 'I know. I know. Today is the last time I touch alcohol until we bring our baby into the world. I promise.'

Om helped me get back on to the chair. 'Okay. Did you have anything to eat?'

When I shook my head, he brought a few snacks from the kitchen and a glass. We drank in silence, just like how we used to before we got married. It was serene, almost surreal. Back in the day, we hoped the solution rested at the bottom of the glass and then, at the bottom of the bottle and another bottle—until we ran out of booze.

We didn't speak much, only exchanging a few words every now and then. Most of the words were slurred and meaningless.

18

I fetch water for Ovya. 'Here, drink some.' She takes a sip, crying. It seems as if her being is being shredded from the inside.

'Look at me. Look at me, Ovya. What happened? Please tell me.'

She glances at me and shakes her head violently. I don't press her but wait for her to regain her composure. It is a while before she tries to open her mouth, but when she does nothing comes out. She struggles for breath. She breathes thinly every time she starts to say something. She takes another sip of water.

She shakes her head again. 'How could he? How could he do this to me?'

I gaze at her, my eyes tight and worried. 'Who? Aadit?'

She nods.

'What did he do, Ovya?'

She hands me an envelope and gestures for me to open it. It contains pictures. One look at it and I know where this is headed. All the conundrum and the indecisions I have had leave in a quick and compelling stroke. I no longer need to spend hours brooding over things. Outstretched in front of me are pictures of Aadit and Saachi from Dr Aashna's dental clinic. It seems impossible that our day-to-day decisions have a lasting impact on how our lives turn out to be. If Ovya lets this go and thinks this is just her husband helping out an old friend, the damage might be contained. However, if she confronts Aadit and accuses him, their marriage could be destroyed.

At present, she sits opposite me, confined to the couch. She is broken, sad and miserable. She is waiting for me to respond.

'I was present too,' I say.

She squints and leans forward. 'What do you mean you were present?'

'I mean I had visited Dr Aashna for my cleaning session the same day. I had seen Aadit and Saachi. In fact, he introduced me to Saachi. Her wisdom tooth hurt badly. He had just brought her there.'

'I'm appalled that you knew but you chose not to tell me anything about it.'

'There was nothing to tell, Ovya. He was just helping her. There's nothing going on between them.'

Ovya shoots back. 'How can you be so sure?'

'I know a good soul when I see one. Just trust me, will you? Aadit is a wonderful husband; he loves you a lot and the two of you make a great pair. It'd be a shame if blots appear in your relationship based on something absurd and imaginary.'

'You have met him once. I have known him for eight years.'

'That is precisely why you need to have a conversation with him and not a confrontation.' She doesn't say anything. I touch her hand and squeeze it gently. 'I can see it in your eyes that you love him as much, and in your core, you do believe he is not a cheat. Just let your instincts guide you.'

'Okay. Okay. I will speak to him and not fight. But

you know, the other day, he also gave her a lift.'

I think about what Ovya said after she left. She too had followed Aadit one day and found him giving a lift to Saachi. Could that be the same day I saw or another day? What if Aadit gives her a lift every now and then... or perhaps every day? I cannot be sure. Is it possible what Ovya is implying might be true after all? My sagacity leaves me as if I am stuck underwater, grappling for air. Everything is slow and wobbly as I try to put things in perspective. But my mind is blank. I bring my diary and a pen, and put down the events in chronological order. The exercise doesn't help. I wonder why I didn't tell Ovya that Aadit had visited me the day I had gone to the dentist and asked me not to tell her about it. Call it intuition or experience of being let down by my husband.

I still believe Aadit is sincere in his love for Ovya.

There is one important question, however, that needs answering. I glance at my reflection in the glass windows, trying to look beyond the backyard. I mutter. '*Who could it be?*' I blink and refocus again. 'Who sent those pictures from the clinic to Ovya? Is it possible the same person has been sending notes to me as well? Only if he or she would have attached a piece of paper along with a note in Gotham. I think harder again. Who is the one person who would benefit from turning the marriage into a shamble? Saachi...'

I search for her on Facebook but can't find her. There are too many profiles with the same name and not knowing the last name makes it hard. I try Instagram. The number of people with the name in the handle is fewer and I spend close to fifteen minutes going through each profile until I finally find her. The profile is private but I send her a follow request with a message, *'Hey, Saachi, Ziva here. We met at Dr Aashna's clinic. I know it might sound odd but I'd love to meet you and talk to you. Let me know, will you? Take care!'*

I don't have to wait as Saachi accepts my request in a minute or so. She replies back. *'Hey Ziva! Yes, of course. Great to hear from you. How does tomorrow evening sound? We can meet for coffee.'*

Her response sets off an explosion in my brain, only this time, it is of the good kind. That she got back to me in a flash makes me nervous and excited about the prospect of meeting her in person and asking her if she is the one behind the notes and the pictures.

I say, *'Tomorrow evening at six at The Hideout.'*

∽

It could have been wine in the glass but it wasn't. It was just plain water. It had been close to a month since I had last had alcohol. I kept telling myself that the sacrifice was totally worth it. My next test was scheduled in a couple of days. I hoped that the treatment plan and the lifestyle change would turn the tide in our favour. Om really wanted this baby and so did I. Having the desire was the easy part, making it happen was difficult.

I stepped out on the empty street that hadn't heard the echo of my drunk laughter for a while. The street lamps shone obstinately in the night. The red brickwork of the walls brought a memory from the past. One day, Om and I had been crazy drunk and were returning from a friend's house. He struggled to walk those few steps to reach the front door of the house. He slipped, smashing his head on the rugged wall. Luckily, the blow didn't hurt him much, but he couldn't stop laughing.

He laughed and I laughed with him for a long time and we didn't step inside for a while.

As I continued my excursion, my eyes fell on the signage: *Drinking alcohol before pregnancy can cause pregnancy.*

I was almost tempted to step inside but I couldn't cheat Om. I couldn't let him down. I stood there, looked at the sign, smiled and started to head back. I saw Om coming back from the opposite side. I waited for him to come near me.

He said, 'I have got two movie tickets.' He showed them to me. 'Apparently, it's just the kind of movie you like watching. The show starts in less than an hour. Shall we?'

I whispered, 'Yes.'

19

I wake up from my afternoon nap in a state of sardonic glee. I don't feel refreshed at all. After a flurry of thoughts, I think of Ovya with the sanguineness that today I will be able to unearth the intentions behind those pictures and notes. A sudden giddiness runs through my veins as I want to run to Ovya and tell her what is going to happen. But I can't, because Saachi might not be the guilty party yet. I am unable to sit down, drink wine or watch anything on Netflix. My mind is like a butterfly—immune to any distraction, fluttering its wings rather wildly.

However, at the same time, my mind also argues against doing this. The apprehension rises from the fear that Saachi might, after all, deny all my allegations and might tell Aadit about it, which could then result in a catastrophe. I put the kettle on for the fourth time since my siesta. The coffee is strong enough, yet I add another tablespoon of coffee powder and swirl the spoon. I take another quick glance at the clock; still a couple of hours to go. It seems as if time is slowing down. My stomach knots as I tremble slightly at the thought of another cup of coffee in the evening.

My phone rings. It is Osheen calling, but I don't answer. She calls me a second time. Every time I miss her call, she gets worried for some reason. I don't pick up and send her a message instead. '*Hey! I am good. How are you? Let me call you later.*'

I tell myself that everything hinges on how Saachi reacts. It's surprising that she has agreed to meet so readily, as if she was looking forward to meeting me. Perhaps, she too has something to share. I scan her Instagram profile trying to figure out through her pictures and captions what kind of a person she is. Deep quotes, serene scenery, pictures with a pup and the odd solo photo of her makes it apparent that she is lonely and probably feels betrayed.

I keep scrolling, and with every picture I see there is a growing concern in my eyes. I am unable to find any photos of her with Aadit or her ex-husband. Like me, she too probably likes to keep her grief private. I have a sudden urge to place my hands lightly on her shoulders and speak with a soft voice so that my words calm and comfort her. I want to tell her that her ordeal will be over soon. Maybe I will in the evening. I want to say the same to Ovya. She's a lovely girl who deserves nothing but happiness. It's time that she too experiences unhindered joy.

I arrive at The Hideout café right on time and look for a corner seat. I anticipate that the conversation might heat up, so it's better to sit in a spot that is inconspicuous and doesn't draw attention. My mind is like the ocean, waiting for the incoming storm—calm at the beginning, with a few ripples slowly transforming into something much more ominous. My eyes are set on the front door and my arms rest on the wooden table. Waiting for Saachi gives me some time, and I find myself swimming in a sea of thoughts about Om. I give in to the redundant yet recurring thoughts, I escape. I remind myself that there are common threads that bind one person to another and common wounds that separate them. My feet run cold and my numb fingers curl over the glass as I take a sip of the icy water.

There comes Saachi. She is dressed in a white floral dress, smiling brightly, dainty dimples on both cheeks. I wonder what has made her smile. Her eyes are black as coal and are bubbling with emotion. Her pencil-thin eyebrows rise slightly as her gaze falls upon me. Her ears and her elegant nose accentuate the innocence of her face. Her thin form makes her seem tall, and she embraces me strongly.

Saachi looks around and sits opposite me. 'This is a nice place for a weary afternoon.'

'Indeed! I too am coming here for the first time. Heard good things about the place.'

She opens her mouth and closes it instantly. 'Whosoever has recommended you has great taste.'

I smile. 'What do you want to order?'

She goes through the menu. 'Did he or she give any recommendations as well?'

I look at her. 'The person said coffee and croissants are a safe bet.'

She puts the menu away. 'I'll have that. And you?'

'I'll have coffee and a walnut brownie.'

She places the order for both of us. 'I want to thank you for inviting me over for coffee.'

I place my hand on hers. 'No, I want to thank you for coming. I had serious doubts that you'd recognize me or respond to my message.'

'Of course, I would. Who wouldn't, considering we

stared at each other the way they do in slow motion in the movies?'

I grin. 'I'm sorry. I was just so shocked to see Aadit there.'

She looks away and then looks down. 'Don't be silly. I understand you were as shocked as a bird that landed on a live wire upon seeing Aadit with me and not Ovya.'

The café is hickory brown in colour with shiny interiors and cute posters and artworks adorning the walls. Jazz pours out from the speakers and the smell of freshly baked bread fills the air. Bright lights are encased in wooden cages and they complement the unsophisticated nature of the place. I take in a deep breath, sucking in the air that carries a hint of coffee.

My lips tighten. 'That is partly true, but I was rather shocked to see Aadit there at the dentist.'

She smiles. 'I know Ovya isn't exactly fond of me. She made it clear to me the last time the three of us had dinner. I get that. Who wouldn't be wary about their husband meeting his ex?'

ॐ

My fear was buzzing like flies in the summer heat. The day that I had been dreading was here. It had been thirty days since we first met Dr Lavanya Parekh, and today we would meet her again. She would check our progress, analyse the new reports and advise us accordingly. Being scared of doctors had become normal for me, almost inescapable. My mind crumbled at the mention of the word 'doctor'.

Our appointment was at 7 p.m. and Om made sure

that we were at the clinic at 6.45 p.m. The air smelt of disinfectant and I had a hard time breathing. It felt as if someone was choking me. My heart was racing; cold sweat glistened on my forehead and the hair at the nape of my neck bristled. My body trembled a wee bit. All I wanted to do right now was curl up into a ball and skip this evening altogether.

I shifted my gaze towards Om who watched me with assured eyes as if communicating that there was nothing to worry about. All I could see was Om and his steadfast gaze, and everything else fell away. All the fears of what the doctor was going to say dissolved into oblivion. I no longer imagined what the report was going to quote. The choked cry for help that had somehow forced its way up my throat turned into a single sob containing the fondness I felt for him.

I put my hand on his and repeated to myself in silence, 'Fear is always vanquished when we have woken to the truth.'

The receptionist called our names and we went inside, hand in hand.

Dr Lavanya Parekh acknowledged our presence with a shake of the head. She studied the reports for a few minutes before turning her attention to us. 'So, Mr and Mrs Wadhwa, the good news is Ziva's reports have shown some improvement. However, since it's only been thirty days, we'll have to continue doing the things we have done for another forty to forty-five days before we see any considerable change. We need to follow the same protocol. No drinking, no smoking, exercise, eight hours of sleep and proper diet and nutrition, along with the treatment and supplements.'

Her statement brought the relief I needed to be free of my ever-present stress. I pinched Om slightly to catch his attention and when he looked at me, I broke into a wide-eyed smile.

20

I wait for her to complete her thought.

Saachi takes a bite of the croissant and a sip of the coffee. 'This is exquisite—right from the heavens. You know, Ovya doubts Aadit a little too much. At times, she can get cynical, almost derisive, and when that happens, she suspects everything.'

I perk up my ears and carefully listen to what she is saying. I am keeping a close watch on her. I am looking out for involuntary body movements—is she covering her mouth with her hand, touching her nose, rubbing her eyes, grabbing her ear, or putting fingers in her mouth? None of these cues come, but I still have a hard time trusting her. Aadit said the same thing about Ovya. Could they be in on this together? Her face has a gentle expression, one of quiet confidence. Maybe she has been playing this game for too long and isn't accustomed to losing. Her words are almost an exact copy of Aadit's. It seems as if they rehearsed everything. I can imagine them going to an ice-cream parlour or a bar, going over each other's dialogues—the way actors do—and perfecting every line, sequence and expression. I hadn't asked Aadit about his little trip with Saachi to the dentist and neither had I mentioned Ovya in front of Saachi, and yet she is giving an explanation I never asked for. I can't trust them. The greater the similarity in their story and the narration, the greater are the lies underneath. Every perspective is different and has its own flaws and quirks, and if these perspectives are polished to similitude right before meeting me, then credence is thrown right out of the window.

Saachi calls the waiter and orders another coffee each for us. She leans forward and says, 'Do you trust me?'

I search for the right words, open my mouth, but close it instantly. 'Under normal circumstances, I would have said that I trust you as much as I'd trust a hyena and walk away. But I am ready to keep an open mind if you can show me some proof.'

Saachi opens her purse and takes out a couple of envelopes. 'Take a look at this.'

She spread both pieces of paper and gestures for me to take a look. I feel like I am being dragged into a territory I don't want to venture into. My eyes run around the café and I notice people sipping their coffees, intent on their own conversations. I hear the occasional laugh and whine.

The first note says:

Hey Saachi!

I just learned about your husband passing away due to cancer and I am truly sorry about it. Do let me know if I could help you in any way, but please stay away from Aadit. I know this must be a hard time for you and you must think I'm a bitch, but this doesn't give you a free pass to spend time with my husband.

Hope you understand. You take care!

The second note is:

Hey Saachi!

How are you doing?

I know my last letter was unkind, probably presumptuous as well. I just have a hard time imagining you and Aadit being just friends and confidants and nothing more. Call me a bitch if you wish, but based on my past experience I can say no two people who have dated seriously in the past and had a falling out can ever be just friends. The passions just happen to reignite, and how do we avoid that? By staying away! I know you're not the brightest girl around.

Now, I am aware Aadit is concerned and cares about you. But you have no right to take advantage of the situation and trouble him in any manner. Like I said in my previous letter, you need anything, I'm here for you, but keep my husband out of your speed dial list.

Your primary objective is to cause a strain in our relationship with your lingering presence, but that won't happen. No matter how hard you try, I can't have you destroy our marriage. However, of course, the easy thing for you to do is to keep away so that you are safe.

You take care and I hope I don't have to write any more of such letters to you.

I read both the notes one more time. 'How can you be sure that it is Ovya who wrote these notes? I don't see any signature here.'

She takes the notes back. 'Do you really need to see her signature in order to know that she wrote this?'

I nod. 'Yes. For all I know, you could have typed this and got a printout.'

She flips the envelope and shows the address of the sender along with the stamps. 'See, it is clearly written, it was sent by Ovya from her residence in Bangalore and the second one is sent from her new residence in Delhi.'

I am startled. I feel like a deer in the woods who looks up at the slightest crunching of leaves. My brain is reeling at the incredulity of it. My shoulders hunch in a vain effort to disappear. The place turns chillingly quiet, as if every table has become still. I rub my forehead. I can't think. I don't know what to make of all this. All of a sudden, I remember the envelopes and notes I have brought along.

I keep them on the table. 'I'll cut to the chase and ask you directly. Did you write these and send them to me?'

She looks at the notes closely for a minute. 'I don't need to even glance at these and you could stake your head on it: I did not send you any notes. I don't even know your address.'

'Now that's a stretch. I am certain Aadit must have filled you in.'

'Aadit told me on the day we met that Ovya is your friend and he would clear the air about us being together so that you don't tell anything to his wife. Are you satisfied now?'

'As a matter of fact, I am not. Do you think we could meet again?'

'You can be as sure as life and death.'

౩

That night, after a long time, I curled my fingers around the hair on Om's chest. At last, I could breathe with peace after quick, uneasy breaths for over a month. I drew in a large drag of air and it seemed as if the edge faded away. All the tension had been leached out the moment Dr Lavanya Parekh said that my condition was improving. Even if it was slow, I had taken a step in the right direction. I felt as if something new awaited me and I was excited about it.

Happiness poured through every fibre of my being, just like the morning rays of the sun on a cold winter morning. My perpetual frown had turned into a radiant smile. I had forgotten to smile for a while but now everything would fall into place. I'd follow the advice of Dr Lavanya, and Om was by my side. *Perhaps, this temporary break from alcohol would make me leave it altogether and boy, wouldn't that be an achievement!*

I opened the window to watch the night sky. I loved watching the distant stars and the moon blending together to paint the sky as if it were a white shiny illustration.

Om left his book on the side table and joined me. He stood beside me. 'Are you relieved?'

I looked at him and chucked. 'What do you think, babe?'

He put his arm around my shoulders. 'Okay. Good! I have been honouring our underwritten rule of watching all the shows together and haven't yet seen the new season of *Better Call Saul.* Do you think we can start watching it from today or is it too much to ask?'

I shook my head and broke into a peal of laughter. 'Only if we watch it in the bedroom.'

He jumped in the air. 'Whatever you say, ma'am.'

Om got some popcorn and a jar full of orange juice. He placed them on the tray and leapt into our bed. The first episode started streaming and Om's eyes were fixed on the screen. I took some popcorn and started watching the show. Every now and then, I'd steal a glance at Om and his focus was on the screen. At last, I put my head on his shoulder and found that I fell into a deep sleep.

21

I can't stop thinking about the possibility that Ovya may not be the victim but the miscreant. I have been thinking about this on the way back, and even now, when I'm at home. If I were to assume and believe that those hostile letters were in fact sent by Ovya, why would she also send me those damning notes about Aadit? What purpose would that serve? Where do *I* fit into the narrative?

I know, from experience, that damaged people often obliviously seek more damage, addicted to being the casualty that they are. Their need for sustained attention often leads them to do unthinkable things and their behaviours ensure they get what they want. The cost doesn't matter. Years of love and trust that are put into a relationship go down the drain as it becomes a game of chess and a form of war. The greater the number of fatalities, the better it is. These broken people, once victims themselves, leave no stone unturned to hurt the people they love and then to play the victim.

All they ever needed was unconditional and devoted love from that one person. But that was snatched away.

Om always said, 'There's very little that you can see with the eyes. Your heart can see a lot more.' His logic was that the eyes can only see the event as it happens, but it can hardly ever comprehend the underlying reason, the intention and the repressed, turbulent emotions that drive the act. The heart, however, paves the way for a deeper understanding and a vision to see the concealed pain, the sadness that exists within waiting for an outlet to escape. I always believed, and still do, that the logic is flawed, for we can't hide what's happening in the heart, even if we are wearing a veil.

For the past four months, the white vinyl window in the living room has been the only way for me to see what takes place inside my neighbour's house. In the morning, through this window, the sun streams in and illuminates the otherwise dark space. The rays warm the couch and get me going. In the night, filtered moonlight adds to the misty setting, making the room drabber. It has been a while since I observed them through this aperture.

I check the watch. It's almost 9 p.m. and time for their customary movie on Netflix with some popcorn in a box. I get my binoculars, kneel down and position myself behind the curtains like always. I run my hands on the rim of the wine glass and take a sip. My insides squirm as if I'm about to witness a crime. I wonder if Ovya had, in fact, confronted Aadit about the pictures and if she had already, how had Aadit responded? If she hadn't, as per my advice, how much longer could she go on without bringing the topic up? I know it is a difficult choice, but I also believe that it's in Ovya's best interest to not make a mountain of a molehill. Perhaps, Aadit was just there helping his old friend and nothing else. Maybe, he is just too kind to say no to Saachi. The flip side, however, is that Ovya has been suspicious of Saachi's intentions, and probably with good reason, and if she doesn't want him to meet Saachi, he shouldn't. He should never meet her in secret. That just makes the whole situation and their friendship more dubious.

Out come the husband and wife dressed in identical blue-and-white striped nightsuits. They are engrossed in their chatter and are laughing most of the time. Ovya grabs the remote while Aadit sulks in disappointment. He goes to the kitchen to bring popcorn and she browses to select a movie. It is a few minutes before Aadit emerges from the kitchen and settles on the couch next to her. She takes a handful of the snack and plays the movie. I can't make out what movie it is, but by the disappointed look on Aadit's face, it's something that he doesn't want to see or has seen before.

It seems as if their love is like tranquil waters upon which there are occasional ripples. It is whole and complete, even with their missing pieces. He places his hand on hers. What is scarred would become soft once more. Ovya's open wounds could be healed by his gentle presence. Even though neither of them speak much, it seems that they are not separate but together. It makes me beam from inside.

I finish the last drop of wine and refill my glass.

Next, what I see takes me by surprise. Ovya suddenly jerks her hand away and leaps up from the couch. The popcorn falls and bounces on the floor before coming to a state of rest. Ovya smashes the remote on the floor. The two pencil batteries come out and fly in opposite directions. I wonder what instigated such a hostile reaction from Ovya, but it isn't hard to guess. It has something to do with Saachi. Perhaps, Ovya couldn't resist and brought up the topic, which resulted in such an outburst. Aadit too springs up from the couch and prevents her from throwing and breaking any more stuff.

In her rage, Ovya becomes blind to the explanations

that are being handed out by Aadit. His delicate touch, it seems, now feels like a burn as she once again pushes him away. Aadit joins his hands together in a pleading move and asks her to sit down, probably to give him a chance to explain, but she is in no mood to listen tonight. She raises her voice in a fit of rage and pushes him away. She is crying. I can imagine her pain, as though she is standing in front of me as tears roll down her cheeks. She doesn't cry silently, but the sound of her wails is muffled by the movie that's still running in the background. Aadit gives her a smile as he struggles to calm her down. His icy temper and his ability to dampen situations by putting out the flames of emotions doesn't seem to be working today. He is likely to have become accustomed to her fiery temper and ways of handling it, but today isn't like the other days. Ovya keeps on screaming and sobbing at the same time, her body shifting due to convulsions while he stands there with a helpless look on his face.

∽

Om had bought a few parenting books from the local bookstore and put them in the library. I was a little perturbed by this. I thought it was a little premature to be buying books like these when I was still undergoing treatment and we didn't even know if I would become pregnant. It seemed to put undue pressure on me, as if I was expected to hold a baby in me at that moment.

My hands shook and my face flushed. I pointed at the new additions to the library. 'What is this? Don't you think it's a little early to buy all this?'

He was engrossed in his mobile screen and gestured

for me to wait. Then he said, 'What? Of course not, it's high time we start preparing.'

I shook my head and snatched the mobile from his hand. 'Really? I'm still under treatment and we don't know what will happen.'

He got up and put his hand on mine. 'Everything will be fine. Now can I please have my cell back?'

I said, 'What if something goes wrong?'

'Nothing will go wrong.'

'What if it does?'

He raised his eyebrows. 'Then we'll find a way to deal with it. Together.'

He took his mobile back from me gently and gave me a look I was used to getting whenever I said something that didn't make sense to him. Om always had a way of understanding my emotional barriers and this gave me the strength to face my fears.

Two weeks remained before we had that final test to determine how effective the treatment plan and lifestyle changes had been. I had done all the hard work until now, and I hoped that the results would be in our favour.

22

I put the glass away and strain my eyes on my neighbour's house and the scene unfolding in front of me. I long for a magic wand so that I could dissipate the searing tension between Ovya and Aadit. I lay my head on the hard surface of the floor, stretch my legs; puffs of warm breaths escape my lips. The floor is stinging cold and my hands tremble slightly along the lined edges of the tiles. The air feels punctuated by her jarred screeching and his deafening silences. Even though I can't hear what is being said, I can still feel the anguish and grief that pulls Ovya down.

The vibrancy of their life, the couple whom I loved to watch and admire from this very window, are being reduced to a black-and-white show. There's nothing that I can do to change that and it makes me feel weak and powerless. Their altercation makes me mute and confused. I can't wait for this night to be over.

With the sunshine and the melodies of the birds, everything will return to normal.

Ovya keeps shouting while Aadit waits for her to regain her composure. I am guessing he wishes to share his side of the story, but she is in no mood to pay any heed to what he has to say. By not sharing the truth earlier, he must have lost her trust. Aadit was supposed to stand by her side, supposed to share every little thing, detail and incident. But he couldn't trust her to understand the most fragile information. For some odd reason, he thought that keeping things from her would solve the issue, but all it could do was delay the solution. The love he has for Ovya is genuine. I have seen that in his eyes. However, the fear of losing her outwrestled that. This fear of his transformed into an enormous pain for her. That's how things go, an intense love almost always results in a massive heartbreak.

Finally, she sits down on the couch and Aadit sits near her feet. He keeps his head on her lap and I breathe a sigh of relief. Things seem to be getting under control. However, she never puts her hand on his hair to caress it. Instead, she keeps sitting motionless, steady as a rock, for a few minutes before she mutters something.

Aadit raises his eyes, as if asking if she really meant what she just said. Aadit shakes his head and tries to put his hand on her shoulder, but she doesn't let him. She pulls away, throws herself back on the couch and doesn't let him touch her. She doesn't look at him as an enemy, but it seems far worse; she stares at him as if he is a stranger.

All emotions and cognitions are pushed away, making space for a heavy sadness. The love, the light and the laughter are now replaced with a throbbing emptiness. Ovya was always full of affection and honesty, more than what Aadit could ever reciprocate. She was soft, kind and with rare energy, but tonight, it is depleted. Aadit stands up, looks at her with wonder, at what is unravelling in front of him. But he doesn't dare speak up. He looks at her one more time, expectation in his eyes, but she keeps her eyes fixed on the ground.

It takes an eternity for Aadit to make sense of what

she is asking and when he does, he takes a step towards the front door. He stops and watches the house, as if taking the visuals with him one final time. He looks at the television, and the movie continues to run in the background, before his gaze returns to his wife. He stretches his arm in an effort to touch her but she is too far away, even though just one stride separates him from her. He pauses, waits for her to look at him, but she doesn't, and then, in a quick, hurried motion, he leaves the house.

When he steps out, he reaches into his pocket and takes out a packet of cigarettes. He holds it in his hand for a moment, possibly thinking about what he's going to do. He lights it and sits on the porch outside, staring as if admiring the house and remembering all the times he has spent with Ovya. He takes a long drag and lets the chemical pervade his insides. The creeping stench and the sickly, purple smoke emanating from the toxic stick fills my vision. Aadit's defeated and crushed presence becomes obscure.

The smoke is all I can witness.

He plays with another cigarette in his hand before lighting it up. The long drags don't stop, and I think, neither do his thoughts. He might be considering ways to fix the situation. I wish I could do something to mitigate Ovya's anger. There has to be a way for Aadit to amend his mistakes. Perhaps all their relationship needs is some time off, and that will be enough to bring things back to how they were before.

He takes out another cigarette, but then puts it back inside.

Silence fills their house like poison. Ovya remains

stationary, almost motionless on the couch, not looking at anything in particular. Aadit is perched on the porch, bouncing the lighter between his hands. The distance between them is a gaping void that needs to be filled with gestures, words, songs and explanations. Their house that once reverberated with music is now a cruel representation of vapid muteness. Aadit gets up, his feet crunching the dry leaves and twigs as he gets into his car. He looks at the house one final time, smashes his hands on the steering wheel before driving away.

I know if this distrust isn't addressed and tackled soon, it will cling to them like a leech and choke the life out of their marriage. But today isn't that day. Today is all about letting the doubts and qualms, like the venom of a rattlesnake, seep into every inch of their being and paralyse them from both speech and movement.

Let that lull hang in the air like the suspended moment before glass shatters on the ground.

I think about reaching out to Ovya. She could use some company and wine. I go towards my bar cabinet, fetch a new bottle of red and place it on the counter. The thud is suddenly accompanied by a piercing scream. My eyes widen and my pulse quickens as I scamper towards my window. I grab my binoculars but I don't see anybody. My heartbeats quicken as if it's an earthquake. The scream comes again—terrified, desperate...final. Blood drains from my face as my legs pound frenziedly on the road that separates our houses. My ears strain for more sounds, but none come. I knock on the door loudly and impatiently, but no one answers. I push the door and to my utter surprise, it is open. I bolt inside. I feel overwhelmed by a wave of emotions, my head is beginning to reel. No one is present. Violent jets of red flow like a river. The walls are covered with irregular splatters of blood. I stagger back at the sight of the crimson. I struggle to move ahead. The colour swirls in my mind while my eyes follow the line. There is so much blood, garish red with a distinct, metallic scent. It is cascading across the floor.

I lean on the couch to regain my balance before taking a step forward. My eyes close and my lips are pursed as I avoid the scarlet pool. *What has Ovya done to herself?*

There is an eerie silence and I can listen to my heart thudding against my chest.

I tiptoe and manage to get close to the face on the floor. I freeze at what I see in front of me.

It isn't Ovya. It is Saachi.

∽

Osheen called me and asked me to meet her and I invited her home for dinner. Om said excitedly, 'How long has it been since I met her? More than two or three years, right?'

I nodded. 'It's been a while, yes.'

He placed the newspaper on the table. 'Are you all right?'

I blink in affirmation.

In the evening, Osheen joined us for dinner. She was draped in a black shirt and blue jeans. She smelled of warm incense, spices and creamy vanilla. We hugged each other before sitting down at the dinner table.

She said, 'Your house is beautiful.'

Om was quick to remark. 'It's all Ziva. I mean, I do whatever she asks me to do without questioning any of the design stuff.'

She looked at me and smiled. 'She really is the Picasso of the twenty-first century.'

He said, 'And I'm the luckiest man of the twenty-first century.'

I interjected. 'Oh stop it, you two. How's your boyfriend?'

She shook her head. 'I broke up with him a couple of weeks ago. Found out he was cheating on me.'

I squeezed her hand. 'I'm so sorry, babe. The good news is that you're only a step away from finding your real soulmate.'

She looked at Om. 'They don't make men like you any more. I wish I could find someone like you.'

Om raised his eyebrows and coughed, probably slightly uncomfortable at the suggestion. He completed his bite. 'I can only say you have great taste. I wonder why you are failing to find a stable partner.'

23

The blood continues to flow through the tiny cracks in the tiles. Every cell in my body wants to scream, but nothing comes out. It seems every wall and corner of the room is filled with the gore and the red. It is hard to make out the colour of her dress. It is soaking wet. Her eyes are open as wide as a church door. There is no beauty left in her. Her body is a mangled mess. She is lying in a pool of blood. I am fixed in position, seemingly losing my ability to move. I want to turn back and run to the comfort of my house, but I can't.

Stress inundates my system and comes with sheer ferocity. My heart pumps and beats as if it's trying to escape. Saliva thickens in my throat and beads of sweat trickle down my brow. The pressure is building in my stomach and it makes me take a leap. I step outside and vomit.

I worry about Ovya, but I am too afraid to step inside again. I feel hot, and with every passing minute, the fear dissipates before it rises back. I get up and my breath quickens as I go in to look for my friend in this godforsaken house. My eyes examine the entire living room from a distance. I walk slowly and carefully, barely moving so that I don't step on the blood. I move into the dining room to look for her.

I breathe a sigh of relief when I don't find her there. This is the farthest I have been into their house.

A paralysing dread spreads through my body like lava. I bring my fists together as I take the next step hesitantly, moving towards the master bedroom. My legs tremble and twitch as I fight the urge to spin around and sprint back outside again. My jaws tighten as I enter the room. I look through it, but much to my relief, Ovya isn't there. I check the washroom and the closet—just in case. My eyes water and hands tremble as I survey the other room. She isn't there either. *Thank goodness for that.* Suddenly, everything seems quiet and serene, as if I have returned to my original state of when I first moved to Delhi.

I am alone and lost.

My hands tremble as I fumble for my mobile phone and take it out of my pocket. I make the call to the police. My voice is shaky, but I manage. 'There has been a murder in my neighbourhood. The name of the victim is Saachi. Please come fast.' I tell the operator the address and he tells me that they're on their way. I don't have it in me to wait inside this house. I step out and sit on the porch, exactly in the spot where Aadit had been sitting not more than a couple of hours ago. Thoughts of worry about Ovya snake inside my head. *Where is she? Most importantly, is she safe?* My mouth becomes uncharacteristically dry. A steady breeze touches my face. *How can an argument between Ovya and Aadit result in Saachi's murder?*

The wind grows stronger, the black clouds gather and rain seems inevitable. I stay put in the same position and the muscles in my neck start to spasm. Within seconds, sheets of rain start to fall, but I don't dare go inside. I let the rain wash over my confusion, woes and worries. The police take their own sweet time to arrive.

I wonder if I should call Osheen and tell her all about it. I decide against it. Then, like a bolt of lightning, it dawns on me that I should call Ovya and find out if she is safe. I scuttle and find a safe spot from the rain as it splatters against the roof. I take out my mobile and call Ovya. My heart pounds against my ribcage as I wait for the call to get connected. It takes a while before I get to know that her phone is out of network coverage. The fear about Ovya that had been obscured amidst the rain now comes back with greater fury. My head is teeming with thoughts, but not one of them gives me any sort of hope.

Is it possible that she might have gone after Aadit?

It is highly unlikely, but there's a slim chance that she might have felt guilty about throwing Aadit out of the house. I don't have Aadit's number to call and confirm it. There's nothing that I can do at the moment but wait for the police to arrive. In the street light, a glimpse of a ghostly sedan raises my heartbeat, but it is not the police. The car turns the corner and disappears. The empty street yawns right before me with no smidgen of cars or street dogs.

I check the time. It is 1.30 a.m.

Suddenly, I hear the blast of a siren and a police car appears on the street, its blue lights flashing brightly in the gloom of the night. The rain too has slowed down to a drizzle. A couple of constables and a senior officer get down from the car. I slump on the brick wall and hold my hands up to gesture for them to come towards me. The door is ajar, but they pause just outside. One of the constables takes out a packet and hands surgical gloves to everyone.

The senior officer looks at me. 'You called us?'

I nod. 'Yes, I am Ziva. I live in the house across the street.'

He says, 'I am Inspector Sarvin. We have a lot to chat about, but first, I'll take a look at the house.'

ᴄ

I knew it was a stupid thought, but somehow, it wouldn't go away. I pushed it out of my head but every time I did so, it returned with greater force: *Had Om approached Osheen that day, would they have ended up married?* The chances are minuscule since Osheen has a history of dumping boys as if they were old shoes. But Om was different. He was sensitive, stable and supportive—just the kind of man she needed to settle down with. But Om chose me, even though Osheen was more attractive than me.

I had once even asked Om about it. 'What would have happened had you approached Osheen?'

He said, 'She would have probably broken up with me in a few months and you would have been my rebound, and we would get married only a little later. No matter what, we would have been together.'

I believed every word of what Om had said that day, and I still do. Perhaps it was just a wave of anxiety before the all-important hospital test that was taking a toll on me. Perhaps it was just me overthinking, plain and simple, for no reason whatsoever. I could try to guess the reasons, but it was just easier for my thoughts to bombard and push me into this negative spiral. It was in my genes to mull over things, events and decisions. My mum did it all the time. I did it as well.

My husband then broke my rumination and startled me. 'Hey! What are you thinking? Still worried about Friday?'

I couldn't tell him what I was thinking. I just whispered. 'Yes.'

'Don't worry. It'll all be fine. I have a very good feeling about it.'

I grimaced. 'Yes. I think so too.'

'Cheer up now. A big celebration is on the cards.'

I didn't say anything. I just hoped that it was only Om and me who would celebrate. I would invite no one else.

24

Sarvin has the usual build of a policeman but without the fat. He must be in his late thirties or early forties, but his innocent face and willowy muscles under the uniform make him look younger. He steps inside the house and takes off his cap when his eyes fall on the body. He takes a quick walk around the house—just to make sure that no one else is there. Then he goes back to the carcass and inspects it carefully. His sharp mind tries to come up with possible scenarios as to what would have happened. He inserts his hand into his pocket, takes out his mobile and opens the recorder.

'Time: 1.50 a.m. I have a single victim, a girl in her late twenties or early thirties. Her name is Saachi. A knife or a sharp object has been used to stab her heart a few times. There doesn't seem to have been any struggle. She must have known the killer. From the looks of it, it appears she would have died within a few minutes due to excessive bleeding, but we'll have to wait for the official confirmation from the medical examiner's report. The forensic expert, Sarthak, and the photographer, Ayu, are collecting evidence now, but I don't feel we'll get anything significant. The killer knew what he or she was doing and must have planned this for some time. Now, I am going to ask Ziva, our witness, a few questions and hopefully, she will be able to help us out.'

He said the last sentence softly, as if assuring me that

there was nothing to be afraid of. I am not afraid for myself but for Ovya in particular, and to some extent, for Aadit as well.

Pointing at my house, he says, 'That's where you live?'
'Yes.'

He gestures for me to take him to my house. 'I can't ask you questions here in this macabre scene. Shall we?' He shouts at his team members, 'Boys, I will be back shortly. Call for backup if you need help.'

The crystal-clear rainwater glistens on my fragile skin, but the rain has abated. My thoughts buzz around, making me anxious and nervous at the same time. A few puddles of water have formed on the road as Sarvin and I change our course every time they block our linear path. The water has washed my pavement and garden. I unlock my door and we step in. It's a relief to catch my breath. There is no stench of blood in the air and I am away from the disturbing sight of Saachi's dead body.

I say, 'Do you want anything? Water, tea, coffee?'

He smiles. 'I'm good.'

I pour myself some wine. 'Sorry, I need this. Otherwise, I won't be able to function.'

'Of course. Suit yourself. I just have a few questions and then I'll be on my way. For now.'

The 'for now' hangs in the air a fraction too long. I know he will be back for more questions. The passage of light slows and the sounds coming from outside are muffled. I can hear nothing but the beating of our hearts. I take a long swig of the drink and put the glass on the table. I think: *The cold steel of the knife had cut short Saachi's life. I never got to meet her again and ask her more questions about her relationship with Aadit.* Her face, that was so beautiful, lit by the café lights, had suddenly turned grotesque—eyes open, mouth slack and expressions frozen. She lay like a butchered animal in the waste of her own blood and here I was, about to answer questions about her death...of which I have no idea.

Sarvin opens the recorder again on his phone.

'Time 2.40 a.m. I'm at Ms Ziva's house. Here to ask her a few questions which I will record for my report.'

He places the mobile on the table. 'Shall we begin?'

I take another gulp of the wine. 'Yes.'

'Okay, then. Did you know Ms Saachi?'

'I have met her a couple of times, yes. I am not sure if that qualifies as knowing someone.'

He pauses. 'Sure. When was the last time you met her?'

I hesitate. 'This evening. I met her at The Hideout café.'

'May I ask what was the purpose of the meeting?'

'Ovya thought that her husband was in some way cheating with Saachi, his ex. She thought that he wasn't being honest about her. So as a good friend of hers, I thought maybe I should look into the matter and ask Saachi directly. That reminds me, shouldn't you guys be looking for Ovya? She is missing!'

'Don't worry, Ms Ziva. The police are looking for Ovya and Aadit. I'm sure we will have found them both before we complete this conversation. Now back to Saachi. What did she say when you confronted her?'

'She told me that there was nothing between her and Aadit and that they were only friends.'

'What did you think?'

'I didn't think anything. I didn't know.'

'Come on, you seem like a perceptive and intuitive individual. I'm sure you would have had an opinion.'

'I am sure you have also sensed that you can ask me the same question a hundred different ways, but my answers would still remain the same. All I can tell you is that Aadit dated Saachi before he dated Ovya and married her. Saachi's husband passed away due to cancer last year.'

Sarvin gets up and walks around the living room, not looking at anything in particular. 'Point taken. May I just understand the layout of the house vis-à-vis your neighbour's house?'

I nod. 'Please, be my guest.'

He ambles towards the window from where Ovya's living room is clearly visible. He says, 'This is Ovya's house, isn't it?'

I say, 'Yes.'

'You have quite a view. The first question I should have asked is if you saw anything. But I'm guessing you didn't, or else you would have told me, right?'

'Of course I would have told you. I didn't see anything. Occasionally, I have peeped into their house, but today I saw Ovya and Aadit have a fight, and then he left in a car and drove off. I retreated back to the couch for a drink and the next thing I hear is a scream from their house. I run as fast as I can and find that Saachi's dead and Ovya is missing.'

His phone rings. He answers. 'Oh lovely. Bring him to the station. I'll be there in thirty.'

He turns his attention to me. 'Good news. We have found Aadit.'

The next day was to be the day I would know whether all my sacrifices have helped cure my condition. The test had been performed the day before and the result was to be out the next morning. We had an appointment with Dr Lavanya Parekh in the evening. I felt a nervous excitement, like a child waiting for their big day.

I had already known that the night would end in a futile tussle of thoughts, which wouldn't help me in any way. The battle between what-ifs and what-nots. I didn't want to sleep yet anyway. Om was snoring next to me. He had had a long day at work since he was taking leave tomorrow to be by my side. At times, I wondered what I had done to get a man like Om as a husband. He was in complete contrast to my late father; my father had had none of his qualities.

The voice deep within cajoled me—the longer I stayed in bed, the better the chances I would have had of falling asleep. However, I was also aware that I always had trouble sleeping, especially before an important day. I would doze off in sporadic bursts, but would mostly be up. Still, four hours remained before Om woke up for his morning jog. I had been accompanying him almost every day since I first met Dr Lavanya. I had been able to lose ten kilos. I was pretty proud of myself having lost so much weight. It made me look younger, a tad prettier too.

I realized that if I didn't get much sleep, I would be exhausted in the morning. Sleeping pills were the first thing that was prohibited—along with the alcohol—when the treatment first began. The downside was obviously that I put on the wrong clothes, left the milk boiling on the gas, forgot my car keys and plenty of other unfortunate incidents. Usually, I managed well enough with six or seven hours of night sleep. I was envious of Om for he never suffered from insomnia. It was probably because he never had the habit of hammering away at some odd thought.

I decided then: I could be irate at my sleeplessness or watch something on Netflix. I decided on the latter. I went to the living room and put on a true-crime movie. I made sure that the volume was low so that Om wouldn't wake up.

Ten minutes into the flick, Om came and sat down next to me. 'Oh, I always wanted to watch this movie. Can you please rewind?'

25

It was hard for me to sleep in the night after Inspector Sarvin left. All I could do was drink wine as if it would free me of all the worries and angst. *Where is Ovya?* The question kept raging all night, and it still does, even though it's eight in the morning. Inspector Sarvin had promised that he would let me know as soon as they found Ovya. For the time being, their focus was to question Aadit and find out what he knew. I don't know if he was a suspect, but I guess the police would seek a few explanations.

I take a shower and change my clothes from last night. I stand at my window and look at my neighbour's house. It had been cordoned off and the police were still going through the property in the hope of finding evidence.

Who would have killed Saachi, and, more importantly, why?

In the soft light of the sunshine and the humid air of last night's rain, my weary eyes are focused on the half-parted curtains of Ovya and Aadit's house, like always. It was fashioned from rustic strings, and on days Ovya slid them open, I could experience the life of their house. I smile as if I could watch Ovya and Aadit going about their day as usual, and listen to their banter and their laughter. Though it's a little premature to think about it: would Ovya and Aadit want to live here after the police are gone, having known that Saachi was murdered here?

Imagining them here, Ovya drinking her morning

coffee and Aadit checking his phone, makes me tremble with joy. It is the same kind of joy Ovya experienced when I met her for the first time months ago. I take a deep breath and my lungs fill with fresh air in an attempt to clear away the longing I feel for them and their happy home. The colours in my life that had just started to appear have been muted by what transpired yesterday. All the hues are now grey, like cement. With it comes the melancholy cloak that I had been able to ward off for a short while. It now clings to my skin, and yet, the warmth never reaches me. My melancholy fixes me in position and doesn't allow me to rise to experience the soft joy of the memories embedded in my heart.

My mood falls, low to lower. I contemplate whether I should start drinking now but I decide against it. In the middle of the room sits a table. It is buckling under the pressure of all the books and DVDs. Inside its drawers are the notes that I have gotten until now. I wonder if I'll receive any more notes now that Saachi is dead.

I aimlessly flick through the channels, not able to focus on any show. My mind hovers back to Ovya and Aadit. It is 11 a.m. and still no call from Inspector Sarvin. Neither has Aadit come back home. *Is he still in custody? Being questioned and grilled by the police? He wasn't even here when the murder happened.* At least that's what I think. And what about Ovya? Have they found her? Is she also being questioned?

I think about calling Inspector Sarvin on his mobile but decide against it. It's probably not a good idea. I have to let him do his job.

I call Osheen instead.

She picks up and says, 'How's everything coming together?'

'It's falling apart.'

She raises her voice a little. 'What do you mean?'

I open my mouth and swallow my words. I look through the window into my neighbour's house and my face contorts. 'It's Saachi.'

'What about her?'

I cover my face with my hand. 'She has been murdered.'

'What?'

'Not just murdered, but murdered in Ovya and Aadit's house. Someone stabbed her with a knife or a sharp object in the heart.'

'Oh my god! Oh my god! That is terrible. How are you holding up?'

'I'll live to see another day, I think.'

'I'm so sorry, Ziva. I know you wouldn't have seen who did it but were you watching through your window into their house?'

I nod. 'I was. Ovya and Aadit had a messy fight yesterday. I think it was regarding Saachi, but then Aadit left the house and I went back to my drink. The next thing I hear is a loud scream from their house.'

'Is it possible that the killer might have seen you lurking at your window and spying on your neighbours?'

'No. I don't think so. I was careful. I was kneeling down the entire time.'

'Just look through your mailbox and see if you have received any more notes.'

'I haven't. I checked.'

'Okay. Good.'

'The thing is... I met Saachi yesterday evening. I thought she was the one who had been sending me those notes, but she denied the charge. I am still not sure if I should have believed her or not.'

'Oh god! What else did she say?'

'She showed me letters that Ovya apparently had sent her. They were threatening in a way, stating that she shouldn't meet her husband or else there would be disastrous outcomes for her.'

'Do you think Ovya is capable of...' Osheen does not finish her sentence.

'No, she herself is missing.'

'Perhaps that explains it. It has to be either Ovya or Aadit. Why would a third person kill Saachi and in their house?'

'I don't think Ovya is a killer. She might have lost her temper at Aadit, and for good reason, but I can't imagine that she could kill anyone.'

'How I wish I had been there with you to help you get through this.'

'It'll pass. I'm worried about Ovya. Thanks to her, for the first time in Delhi, I had started to feel like I had a friend who I could rely on. In her own way, she was helping me navigate through the contours and ridges of life.'

'When this is all over, come back to Mumbai. We could share a flat. Like old times?'

'Yes, that would be nice. But I have a feeling that this won't be over any time soon.'

Om and I were back again at Dr Lavanya Parekh's clinic after a gap of three months. Surprisingly, I wasn't nervous or anxious. Perhaps my mind and body had gotten tired of all this and had chosen to behave uncharacteristically that day by being a little more courageous.

After waiting for about ten minutes, we were asked by the receptionist to go inside. Dr Lavanya bore a face like a brick wall. She was going through the reports, and Om and I could not comprehend them as the medical jargon they contained went past our head. All we knew was that there was a good amount of highlighted text, which was probably a good thing.

We sat in silence over the next few minutes as she went through all the reports, her expressions not giving away their content.

At last, she looked up, nodded and said, 'Mrs Wadhwa, your reports are good. I think there's a bright chance you can become a mother. However, the things we have been following will need to be followed with the same adherence levels, at least until you both become parents. You understand me?'

In the car, I felt fireworks. I considered the possibilities of the future and the things that were in store for us. I couldn't stop grinning at what had transpired in the clinic. Om too was as happy as a blooming sunflower. He kissed me in the car, not a short peck but a long, passionate kiss. I didn't remember the last time when we had shared something like that in the car.

The air conditioning ran its icy fingers through my mouth as I opened it for the first time since we had gotten out of the clinic.

'Today we can celebrate,' I said.

Om smiled. 'Yes. We should head to our favourite restaurant.'

I said, 'And we will drink a lot.'

'No. We'll drink just a couple of glasses at most, just as Dr Lavanya asked us to. Not a drop more.'

I nod. 'Of course. We'll stick to the rules.'

26

Looking at the same concrete walls, I find relief when my eyes drift to my garden. It has been flourishing ever since Ovya and I last worked on it. I know it demands another session of the same care, but I don't have the strength or the desire to work at it. I'll probably consider it a couple of days from now when Ovya and Aadit are back home. We could get together again for dinner, this time at my house. I would make coffee sangria, zoodles and tacos for dinner and we'd spend the entire evening chatting and playing games.

Even though it has been only a few months since I met Ovya and less than twenty-four hours since I last saw her, a feeling of abandonment envelops me. Reasons and logic slip through my cold fingers. I am left with a huddled heap of broken things and unsaid feelings. I sit alone in my living room and the sun is bright and blazing, but a darkness shrouds me. Osheen isn't here to soothe my fears, nor is Om here to tell me stories.

It is just me, alone in my house, and that suddenly feels strange.

I peep through the window. The police are still inside, looking for clues and evidence. They have been inside for almost sixteen hours and Ovya has been missing for a shade over that. I read somewhere that the chances of finding someone drop if the person is not found within the first seventy-two hours of them going missing. What

Osheen said about Saachi's murder, that it had to be either Ovya or Aadit, does make a lot of sense, but I don't believe that either of them is capable enough of doing that. They aren't twisted or unhinged enough to be *killers*. Moreover, it's just an easy answer, and in life and death, there are seldom any. It could be the work of a third person who would benefit, not just by killing Saachi but by pinning the blame on Ovya and Aadit. It happens all the time in the shows and movies I delight in.

What if Ovya isn't hiding at all but has gone to a friend's house or her parents' house? What if she witnessed the murder and is now too scared to come out in the open? *Oh, the things I am capable of thinking!*

All of a sudden, I realize that I haven't had anything to eat since last night. My stomach churns as I head to the refrigerator to find something. However, it is as empty as the dead woman's eyes. I go to the kitchen and prepare corn and spinach sandwiches quickly. The urge to drink wine dominates my thoughts but I quench my discomfort with ice-cold water. I look around the disarray that my house is in already—dust has settled on the furniture and unwashed clothes lie on the countertops. It makes me irritable for a second, but my thoughts gravitate back towards Ovya and to Aadit.

I try to think what Om would have done in such a situation? How would he function? He'd probably be calm and let things play themselves out. My brain, on the other hand, is in overdrive as I think about all the possibilities and outcomes. I hope that what feels most desirable becomes the most likely end result. I go towards the window again in the hope that, by some strange magic, Ovya would have appeared.

That isn't going to happen.

The police are winding up after close to eighteen hours. I wonder if they have found all the evidence they need to prosecute the culprit, or if they have not gotten anything at all. Maybe they have been at it for so long because they were trying to find something until they gave up. Whatever the case might be, I just want to know about Ovya.

I rush outside and catch one of the police officers now boarding the Gypsy.

'Hey, officer. I do not wish to bother you, especially not after you guys being in there for almost a day...but would you happen to know anything about Ovya? Have you found her?'

He looks at me with caution. 'I'm sorry, I didn't catch your name yesterday...'

'I'm Ziva. I'm the one who called you guys last night.'

He breaks into a smile. 'Oh, of course. It's just the lack of sleep that is affecting my faculties. I don't think they've found Ovya yet, but rest assured, we will.'

He pats me on the shoulder and boards his police car. He drives off with three other officers. My eyes are fixed on the car until it makes a right turn and moves out of my sight. It is as if an invisible spectre is blinding me; my eyelids are too heavy and my pupils don't stray. The rest of my face too feels as immobile. It stays that way until the sharp, discordant bark of a street dog breaks my daydream. Normalcy returns as I look at Ovya's empty house.

I check the mailbox again just to be doubly sure that no envelope has been dropped off again. I put my hand inside and suddenly, I sense the same kind of silky paper that has been used in the envelopes before.

My face falls, faster than a cup that has slipped from the hand. My heart shatters with as much sound and impact. I turn as white as plaster and I glance nervously at my neighbour's house before I run back inside. I do not wait. As I try to tear open the envelope my hands tremble, yet I can't wait to read what's written.

DIDN'T I TELL YOU THAT AADIT IS NOT WHO HE MAKES HIMSELF OUT TO BE? SAACHI IS DEAD AND OVYA IS MISSING. WHO DO YOU THINK IS GUILTY, ZIVA?

∽

Drinking wine after months felt like the greatest luxury on earth. When it touched my palate and glided down my throat, my skin tingled and butterflies flew wildly inside my stomach. I had taken this activity for granted for the last few years, but having to take a break from it had made me value these joys in life. Having received the great news by Dr Lavanya earlier in the day made me want to drink through the night and celebrate, but I couldn't do that. And for good reason. I couldn't risk months of hard work being spoiled by one night's madness. Moreover, it made life easier when Om didn't drink in front of me.

The loud music pierced through my bones. I could see that Om too didn't like the noise. Had we been five years younger, we would have been on the dance floor. Then, a wild thought struck my head and I dragged Om to the dance floor. Despite his best attempts to not join me, I made him shake his body and when he did, I could picture us in our twenties, drinking and dancing away the night.

Times had changed, and so had we.

The music moved us as if we were puppets on strings, our heads were pounding because of the music but that didn't deter us. We spun around the dance floor, sweat on our skin. We had already downed two glasses of wine, but the high had not kicked in yet. However, we let loose. Tomorrow, we'll have hell to pay. I might miss my yoga session and Om his jogging, but the good vibes of the club keep us flowing.

Out of the blue, Om said, 'I'm too tired and thirsty.'

'We can order another glass of wine.'

He eyed me with a frown. 'I'm thirsty for water, not alcohol. Moreover, I think it's time to go. I don't want to miss my jog.'

I said, 'Can't we stay a while longer?'

He looked at me and said, 'Do you want to stay here and waste your night away dancing or would you rather go back home for Netflix and chill?'

It didn't take me even a second to reply. 'Well, the choice is obvious, isn't it? Let's go home, babe.'

27

I open my eyes in complete shock and read the note again. I want to scream but no sound escapes through my mouth. My perception of time is distorted as everything slows down to a crawl. I fall. Nothing separates the wooden floors and me. They seem ready to swallow me. My hand reaches out in a vain attempt to hold on to the counter for support. But I hit the floor, it cracks, and I descend into an endless abyss. Everything is a blur, a blur that blankets everything. I close my eyes and surrender myself briefly to the paralysing nature of the note.

While on the ground, an epiphany strikes me. 'The police are doing their job, but what if I too could contribute in my own way to help find Ovya?' After all, I had found out what Om was up to in the past when things had gone awry between us. There's no reason why I can't wear the same hat again.

But first, I needed to meet Inspector Sarvin.

I pick myself up and give him a call. 'Hello, Inspector Sarvin, Ziva here. I want to speak to you. Could you please come to my house?'

'I'll be there in thirty minutes. See you.' There is absolute stillness within my neighbour's house. The lights are switched off and the curtains are pulled apart. The wind doesn't stir the grass, or the leaves. Not a sound arises from the deserted mess of their residence. Even my own breath doesn't quite seem to travel far. It dies as soon as it leaves my mouth. The house has transformed into a space where even if a leaf falls, it will do so without drifting. Not a single bird is perched on the branches of the trees outside their house and the grass is straight and hushed. Too often what I see outside is reflected back inwards, but today is different. The stillness is tranquil. It makes me feel wary. I feel as if a predator is waiting just around the corner to shred me to pieces. My little world seems like a cocoon with no way out.

The bell rings and Inspector Sarvin is at the house. He comes in and sits on the couch.

I have a smile on my face. 'Any news about Ovya?'

He shakes his head. 'No, nothing yet. Our team is looking for her 24x7 but we haven't been able to locate her. I'm certain we'll find her soon enough.'

My lips quiver in fear. 'I am sure you and your team are doing a phenomenal job. I am just so worried about her.'

'Trust me, Ms Wadhwa, you are not the only one. We are as concerned about her well-being and are committed to finding her. We'll let you know as soon as we hear something.'

'Why is Aadit being held in custody? Is he a suspect?'

He smiles but the smile disappears almost immediately from his face. 'He's staying in a lodge near the police station of his own accord. He is not required to visit the station every day, but he insists. He wants to help us locate his wife.'

'But is he a suspect?'

'I'm sure you know we can't share details with you. If my interrogation is over, can we get to why you wanted to meet me?'

'Oh, I am so sorry. I didn't realize I was being nosy. Yes, let's get to the point.'

I take out all the white envelopes and spread them on the table in chronological order. 'I have been receiving these notes ever since Ovya and Aadit shifted to that house.'

I point to the last envelope.

'This one, I received today. I don't know when it was dropped but it was here when I checked my mailbox in the evening, right after the officers left.'

He takes his time studying the notes. He massages his throbbing temples. It is possible that he might not have slept at all or gotten very little sleep. He groans and glances at the notes. He blinks rapidly, his feet begin to shake. He glimpses at the ceiling before bringing his focus back to the notes. He leans back in his chair and rubs his bleary eyes before casting them upon me.

'Why didn't you tell me about this before?'

I said, 'I didn't think it was related to the case.'

'Please allow us to decide what is important and what is not,' he retorts. 'What else do you have?'

I shake my head. 'Nothing.'

The next moment I remember the notes Saachi had showed me the day I met her. Notes purportedly written by Ovya. I tell Inspector Sarvin about them.

He says, 'Yes. We found those in her purse, which means she never went to her house after meeting you. Do you think Ovya could have written them?'

'I thought that the police rely on facts and not opinions.'

'Very well. Is there anything else you want to talk about Ms Wadhwa?'

'Can I meet Aadit?'

He said, 'Why would you want to come to the police station?'

He waits for me to say something but I don't. He gets up to leave.

I stop him. 'How is Aadit doing? Is he coping well?'

He turns around. 'Oh, he'll live. We can't say the same about Saachi. Can we?'

I hold back my reaction to preserve my sanity. Tomorrow will be a new day, and I am certain my survival instincts will allow me to come up with ways to find Ovya.

∽

Back home, we didn't sleep at all. Instead, we watched a movie and had sex, as we had decided to do while at the club. Today, Om's touch electrified every nerve and cell in my body. Being together in that moment brought intimacy into my thoughts, dreams and wishes. With my imagination running wild, we had the perfect play in bed. I had a feeling that it wouldn't take me long now before I got pregnant for the first time. I could anticipate the absolute joy that would come with it. Of course, I knew the precautions that I had to take would only get stricter. But that was a small price to pay for my baby.

I was beaming from inside and the smile was hard to conceal. Om said, 'What are you thinking about?'

I caressed his chest with my hands. 'You know, just dreaming about our baby.'

'It's no longer a dream, hun, it'll soon be a reality.'

My eyes twinkled and tears flowed through my half-closed eyes. I held my breath, but my voice cracked. 'I can't wait to see you become a father.' A gale of laughter followed the announcement.

'You think I won't be a good father?'

'No, I think you'll be a great dad. I just can't imagine you playing that role.'

'That is true for you too. My brain fails to imagine a maternal version of you.'

'That's just because you have a cramped imagination.'

He burst into laughter. His laugh tickled my ears and I was left with no choice but to join him. Despite our age, we laughed like children, and we waited to have one of ours.

28

I didn't sleep well today again. Not sleeping well is a curse that I have carried through my life. For the six hours that I was in bed, I must have woken ten times. Each time wasn't long, but it was enough to disturb the shut eye. With every disturbance came perturbing thought about Ovya. I'd rather not think, but I guess I am flawed. I cannot stop worrying about her. My psychiatrist had suggested that I try meditation to be more present and aware of my thoughts, but I didn't have the patience for that. Does lying in bed in silence count as meditation? The wine helps. It makes me more watchful of my thoughts. So far, that has been the only medicine that has worked for me. I hope things work out for Ovya too. I hope we find her. I put my feet on the ground but they are wobbly. I dally. Finally, I step outside to check the mailbox. There's nothing in there today. I breathe a sigh of relief and look at the heavens above to thank them for the empty mailbox. But I see no fairness, no remorse, or responsibility. Saachi is dead, Aadit is at the police station and Ovya is missing. Does there have to be a grand plan? One no one is able to comprehend?

The calm and serene days of bright sunshine and fluffy clouds are behind me. Now, all I have to face is dark and angry days that spit sheets of rain and hostile fire.

I step back inside and sit on the chair and watch

the garden that has turned a shade brighter. Ovya had said that it would take a couple of months before all the glory was on display. It seems as if that day is here today. The dahlias are blossoming, the buttercups have turned golden, the grass is the colour of dreamland's meadow, the soil is renewed and the leaves are perky. Every now and then, a few butterflies waltz around, and the air is mixed with bursts of birdsong. My heart rejoices at the sight in front of me only to become wistful moments later when I think of Ovya.

My phone rings. I have a funny feeling that it might be Ovya who has finally found the time or signal to get in touch.

However, I am surprised to see that it is Sasha calling me.

'Hey, Ziva! How are you?'

I say, 'Hey Sasha! What a pleasant surprise. I'm okay. How are you?'

Her voice becomes high-pitched when she says, 'I'm in the city. Do you think we could meet?'

'What? You're in Delhi? How? When?' My excitement fades the moment I realize that I had resolved to put all my focus and energy into finding Ovya. 'How long are you here for?' My voice quivers.

She says, 'Is something wrong, Ziva? You can tell me.'

'No. No. Nothing's wrong. I was just a little caught up today.'

'Oh, darling, I leave tomorrow morning. I wanted to catch up, drink some wine, share possible ways that we could work together again. You know, the usual.'

'Oh yeah, that would be so nice.' I think for a few seconds before saying, 'Let's do lunch?'

'Lunch would be lovely,' she says.

'See you at two at The Delhi Hive.'

I look at myself in the mirror and stare for a long time, determined not to get distracted by anything else. I try to remember if Ovya had ever tried to hide something behind that lovely smile of hers. Did she ever try to fool me? Did I ever notice that the expression on her face wasn't genuine? Did the smile on her face not reach the eyes? Did she conceal her depression behind her pretty form and pray that no one would notice? I am not sure why I am thinking about these things when the only priority should be to find her.

I know I can't tell Sasha anything about what has happened in my neighbourhood. I would have to plaster a smile on my face and not give anything away. I tug on unfaded blue jeans, pair them with a pink top and ballet flats. I gather my hair, twist it and then raise it up against the back of my head. Then, I use a grey and gold-toned embellished hair grasp to keep it together. I spray a subtle scent with notes of kumquat, lemongrass and pear blossom and head towards my car and drive away.

Upon reaching the restaurant, flashes of the day when I had coffee with Saachi flood my mind. Suddenly, it seems like a bad idea to have agreed to meet Sasha. I stay in the car and try to calm myself by taking deep breaths, but it doesn't work. Panic grows in me like a ball of fire and thoughts run over one another like a hare running' to save its skin. I want them to slow down but they don't listen. My breathing becomes rapid and shallow and the breaths come out in gasps. My heart hammers inside my chest and I fear I will black out.

I increase the volume of the radio in a vain effort to

divert my attention. I want everything to slow down so that my body and brain can cope with what is happening. Blackness creeps like a slithering monster, waiting to gobble me up. I decide to call Sasha and tell her that I must call the lunch off. I am aware it would be terrible on my part, but that seems the only way out. I pick up my phone and dial her number but she doesn't answer. The next thing I know, she is knocking on the window of my car.

I put on a fake smile—the way they do at reception centres. I try to conceal the panic attack. I turn the music off and get out of the car and embrace her in a tight hug.

We hold each other for a moment extra.

When we let go, I say, 'This felt good. I've missed you, Sasha.' Teardrops find an opening in my eyes.

∽

It had been more than three months since we had last gone to Dr Lavanya's clinic and the same amount of time had passed since we had started trying to have a baby again. However, this morning when I woke up, I experienced nausea and I threw up a little. My first instinct was to take medicine for it, but then I took a home pregnancy test.

It came out positive.

My body tingled from head to toe. I bounced on my feet and rubbed my hands together. I was ecstatic, unable to control my joy. Om too had the expression of a child who had received a big birthday present. The excitement wired us together as we put on some music and danced our way through the morning. All the prosaic worries of the day had been muzzled under the weight of this news. The past didn't matter now as Om and I looked forward to the future. In one adrenaline-filled moment, he picked me up and swirled me in his arms before we crashed on to the bed. He kissed my mouth and my stomach before calling Dr Lavanya's clinic for an appointment.

We were lucky to have gotten one for the same evening at 7 p.m.

Om whispered, 'I love you.'

'I love you.'

In the evening, we were back again at Dr Lavanya Parekh's clinic for an abdominal scan. It was performed by a doctor from her team. She sent the reports directly to Dr Lavanya's cabin but before that, she confirmed that I was, in fact, pregnant.

Inside her cabin, Dr Lavanya looked at the reports and broke into a grin. 'Congratulations, Mr and Mrs Wadhwa. You guys are on your way to becoming parents.' She looked at me as if I was the only person she was addressing. 'You're in your first month. I don't want to repeat this again, but things we've been doing need to continue. They are clearly working. Monthly check-ups are mandatory. Until you conceive, adherence to a healthy diet and exercise is critical for your overall health and baby's health. Also, in case of any sickness or any discomfort, you need to come to the clinic without wasting any time.'

Om and I nodded and said in unison, 'Thank you, doctor. Thank you for all that you have done for us.'

'Of course. Congratulations once again. I'll see you guys in a month.'

29

The gleam in Sasha's eyes is as vivid as I've known it to be. She orders her staple—chicken breast with mushroom sauce and grilled vegetables—while I surprise myself by ordering some penne alla vodka.

I say, 'How long have you been ordering the same dish for lunch?'

She laughs. 'In fact, I have ordered this after a long time. I was just checking if you remembered.'

'After having seen you eat the same chicken breast for over four years for lunch, even if I get dementia, I probably won't forget this one thing.'

She cackles. 'You're the same. Same deprecating sense of humour and the same obsession with pasta and wine.'

'Some things hardly change.' I sigh.

She leans forward. 'Did you finally start liking it here in Delhi?'

I lock my gaze on the door and watch a couple enter the restaurant. They are holding hands and, for a moment, I think of Aadit and Ovya. The couple pass our table and sit behind us.

I say, 'I see Delhi and it disgusts me to the bone. I can't wait to get out, but I have a few things that I need to do and after that, I'll move. Probably go to London and stay there for a few years. Who knows.'

She slices her chicken with precision using a knife and ingests a small bite. 'You should have never left

Mumbai, but I understand why you took that decision at the time. What's stopping you from coming back? We can work together. We'll start our own agency. I'll get the clients and you'll do your magic with the laptop. It'll be like old times, only this time it'll be better than before.'

I look at her in wonder. She still has the same passion and drive for work. A few months ago, I was looking for freelance work just to keep me busy. 'It all sounds exciting, Sasha, but it's just not the right time. I have to do a few things. Perhaps after that we can talk about it.'

'Of course. I was just planting the seed. You sleep over it for as long as you want to.'

I smile. 'What work did you have in Delhi?'

'Oh yes, I had come for a meeting with a new client. Before I forget to ask, would you like to freelance with the firm on this one?'

I chuckle. 'What's it about?'

'Oh, don't worry. It'll be a walk in the park for you. It's a new satirical website and they need designs. They want us to create new illustrations, and in some cases, we'll have to photoshop real people's faces on to the things. I'll send you a proper brief by email and you can decide. What say?'

I nod. 'Sounds interesting.'

'Perfect. You know I would have loved to stay in Delhi for a few days, but I have another meeting tomorrow in the office at 2 p.m. You know how it is.'

'Don't worry. I am glad we could meet for lunch. What does your schedule look like for the evening?'

'I have another meeting at 4 p.m. in Noida. After that, I'll come back to Delhi and meet a few college friends, go out somewhere and tomorrow morning at 7 a.m. I have a flight back to Mumbai.'

'Look at you go. No, fly. You're crushing it, babe.'

She looks at me in the eye and blinks. 'I learned from the best. I learned it from Ziva Wadhwa.'

I chuckle. 'Hardly. Nowadays, it is terribly hard for me to even get to the bathroom from my bed. I have become as lazy as a toad at the bottom of a well.'

We finish our lunch and it is time for Sasha to leave for the time being. I don't know what is going on inside me, but I don't want her to leave. From not wanting to meet Sasha at all to wanting her to stay longer...I am caught up in uncertainties. The way I confronted Saachi, the way Ovya and Aadit fought, the way Saachi was murdered and the way Ovya went missing. I only have questions and doubts, but no answers. It is painful to be stranded in the middle of this puzzle and not be able to find the missing pieces. This is the time for me to protect my own heart and my own self, but the damage has been caused. Ovya's disappearance is too grave for me to ignore. I had thought that I would walk with her through every storm but somewhere, her hand slipped out from my grasp.

It's up to me to try and locate her.

Sasha hugs me and I hug her back more tightly than before. The warmth of her breath on my shoulders comforts me, and I feel my broken pieces coming back together. The restaurant door opens and with it comes a jangle of tunes. At that moment, the air becomes water; I find myself drowning inside, desperate to swim and get a whiff of the surroundings.

I realize there is someone else who needs such unconditional support. He probably is the one who is suffering the most because of everything that has happened over the last few days. I decide to go and meet Aadit.

I park my car outside the police station and stare at the old crumbling building built of stones during god-knows-which era. It is nothing like the steel and concrete monuments around it. The walls are thick, like those of an archaic castle, and the windows with iron rods are dingy. There's no flicker of light from inside and the heavy wooden doors are shut, giving nothing away about what goes on inside.

I get out of my car and head straight towards the police station. I am stopped in my tracks by an approaching car that swishes past me, only to reverse back to next to me.

The window comes down. It is Inspector Sarvin. He says, 'I thought it was you, Ms Wadhwa. How are you?'

Startled, I say, 'I'm here to meet Aadit.'

He says, 'Of course. He's inside. In fact, I will join you in a while. I just have to follow up on this lead.'

I nod.

'Okay then, see you.'

I let his car leave before resuming my walk towards the police station. As I enter, I see a bench on the right-hand side. Aadit is sitting on it and smoking a cigarette. He is absorbed in his own thoughts and does not notice me until I sit down beside him and place my hand on his. The cigarette drops from his hand and we sit beside each other for a short while before the silence between us breaks with Aadit's cry. It starts slow and gentle before it turns into a wail that tears through my heart. I embrace him and fold his crumpled form into myself. He collapses on my chest, his voice full of sorrow. The weight of his agony pins me down as I struggle to keep him together.

I say, 'It's okay. It's okay. We'll find her.'

က

I had two hearts now—my baby's and my own. My love had expanded and converged into my baby's tiny form. It wasn't just joy but a privilege to carry him or her around as I placed my feet upon the ground. As I giggled and wiggled, I felt serenity and comfort from the being in my stomach. I liked knowing that someone else shared my joy in the most literal sense. At times, when I became quiet, I knew my baby was listening to my silence, absorbing the world around me. We were always connected and we shared an unimpeachable bond. This fact then marked the beauty of my existence.

It was my eighth week and Dr Lavanya told us that the foetus's sense of touch would begin to develop now. I always had a problem with the medical term 'foetus'. It just seemed inhuman to me to call a baby in the womb a foetus—as if it is just one of the many things present in the human body. I always preferred the word 'baby', or 'child'. The point was anything seemed better than foetus.

Regardless, Om had found a spring in his feet and he tried to make me laugh.

He said, 'It's important that you're always in a good mood and the environment of the house is hospitable. It works like a charm for the baby.'

I was in this space where I had stopped disagreeing and arguing with Om. Even though this statement was true, he otherwise also made a lot of unfounded statements that were so utterly false that you'd fall laughing off a cliff. 'Eating peanuts and dairy will make the baby allergic to them,' he would say. Or 'You should be eating for two lives'. And the best of the lot: 'You shouldn't touch the neighbour's cat'. The thing was that Om had started caring about me way more than he had before and I'd be lying if I said I didn't love and enjoy it.

30

Words leave me when I stare into Aadit's brown, misty eyes that shimmer with teardrops. On my way to the police station I had thought about the things that I would ask Aadit, but on seeing him like this, my heart falls silent. I can't open my mouth. It seems as if we are stuck underwater and everything is slow and warped. His gaze shifts from me to the ground. He hasn't said a word in the ten minutes we have been sitting together but his eyes appear to speak, to shout and ask about the whereabouts of his wife. My mind is blank and my eyes are wide open as I watch him with horror. His expectant eyes look at me as if he is waiting for me to spill the good news. But I don't have any.

All I say is, 'How have you been?'

He takes out a crummy handkerchief and wipes his eyes. 'What do you think?'

I nod slowly and communicate in the most subtle way that I understand how hard it must be for him. 'Yeah. Does the police think you might have something to do with the murder…and the disappearance of Ovya?'

He tries extremely hard to say something but fails. I fetch him water and he takes a sip, and I stroke his shoulder while he gathers himself. At last, he manages, 'Inspector Sarvin thinks anything is possible. I don't like the fellow. I think he is too cunning, but he is good at his job. That's all I want, someone smart to find Saachi's killer and find my wife. What do you think?'

'I don't know, Aadit. Clearly, I am not as smart as Inspector Sarvin, but I don't think Ovya killed Saachi and ran away, if that's what you are asking me.'

At that moment, Aadit breaks into a chuckle. 'The police think that it's highly possible that Ovya—my Ovya—brutally murdered Saachi and wriggled out of the city, the country. Who knows...?'

I place my hand on his. 'You know it's not true. I know it's not true. We'll find Ovya and whoever killed Saachi.'

He says, 'The police showed me letters. Letters written to Saachi by Ovya that were filled with so much hate and disgust. I didn't know that Ovya was capable of so much hostility. I know she had problems with Saachi, but to write something so vicious without ever telling me. It came as a shock. I don't know if I know Ovya any more.'

'I know it must be terribly difficult for you to think straight and make sense of what is happening, but for all we know, Saachi wrote those letters to herself to pull Ovya down in your eyes.'

He retorts, 'If that was the purpose, why is it that Saachi never mentioned anything about them to me?' With that it is confirmed that the two letters Saachi showed me were, in fact, written by Ovya. Perhaps, she wrote more. The police might have found them at Saachi's house. To think of Ovya in a negative light seems like a betrayal of the friendship we have shared. It is easy for love to turn into hate when you don't put up a fight. I can't let just one bad action of hers swallow everything that is good about her. I won't pour acid into my soul. *She might have written those letters, but she isn't capable of murder.* It is my duty to fight for good memories and save her marriage. I will fight to keep myself empathetic even when the police say and believe terrible things about Ovya because if I don't, there would be no difference between Om and me. The unwillingness to put up a fight and think the worst of Ovya, despite all her qualities, is a betrayal to me.

Aadit might have started doubting his own wife but I will not. Not unless I hear it from her own mouth.

I say, 'Doubts are dangerous, for they cloud everything that is real. I understand the precarious situation that you are in, but I would advise you to have a little faith. The police want to solve this crime quickly and move on to the next one. They don't care who the murderer is, nor are they interested in finding Ovya. Hell, seventy-two hours have passed and we haven't heard a thing from the police about her. They want someone to take the fall. Who better than a person who is not here to defend herself.'

He twists his engagement ring. 'You're right. I think you should find out about Ovya. Do your own investigation. One that is separate from the police. She loved talking to her college friends. Perhaps they know something. Although the police have already spoken to them, they might have missed something. I will also share her social media credentials. Maybe that will prove useful.'

I lift my head and look at the lone tree at the end of the road. It stands mute. With every gust of wind, the leaves dance to the music of the bird. The bark shines like gold, the kind that fills me with exhilaration, opening the doors to reckless and unflinching boldness.

I say, 'Don't you worry. It won't be long before you are enjoying Netflix and popcorn with her.'

We do not realize it but Inspector Sarvin is standing in front of us.

He speaks up. 'Ms Wadhwa and Mr Malhotra, I come to you with bad news. The last live location from Ovya's mobile phone was near your house. It is possible that she last used it just before the murder, but it hasn't been turned on ever since.'

I say, 'All you have done in three days is to run from one dead end to the other. You don't have the slightest idea about where she is, do you?'

Inspector Sarvin sits down next to Aadit, looks at me and then stares at the ground. 'We know for sure that Ovya is still in Delhi.'

∽

I called up Osheen that day and broke the news that I was in my fourth month of pregnancy. Om and I had decided to keep the information within the family, but I couldn't keep it from Osheen for too long. He said it was okay for me to share it with her and that he would share it with his best friend, Mihir, as well.

Osheen must have jumped in joy. She said, 'What? You're pregnant and you're into the fourth month? You're telling me this now? This is the best news I have heard since I learned I no longer had to pay for booze. Congratulations, Ziva. I'm so fucking happy for you.'

I smiled. 'Om and I had decided not to share it with anyone as of now. After a brief discussion, we decided I'll share it with you.'

'That's amazing. I still can't believe that my best friend is pregnant. We need to celebrate. Today.'

I laughed. 'We can celebrate with green vegetable juice, dry fruits and egg chaat.'

She said, 'Oh, come on. I mean a celebration, not a session of dieting. We'll eat pizza and drink alcohol. Oh, I forgot to tell you. My company pays for my alcohol as well. Monthly expenses of up to ₹1 lakh are covered. Now, isn't that a sweet deal? Today is 1st August.'

'It all sounds exciting but I'm not supposed to drink during my pregnancy.'

'One night of drinking can't hurt.'

'According to Dr Lavanya, my gynaecologist, it could. I can't take that chance. Om and I really want this.'

'But we can still meet up and I could congratulate you?' she said, a bit disappointed.

'How does tomorrow at 7 p.m. sound?'

'Sounds as good as the first cry of your to-be-born baby.'

31

Ifeel like a ghost in a world of paper dummies. I am a ghost that needs to work like a machine. I am the spectre that has to run through the darkness, through time and space, to find one particular spark. The police are like unwanted noise who will try to distract and derail me from my mission, that of finding Ovya. She had gone into the dark alone. She is a fragment of fire and all I have to do is become her fuel.

There is silence in my soul. I am wrapped in hope. I feel the chill in my blood as I open my notes where Aadit had written Ovya's Instagram credentials. He told me that she spent a lot of time on the platform and it was possible that I might be able to find something. I am not sure what I might uncover on the platform, but it is worth a shot. I put in her credentials and I am in.

Getting lost is simple. You just need to have the heart to walk away from everyone and everything. Most people are so busy that they won't realize that you're gone. There's no need to wipe your digital footprint in order to erase yourself. You just need to stop sharing stuff and people will forget that you're still breathing. You don't have to buy a cabin in the hills in order to cut yourself off from people. You could do it within the bustling city of Delhi; you could fall off the face of the earth.

However, this isn't the case with Ovya.

I see a number of unanswered messages on her

Instagram since the last three days. I carefully read parts of them without opening the messages. Most of them pertain to her whereabouts. However, there is one, from a certain Omkar, that reads: 'Hello, homeslice. I like your face and I can't wait to see it. When are we meeting?'

I immediately open the message and go through her other conversations with him. Ovya had only recently started conversing with him. About a month back. He was flirting with her quite brazenly. However, she never stopped him from crossing the line. She didn't reciprocate as enthusiastically, but she didn't stop him either. This is strange. I can't imagine that Ovya would ever even think about anyone other than Aadit. Could it be just a way for Ovya to get back at Aadit for not being honest with her about Saachi?

There's only one way to find out.

I message the guy. I am careful to write in Ovya's tone and voice.

'Hi! What's up?'

And I wait for him to get back. I prepare coffee and toast for myself, but he has not responded. I take a bath, dress up, and come back to the phone. There's no response. The kind of messages that he'd been sending, he should have been jumping in joy to see a message pop up from Ovya.

My eyes fall on the cobwebs that hang loosely from the roof. In the darkness of this old house, I am unlikely to spot any spiders. I can't even see my own feet. Even though the spiders can't reach me, they set my heart racing.

I bring a broom and climb on to the couch.

The webs seem to cackle softly as the broom sweeps

them off the top. The broom is now encased in a layer of dust, and I make a note to call the cleaning service again. My eyes settle on a red toy car; I had bought it what seems like a lifetime ago. For some reason, I had decided to keep it and not throw it away with all the other toys I had got when I was pregnant. I get down from the couch and observe the headlights of the toy. Something seems off. It is as if the car is watching me. I bring a screwdriver from the toolbox and unscrew the lights.

There it is—the spy camera that I had searched for desperately.

Sometimes, when you're looking for something in particular, you end up discovering other things that you had longed for in the past.

I wonder who could have put it there. Apart from the cleaning service, people rarely visited. That one time that Aadit visited and Ovya had come often; no one else had visited the house. I had always been with the employees from the cleaning service, no matter which part of the house they were in; Aadit had been here only for a little while and I had been sitting on the couch with him. It was Ovya who had been a regular to my residence and I'd leave her alone in the living room while I prepared things for her in the kitchen. It would have been easiest for her to plant the camera, but why would she do it? Why would she want to keep an eye on me? It didn't make sense.

My door was always open for Ovya. She always walked in without any inhibitions, and greeted me with a hug that could melt winter snow. I always felt blessed to spend time with her. When she talked, it was like dew falling on the morning grass, and it seemed like her words allowed me to let go of my past. I was drawn into her vivacity, her carefree attitude and respect for relationships. Perhaps it was my inability to remain isolated and cold that let me welcome her in my life.

There's no doubt that she had healed me through her constant and endearing presence.

I return to the phone but Omkar hasn't responded yet. It's been more than two hours and the guy is playing cool. I open his Instagram profile and there's only one picture of him. He is holding a glass of whisky. The layout of the room—the sitting arrangement, the table, the rug, the plants—suggests that it is a living room, probably his. His bio says, 'Here for you.'

Could this 'you' be Ovya?

∽

Osheen picked me up from my house after work and we reached the restaurant at 7 p.m. The place was pulsating with infectious energy, and seeing it more than half full in the early hours of the evening had heightened my curiosity. I couldn't wait to try the food. I would come back again after my baby was born to get the complete experience.

Osheen said, 'Look at this place. I am already falling in love with it.'

I said, 'You do fall in love quite often. Is it not time to settle down?'

'You know I have been giving it serious thought, but something or the other stops me in my tracks. It's possible that I haven't found someone as gentlemanly as Om.'

I ordered myself a glass of orange juice and some grilled chicken to go with it while Osheen ordered a glass of rose wine and pizza. Having abstained for so long, I had built a wall of steel around my craving for alcohol. It was hard to breach. The server brought the items ordered and placed them on the table.

Osheen pointed at a couple and giggled. 'Looks like they have been drinking since yesterday.'

I laughed. 'They have age on their side and must not be married. Om and I were exactly like that. You have witnessed us on multiple occasions in the past.'

She nods. 'Yes, do you remember that day when we had booked an Uber and the three of us puked in the car—all at the same time?'

I smile. 'How could I forget that monumental day? That was the only time Om puked after drinking. On every other occasion, he could go on and on.'

'Those were the days. I miss them. Those unbothered times.'

'Who doesn't?' I said.

'But why didn't you tell me about your pregnancy? I thought I deserved better.'

I take a sip of the orange juice and a slice of the pizza. 'It was super hard for me to carry this child. There were uterine issues. The kind of treatments I had to endure and the kind of sacrifices I had to make...Om suffered along with me. It was an extremely hard four or five months, but eventually all the hard work paid off when the news of my pregnancy was confirmed. However, it is critical that I keep up the good work and continue following the doctor's instructions to the last letter. This means that I can't drink or smoke. Why do you think I am not getting drunk with you.'

'I understand. Who would want to take a risk after so many sacrifices.' She paused before asking, 'You can't even smoke up?'

'I don't know, but in any case, I hardly enjoyed it back then.'

'Back then, we didn't have good stuff. Now I do. You want to take a puff?'

I resisted the temptation and declined.

It wouldn't have been fifteen minutes when Osheen asked me again. 'Don't you fancy a puff?'

By now, she was wasted, having drunk more than a few glasses. She had also been slyly taking a few puffs of weed in the washroom. I was getting agitated and wanted to return home but she wouldn't listen to me. I guessed she was in that zone. She only listened to the alcohol.

I said, 'Can we please go back?'

She murmured, 'What is the time?'

'It's 11.00 p.m. We should head back.'

'We'll only return when you take a puff or drink with me.'

'Neither is happening, Osheen. Let's just go. Om must be worried.'

She grabbed my hand, pulled me close and locked her eyes on me. The next moment, she started to laugh as if she had heard the most amusing joke of her life. 'The number of times a day you say Om makes me believe that you have started chanting the name.'

'Come on, like always, you drink and then you can't control yourself. Let's go.'

'Puff or a drink?' she asked.

I thought of calling Om but I had no signal on my

cell. I couldn't possibly leave her alone and get out to make the call. I didn't know what to do. Agreeing to meet Osheen in the evening had been a bad idea. She started humming the song that the DJ was spinning and waited for me to decide. I thought about all that could go wrong, and in a jiffy, I knew what I would do. I grabbed the joint from her and took two long puffs before crushing it into the ground.

'Now are you happy? Shall we?'

My head started to spin as I called for the bill.

32

A touch short of ninety-six hours have passed and there has been no news of Ovya. The police are as clueless as my drunk father pointing the television remote at the microwave. Their abandoned house is quiet. It stands still in a composed manner, as if it has chosen solitude for the time being. It waits for its owners to come back, and with them, all the life which had gone amiss. The walls stand firm, the windows are shut and the porch is covered with dried leaves. The perimeter of the house is still lined with the dreaded 'Do Not Cross. Crime Scene' boundary. There is something wrong with this particular house—as if it had been cursed by a witch or an occultist. In the six months that I had lived here before Ovya and Aadit joined, it had been empty. At least two families had moved in before Ovya and Aadit. However, both the families did not stay for long, and the house was vacated within a couple of months.

When Ovya and Aadit moved in, it seemed as if the curse had been lifted. But it didn't take long for it to strike again, and this time, it struck with fury.

Just like a stain that vanishes upon cleaning—like it was never there before—Ovya has been missing as if she wasn't even there. The whole thing has been a joke. I run my hands over the thriving flowers. The day the two of us had worked here, the plants had been dying, withering away. The decay has faded, and now remains just in memory and history. She was here and used her soft, supple hands to tend to my little garden. The garden remains, but her hands are gone. I cast my eyes around, listen to the birds and feel her presence. I close my eyes and imagine her sitting on that chair, coffee sangria in hand, talking about trivial things and laughing at something stupid. The moment I open my eyes, she is gone.

I release the white petals of the daisy I am holding, and watch them float away in the breeze.

I get my phone to check if Omkar has responded to the message. He hasn't. I call the few numbers that Aadit had given me—numbers of Ovya's college friends and a few relatives. Her parents had passed away a few years ago in a car crash. She didn't have any siblings and she was cut off from the extended family, except for minor exchanges with an aunt and a cousin.

I start to call the people, one by one, and attempt to find information. Those itsy-bitsy pieces that might prove decisive in solving the puzzle of Ovya's disappearance. I am not the type of person who chit-chats, but I'd have to do that in order to gain their trust. I want them to share things they had not shared with the police.

I first call Arunima. The way she talks about Ovya gives away how concerned she is. I have to say, she is not very concerned. The evidence lies in her words and lack of emotions. I couldn't listen to her prattle for too long. She was loquacious but her words didn't hold any value.

Next on the list is Devika. She seems egocentric, just like a child. The conversation revolved more around her than Ovya. Every time I try to bring the topic of discussion back to Ovya, she comes up with a way to steer the topic back to herself. All her pains are front and foremost and Ovya's don't matter. She doesn't even care to hide that it didn't bother her that her friend from college is missing. She keeps on talking about what ails her and what could be the quickest escape from that ailment. The only relevant piece of information she shares is that Ovya used to meet a psychiatrist for her OCD in college. Devika adds that she too is considering seeing the doctor for the anxiety that afflicts her.

After Devika, I call up Sukoon. She is keener to seek information from me than giving out any. It begins with slight coaxing and chatter follows. She wants me to relax. It doesn't work but my need to extract things, anything, out of her, makes me tell her that Ovya disappeared four nights ago and hasn't come back since. Once I answer her question and satiate her curiosity, she tells me about incidents from college that don't shed any light on Ovya as a person in the current scenario. After that, follows another question about Ovya. I half-answer it without sharing any details. At one point, it seems as if she herself is conducting her own little research and investigation on the disappearance. After about twenty minutes, I disconnect the call without feeding her nosiness any further.

The last friend on the list is Mani. After talking to a few people for more than a couple of hours, it seems impossible to continue this crusade. I don't feel like myself. I am doing things that are alien to my nature. But I persist. I continue doing what's uncomfortable because that's the only way to find Ovya.

I call Mani. He answers after the first ring.

I say, 'Hi Mani! I'm Ziva, a friend and neighbour of Ovya's. Could I have a few minutes of your time?'

He says, 'Hi Ziva! Of course. How's Ovya? Have the police found her?'

'Nothing yet. The police haven't been able to do much except run here and there and hope that she falls in their laps, but we know this isn't how things work.'

He says, his voice dripping with concern, 'What? They haven't found her? That's incredible laxity. What do you need from me? How can I help?'

At last, someone who knows what to talk about and how to talk.

I say, 'I mean I don't have any specific questions as such. Just want to understand if Ovya had made any enemies in college?'

'Enemies? God, no. The girl couldn't hurt a fly. She was always so grounded and humble about everything. She didn't have any enemies, as far as I know. She could have people who were jealous of her but enemies, that's a stretch.'

I say. 'All right. What about a jealous ex?'

'When Ovya dumped Harsh for Aadit, there was a scene. I believe Harsh even threatened Ovya and Aadit, but she was fearless. If she had decided to date Aadit, that was the end of it. Nothing and no one could change her mind.'

'Where is Harsh now?'

'I think he moved to Canada right after college. That was a long time ago. I think he got married right after Ovya married Aadit. I am sure he is over it by now.'

I say, 'Do you have his phone number?'

He asks, 'Do you think he could have been involved in any way?'

'Old wounds never heal. They begin to fester at the slightest pain.'

∽

I didn't let Osheen drive. We booked a cab. On the back seat, Osheen drank the beer she had bought from the restaurant, breaking her momentum with long drags of the doob. She asked the cab driver to put on some music and started singing and swaying to the songs being played on the radio. Her singing was guttural and tremulous and made my ears bleed. I wanted to open the door and jump out of the car, but I couldn't. I tried to stop her but she wouldn't listen. She was in her zone and when she's in that place, she only listens to herself.

The only thing I could do at that moment, the only thing that I thought I could do, was to take a few more drags and numb myself to the noise. My already spinning head went into overdrive. I collapsed under the stench and strain caused by the weed. My eyes started to become rotten with every drag and lured me into the morbid end of my abstinence. I saw my mother who had suffered all her life at the hands of my always-drunk father. The lack of love in her life wasn't replicated in mine. All my life I had believed that I would die single and lonely, until I met Om. He changed how I viewed life and made me whole. He made me a better person. Now with every drag I took, his love dissipated and disappeared into thin air.

I never returned the doob to Osheen.

Her discordant singing had stopped. I struggled to breathe as my chest burned like wildfire. My chest tightened as I coughed and wheezed incessantly. I peered out of the window, desperate for some fresh air and light.

It never came and I succumbed to a long, dreary sleep.

33

I have Harsh's phone number now, but I don't call him. First, I do my research on him on social media. Come to think of it, I have become quite adept at finding information about people on different social media platforms. I learn that he's been working at Bank of Canada in Vancouver in the marketing department. Ovya and Aadit married each other eight years ago. Ovya is the only mutual connection that I share with him on LinkedIn. On Facebook, I find pictures of Ovya and him from college, from when they were dating each other. I also see pictures of him with his wife. Her name is Shireen. From the pictures it seems like he would dance to any tune that she played. The way he looks at her, the swoon oozing out of his large, round eyes makes it pretty clear who would have proposed.

However, the question is: why did Ovya break up with Harsh? Why is it that after she did it, it didn't take him long to find his bride?

Questions simmer inside my head and stir up all kinds of conflicting emotions. I scroll on his timeline and find that he had come to Delhi only a week ago. I wonder if he is still here or if he's flown back to Canada. I keep scrolling and find quotes on longing, death and sadness filling his page until I reach the post where he's talked about how he misses his wife. Shireen has passed away.

The news hits me like a slap and punctures my curiosity of finding out more about him. I feel sad and apprehensive, but also excited. All my feelings mix together like colours on a blank canvas. I want to call Harsh but I can't seem to come up with what to say.

I call Aadit first. 'Hey! Did you know Ovya was dating Harsh before she married you?'

He says, 'Yes, I am aware. The guy was batshit crazy. He should have been in an asylum and not in a design college. He stalked and threatened Ovya long after we had started dating. I had to go to the police and get a restraining order. I guess that brought the guy to his senses. He went abroad somewhere, Canada I believe, and he married someone there.'

I say, 'The screwball lost his wife three months ago and he came to Delhi a week back.'

He says, 'Are you suggesting he could be involved?'

'It doesn't harm us to check.'

I need wine to make myself steady. I open a new bottle and fill the glass up to the rim and finish it in a few large gulps. I fill the glass again and bring it to the couch and take a sip. I feel as unsteady as a leaf in a storm. I hope it is Harsh. Perhaps he had gone all psycho and had approached Ovya and at her slightest rebuttal, kidnapped her. If he still has feelings for her, he wouldn't harm her.

My shallow heartbeat grows stronger and it seems as if my chest will explode. I dial up his Canadian number. The phone rings a few times before he answers it.

He says, 'Who is this?' The baritone of his voice reverberates through my bones as I slide my arm on the table. The low rumble of his voice is discomforting as it alerts me to the danger ahead.

I say, 'Hi, I am Ziva, Ovya's neighbour and a good friend. Could we talk, Harsh? I just had a few questions.'

He speaks with an air of authority. His voice thunders down the telephone. 'I have nothing to do with her. I don't want you to call me ever again.'

'Please listen, Harsh. I know you are going through a difficult time. You have just lost your wife and to speak to someone inquiring about your ex is, well, unpleasant to say the least. I get that, but we are in a crisis and I wouldn't have called you without reason.'

There is a brief pause. He must be examining my words. Then, he breaks the silence and says, 'What do you want to know? Make it quick.'

'The thing is Ovya has been missing for more than four days and we don't know where she is. I learned that you had come to Delhi only a week ago and was wondering if you had spoken to her.'

'Goddamn it! Are you out of your fucking mind? Why in the world would I speak to her? She cheated on me with that godforsaken lecturer. She left me in the dirt while she sang and danced in every corner of the city.'

'I understand that you're still hurt but it is critical for me to know if either of you contacted each other after your wife passed away.'

'I never did. She sent me a condolence message when she learned that Shireen died. She checked on me about a month ago and asked how I was doing. I was shocked when she got in touch with me after how things ended with us. It wasn't nice. I could have behaved a bit more responsibly. But I never responded to any of her messages. The last she messaged me was when I landed in Delhi.

She asked me if I could meet her. Like before, I never got back to her.'

'Could you please send me the last text she sent you?'
He did.

The last text read: *Hi Harsh, I guess I know that you are suffering after having lost your wife. It must hurt, like walking barefoot on pins and needles. However, I hope you can find some sort of peace knowing that Shireen loved you till her last breath. I can't say the same about myself. Do you think we could meet? I'd like to apologize to you for all my misgivings from eight years ago.*

I say, 'Thank you, Harsh. We'll be in touch.'

∽

I was on the bed. I did not move or say anything. I kept my eyes shut and synchronized my breaths to the beeping sound of machines that surrounded the cramped bed. My hands and legs were numb while my lungs still burned. Curiosity made me open my tired eyes. I was met with a peach-coloured hospital room. I sank into obscurity, overwhelmed by a sense of gloom.There was a lone window, the size of a Parle-G biscuit. The room had a stagnant smell as if it had been cleaned with mud water and not disinfectant. The bed was low to the ground and the mattress was pencil-thin. The frame bore signs of rust. I wonder when was the last time the room had seen a change of interiors and furnishings. I bit my lip.

My mind drifted back to my uncluttered, spacious home. Everything pristine and calming. Home, where I could pull the blinds, switch off the lights, spray lavender room freshener, eat strawberries, play jazz, browse shows on Netflix and kiss Om. Here, I was in a hospital bed. I was stuck because there were "problems" that needed "fixing" and "tending". Whatever! I didn't feel safe or right here. I let my hands fall and discovered a bell on one side of the bed. I pressed it and in came a nurse, followed by Osheen and Om.

I was confused as to how smoking a doob could land me in a hospital bed. Om and Osheen stood behind the nurse as she checked my pulse, temperature and blood pressure before excusing herself.

Om's eyes were as red as a ruby. He looked at me with concern. 'How are you?'

I tried to sit up on the bed. 'I'm okay. What happened?'

Tears rolled down his eyes as he tried to say something, but words didn't accompany his laboured breaths. He retreated back and broke down. His face dropped. He burst into wails, the sound of which echoed through the halls of the hospital. Osheen stepped forward towards me. She couldn't look me in the eye. 'I am so so sorry, Ziva. I am responsible for all this mess.'

'Would either of you tell me what's wrong? I don't get it. Please, either of you...'

Her eyes were also filled with tears. She whispered. 'Had we not gone out, none of this would have happened. I was out of control and I made you smoke up and drink beer and you fell face first on your stomach. I am so sorry, Ziva...but the baby is no more.'

34

The problem arises when we are made to tread a path strewn with lies and schemes, when our own team has been compromised. That is when we need to question if it's worth fighting.

There were things Ovya wanted to give up, but Aadit surely wasn't one of them. Even when she had found out that Aadit was lying about Saachi, she still wanted to stick by his side. She would linger on like an unfulfilled desire. She wanted to grow old with him, even though it might have meant crying harder and harder with each passing day, her suspicions growing like creeping weeds. When I look back on the day I saw them fighting, Ovya appeared to be a shadow of herself while Aadit, on the other hand, looked like a boy who had been caught streaming porn on his dad's laptop. He had stepped out of the house after the fight. Sitting on the porch, he had smoked, and then he left. He never went back inside to explain his side of the story.

The moment he drove off and she didn't stop him, their relationship shattered, and the fragments from that damage were way too many, so much so that they could even outnumber the stars in the sky. He should have begged, pleaded, got down on his knees, just the way he would have done when he had proposed to her. He should have explained how their love was unique and that there was meaning in that. However, he never made an effort.

He closed his mind and heart and put barriers. He did not relay any information. That day, they let a minor spark become an ominous storm. That indeed was the beginning of the end, a precursor to all the carnage that followed.

I call Aadit.

He sounds tired. 'Hey, any news about Ovya?'

I say, 'Hey, I think I might have found something but I'm not sure yet. Will have to explore it in detail. What are the police saying?'

'They are like untrained dogs. They bark the moment you ask them something. They don't have anything. They are stuck in a rut and don't know which direction to take.'

I say, 'Do you think it would be wise to come back home for the time being and let the police do their job?'

He pauses and considers my suggestion for a brief moment. 'No, I'll be here for the time being. You let me know if that lead of yours proves any good.'

I need to get away from the house to think. The neighbourhood looks like an inescapable labyrinth of gloom. All the houses are mirror images of each other; the street lamps, the cars, everything looked the same. With every step that I take forward, it feels as if I'm being absorbed into a never-ending abyss of sameness. I pause for a moment before starting again. A sinking feeling overpowers me as I reach the coffee shop at the corner. I order myself a latte and a walnut brownie.

The sounds—of people talking to each other, the coffee machine and the staff working at the counter— are a little louder than usual. The staff serves my coffee along with the brownie. I take a sip and it feels as if I'm in a dream. The caffeine silences the sounds in my head for the time being.

I see two twin sisters sitting at the far end. There is something about twins that's enchanting, their warmth and joy reflect off each other. The way they have grown with each other is apparent. The relationship is different from other siblings. I know this because I knew a pair of twins at college.

I observed the two of them at the shop as they giggled; they were likely talking about boys. I am seeing them for the first time.

Perhaps they were just passing by. Aren't we all just passing, moving from one place to another? Without an inkling of when the journey ends?

I call Harsh again. He isn't pleased to have me call again. 'What do you want now?'

I say, 'You know what I want. I want Ovya to return home without her losing a single strand of hair.'

'Let me tell you something about Ovya. She's a little conniving bitch. She'll make you believe she is the sweetest girl on the planet, but the truth is that she is as bitter as the bile that rises in the mouth. You are forced to swallow it. Now, if you'll excuse me—'

I say, 'Do you want to hear something funny? There was this guy whose girlfriend cheated on him years ago. He married someone else, I mean, he had no other choice. So, he marries this new girl who then cheats on this poor guy with another married man—only a couple of years after they are married. The guy learns about her infidelity. He gets mad about it. Who could blame him? He, however, never shares any of it with his wife. He never confronts her. He lets things remain as is. He waits and waits until he finds that opportune moment and then he turns his wife's car upside down. She dies on the spot. The husband fakes bereavement for a few months before returning to India. Do you know the rest of the story?'

He loses his deep voice and strong demeanour. 'What do you want from me?'

'Just the truth.'

∽

The warmth from my body faded as the world around me grew old and rotten. *This too shall pass.*

More than a decade ago, I had experienced decay and dust when I killed my father and my mother had taken the blame upon herself.

All of a sudden, the room felt cold and I shivered. It occurred to me that this was just a nightmare and I had to play along. The world would right itself when I woke up in the morning. I thought of the toys I had bought a few days ago for my unborn child and started crying.

I said, 'You are lying, Osheen. You're a fucking liar. This is one of those stupid pranks. Isn't it?'

She shook her head and fell to the floor. 'I wish it was.'

I looked at Om. 'Well played, guys. Now can we please stop this game. It's hurting my head and I swear to god, it isn't good for the baby.'

Om never uttered a word. He just turned away and left the room. He was consumed by grief and anger. When he got like that, he usually went on total radio silence.

I said, 'Where did he go, Osheen? Please bring him back.'

She got up and caressed my head. 'Don't worry. It'll be fine.'

I wanted to shout but I didn't have the energy to open my mouth and strain my muscles. She kept kneeling, stroking my head. I caught hold of her hand and jerked it away. I turned on the bed so that I didn't have to face her any longer.

She stood her ground, waiting for me to look at her, but I didn't.

Before she left, she said, 'I'm so sorry, Ziva. I can't bring your child back, but it's on me to bring Om back into your life again.'

35

Aadit is coping by remaining where he believes he will find answers. That's why he hasn't come back home. He still sticks by the police station in the hope that Inspector Sarvin will use a magic wand and bring Ovya back in front of his eyes. However, that hasn't happened yet. The chances of it happening any time soon are rather slim.

Being drunk has been my coping mechanism for years now. A bad day at work or a fight with Om, and I'd be downing bottles of wine until I couldn't hold a glass straight. Even now, my hands grip the wine bottle as my eyes swivel and examine the empty house. I tilt my head back and take a long swig from the bottle. The walls seem to move closer to me, changing features with the slightest distance they cover. I have a bitter taste in my mouth, probably because of all the wine I've had since returning from the coffee shop. I clear my throat and stand up, only to fall down back on the couch. I struggle to walk towards my bedroom, as my wobbly legs refuse to cooperate. Every step I take comes with possibility of a great fall. I am thrown off balance on more than one occasion, almost tripping at times. My bed beckons me where I hope to overcome my state of inebriation. I begin to walk again, leaning on the bookshelves and walls for support. As I disintegrate into the bed and close my eyes, I remind myself that I have to confront Harsh tomorrow and find out whether he had met Ovya since his arrival in Delhi.

Scars offer a road map of what a person goes through and how they go through it. I don't know what Ovya had suffered while growing up. Was she also as unlucky as me? Did she have to grow up with one dead parent and the other in jail? My scars are nasty. They looked as if something has smouldered the skin. With time, they have faded to a soft pink before coalescing with the skin. However, the sensation of the pain lingers on and rises like sunlight from water. These reminders of agony and trouble shape the person we have come to be. *Is Ovya too fashioned by such torments?*

Osheen calls me. 'Hey! How's it going?'

I immediately understand the subtext. This is Osheen's way of expressing her concern for me with a veiled question. What she is really saying is this: 'Are you having more wine than you should?' I say, 'Don't worry. I'm not in the zone.'

She says, 'Doesn't appear that way to me.'

I say, 'I know what I am talking about.'

'Have the police found Ovya?'

I sigh. 'When they do, I'll be happy, drunk and in the zone.'

'What are they doing about it?'

I say, 'The usual. Hitting dead ends one after the other.' I chuckle. 'They don't have a clue, Osheen, and I think it will remain that way.'

She says, 'I wonder if you are wearing your Sherlock hat and have assumed charge of the investigation.'

'I have been digging and have been able to recover a few dead bones from the past.'

'What do you mean?'

'Ovya had a crazy ass boyfriend, Harsh, many years ago. He came back to Delhi only a week ago.'

'You think there is a connection?'

'I don't know. I guess I'll find out when I meet him in the evening today.'

She sounds concerned. 'Why don't you let the police take it from here? You've found a piece, let them fit it together. If the broken-hearted man is crazy, he could be dangerous as well.'

I say, 'Don't worry. I'll be careful.'

'When and where do you meet him?'

'At 6 p.m. at Burn Out.'

A thought is nothing but an entry into the otherwise invisible expanse of the mind's journal. It is a safe place to explore and experiment with different ideas before giving them form in physical space. It is a dancing hall for dances that will never happen, a playground for the wildest desires and imaginations. It gives oneself the freedom to get lost without having to worry about coming back, to reality. I am studying Harsh's picture again. He does look a bit wretched, as if he is always filled with untapped rage. I wonder what Ovya saw in him to date him in the first place. Perhaps she was just afraid of him and that's why she agreed to date him. When I find her, it'll be the first question I ask. If beauty and beast ever were personified their, relationship would have looked like this. It is surprising that Shireen agreed to marry him.

Karl, the private detective whom I hired from Canada, did tell me that Harsh was in fact a nut job. During the five years of his stay in the country, he had been fired from seven jobs, all due to anger issues. The mad-as-a-maggot face, narrow eyes, twitching facial muscles, spewing and putrid mouth and his clenched teeth show me that's how he is. He would have thrown a tantrum after returning home, broken mugs on numerous occasions, and his face would have turned red in anger.

I have no intention of squabbling with him and getting into an argument. I just have a few questions that need to be answered by him with cent per cent honesty. Instead of meeting fist with a fist, I go with the firm resolve to diffuse all anger and discomfort with clouds of familiarity. Although argument and confrontation are ways to learn how the other person is, I have a fair idea of how Harsh is.

All I need to do is tame the monster inside him.

∽

After staying in the hospital for the next two days, breathing the stench-laden air of my room and thinking about different possibilities and how things would go with Om, I realized no option was pretty. I found the resolve to return home. He didn't come to pick me up and I dared Osheen to not come either. I could manage on my own, even if it meant that I would have to take an auto. I didn't remember when was the last time I took one. The air brushed over my face and whispered in my ears about the looming danger. The journey flustered me to such an extent that I stopped by at a local coffee shop near our house.

I ordered a cup of cappuccino and some chocolate truffle cake as that seemed to be the best way to dissipate the stress I was under. As I was savouring them, I ran my fingers over my stomach, and like a bolt of lightning, I was reminded about the baby that was no longer inside my womb. The cries came out in ragged motion and I was sure the people at the neighbouring tables saw me crying and breaking down, piece by piece. I wasn't able to finish the items on my table and ran towards the front door and exited the shop.

I stopped just outside our main door. My breaths quickened and I felt like an alien as I stepped into my own house. The door wasn't locked from the outside, which meant that Om was home. I pressed the bell and my heart raced. It was as if someone was typing words at a rapid speed on a keyboard.

I didn't want to face Om. How could I?

He opened the door and returned to the couch. He didn't face me, never asked me how I was. The burning rage ran through his body like poison. He almost demanded release. Though on the surface he was calm, a volcano was erupting inside him and I could see that the fury was erupting out of him occasionally. The wrath was strong enough to consume me and our marriage and there was nothing I could do to make it right at the moment.

I sat on the couch opposite him and waited for him to look at me so that I could begin a conversation. He continued to type something on his laptop, his eyes fixed on it while mine were fixed on him.

After sitting in silence for ten minutes or so, I said, 'Hey.' The simplest word to begin any conversation.

It took him a few seconds to say. 'Give me a couple of minutes more. I'm working on something.'

I waited and when he was finally done he said, 'Hey. How are you?'

I said, 'I'm okay. You?'

He said, 'I'm sure you can guess.'

I nod. 'I don't know where to begin. All I want to say to you is I'm really sorry. Both of us sacrificed a lot for it to happen and somewhere, in one devilish moment, I lost it. I lost it, Om. I'm so sorry. I'm so sorry.'

I was wailing. I waited for him to get up and comfort me. He never left his seat. He remained fixed on the couch. Then, fixing his gaze back on the laptop, he got back to what he was doing before.

36

I am not worried about my meeting with Harsh. In fact, I am looking forward to it as I drive down the roads and think about the last few days. My life is now a tiny speck, marked by things I had never imagined. My old abundance of wisdom has always told me that the answer is always simple. It's just that we forget to look at the question with the care it demands. I also believe that we always have time. Enough time to let things slide through the fingers like sand. Even if today is our last day, we always have time to fix things that are broken.

The road stretches onward like a never-ending ocean, circling the land. The turns are easy as my car steers along the road, which has welcomed the sun, rain and the occasional hailstorm. I let my eyes run over the buildings and observe the hues that encompass them, their imperfections, and yet, they stand close to each other and stick together. These details make me wonder why people cannot learn to resolve their differences and be together. Shireen and Harsh, Ovya and Aadit, Om, and I—we are all the same.

The restaurant is almost full, which is perfect. I look around the busy tables. Young couples are drinking beer and munching on appetisers. Older couples are drinking wine and are enjoying their meals. A group of young women keep dissolving into giggles while they clink their gin glasses and a flinty man is dining alone; he is getting irked by the sound, and the mischief. The wait staff direct me to an empty table. I order a glass of wine. As is my habit, I'm a tad early. It gives me the opportunity to study the environment. The last time I met someone for the first time in a restaurant, they ended up dead. As much as my disdain is for Harsh even before meeting him, I sure hope he doesn't meet the same fate.

He walks in. His tough skin is pressed neatly to his black suit, tailored to perfection, and made of the finest cotton. He did make good money; Karl has told me. His eyes have a look of irritation that seems to be spreading to his face. He walks with a slight stoop, yet moves quite briskly. He greets the staff and I guess, he asks for me. He nods as he moves towards my table. His smile wanes the moment his eyes meet mine. The jovial nature of his show is over and it is down to me to control the beast that lies within him.

I get up and shake his hand. 'I hope you didn't have any trouble finding the place.'

A burst of raucous laughter erupts from him. 'I have lived in this city before and this restaurant has been here for the last twenty years. The older staff knew me by my name.'

I take a sip of the wine. 'Indeed. A great place to be known by your name. I wonder if these innocent and almost ignorant souls are aware of the mischief you have been up to in Canada.'

The waiter comes to our table with a glass of whisky and places it in front of him on the table. He looks at me with suspicion.

I say, 'It's not just them who know you. I have done plenty of research and I think I know you too.'

He takes a long gulp and coughs. He clenches his teeth and whispers. 'What is it that you want?'

'I just want Ovya to return home safely. I believe I communicated that over the telephone.'

He finishes his drink and orders another glass of whisky. 'The thing is, Ms Wadhwa, I have no idea where she is, but considering your violent history, I can only guess.'

'I wouldn't cross that line, but you, Harsh, your acts of violence are as fresh as the morning dew and somehow, the cries of your dead wife do echo in my ears. It's as if she engages with me in telepathic communication. You know, it is strange but she seems to be shouting from the rooftops that her husband killed her. The good thing for you is that only I can hear her.'

He swallows all the anger arising out of accusations. His eyes are bloodshot while his body trembles ever so slightly. He regains control of himself by closing his eyes for a second and then downing the second glass of whisky. 'What makes you think that I have anything to do with Ovya's disappearance?'

I say, 'I believe that after the untimely death of your wife, you started feeling alone and lonely, and for good reason too. Ovya here was questioning her wedding. Like a good person, she got in touch with you to console you and offer her support in your difficult times, and that gave you the opening to crawl back into her life. Isn't that so, Harsh?'

He looks at the menu, wondering what to order and how to answer my question. He is buying time, distracting me. I stay put on the matter and press him for answers. He calls the waiter and tells him to get another glass of whisky, a glass of wine for me, and a plate of chicken tikka.

He says, 'I had gone to Egypt a couple of years ago with my wife and we were dining at this restaurant. I don't remember the name. Anyway, as we began our meal, I felt that salt had been added to the meal conservatively. I asked the waiter for it and he looked me in the eye as if I had asked to sleep with his wife. He made faces, consulted with the manager, and then, he brought me the salt. Later, I learned that asking for salt and pepper is akin to slapping the chef across the face in Egypt. Guests in India are treated with great respect, but here you are, sitting at the same table across from me, disrespecting me by making all kinds of allegations.'

The lighting dims and I notice that the air is thick with the smell of different kinds of dishes. A waiter passes by our table carrying seafood. I have never fancied fish or crustaceans. The noisy chatter of the people has begun to fill the space and I feel more confident about Harsh's guilt.

I lean back on the chair. 'Growing up, my father was never any good, but my mother, she was able to teach me a few things. There's one lesson which I will never forget. She said, "You can only correct what you confront". The time has come for you to correct all the wrongs you have done all your life.'

He starts playing drums on the table with his hands, which despite the noise, is rather too loud for me. Every beat on the table echoes the turbulent thud of his heartbeat. His face becomes rigid with tension as he says, 'When Ovya messaged me after Shireen died, I was taken by surprise. I didn't respond for a few days since I didn't know what to say, but when I did, she told me how sorry she was for my wife and how our relationship ended. I didn't think much of it at first, but then, like a sudden gush of water, old memories started coming back. The fire I used to feel for her rekindled and I wanted to talk to her, just like old times. I didn't know how it was going to happen but about a couple of weeks ago, I messaged her and she responded immediately. We would chat every now and then like old friends, and then one day, she said it'd be nice to see me in person and catch up. That is when I decided that I'd come to Delhi and meet her. God knows how much I missed her when Shireen was sleeping with her boss. How much I still cared and loved her. I booked a flight and came to my uncle's house in Delhi. We were to meet the day after she disappeared, but as you can guess, that never happened.'

I look him in the eye and almost feel sorry for him. I know he isn't telling the truth. I can smell a lie when it's being cooked in the head. 'You are a good actor, Harsh.' I raise my hand to order a glass of wine. With my eyes on the waiter who is swiftly walking towards our table, I say, 'Here's what happened, and denying this will have serious repercussions.'

∽

For the past month, even though Om and I had been living together, we had been separated. The only time he ever spoke to me was when he had to leave the keys of the house to me or when the landline rang and he picked up and the call was for me. The sun hadn't shone on us, the breeze hadn't touched us and birdsong hadn't glided through our windows in these dark and twisted days. The comfort of the relationship and love we shared had been forgotten.

Om didn't look at me like an enemy; far worse, he looked at me like I was a stranger. The truth is that I never intended to hurt the baby or him. In fact, I had wanted to become a mum as badly as he had wanted to become a father. I knew I had fucked up and there was no way I could correct my mistake. There was no undo button waiting to be pressed. My fragile soul cried in agony, but he never paid attention and listened to it.

Every time I tried to have a conversation with him, he would shut me up like you shut a stereo when it makes a discordant sound.

It was as if the love we had shared was transformed into pain, and that pain had become fear and that had sowed enough doubt in us for us to break apart. Strong hate was needed to break a strong love. Walls were erected and boundaries were drawn between two seemingly inseparable people. Perhaps that was how he wanted to maintain his sanity and protect himself. I wondered if that was the end of our story. Surely, we could find a fragment of love to hold on to and build the old repository of trust and affection back. A seed that could propel new life into our dead relationship and bring us back together.

He still saw me for the person I was before the tragic day and I could still find the old him, I believed that. I knew he was hurt and I was sorry, but he had to know that a part of me was bleeding too. If only he could be a touch softer. I could have taken down the walls one brick at a time.

But he wasn't ready for that yet.

To trust the person who shattered your dreams wasn't easy. I got that. The problem was, however, that this path that he had forced me to take was untrodden and foreign. It twisted out of sight with every step. I wanted him to take my hand and not let go of it. If only he would have allowed me to move towards him, we could have figured it out and found a way out of this labyrinth. The new vista out of this shithole would be prettier, I knew that. Things always got better with time and Om would come along to walk beside me, hand in hand. The only problem was I was having a hard time making myself believe that would actually happen.

37

Waking up can be bitter, especially when you have been sleeping all the time, ignoring the truth, thinking dreams are better than reality. The memory of the dream might fade away with time, but the experience of it doesn't. You are reminded each day of how you fell into the trap and believed every illusion it offered. Here comes the sad part—you are left alone with this feeling of rupture and withdrawal. You search through this empty pit of emotions for proof that you even had the dream at all.

Yesterday, after a few more rounds of whisky and persuasion, Harsh confessed to me that he had, in fact, met Ovya in the afternoon and was planning to stay in touch and explore the idea that they could get back together. I believed him and it wasn't the wine that was responsible for my feelings. It was the undeniable proof that Karl had discovered that made him culpable for the death of his wife. That made him admit to the truth. I do not know how to break this all to Aadit but it needs to be done.

Choices are seldom between left and right. With eyes open a little wider, numerous pathways appear, some ragged, some straight. The correct path for everyone is different; the inner compass in each human being leads them to the desired destination. Ovya chose a path that I couldn't have predicted in my wildest dreams, and I'm certain Aadit will be as shocked as I am, shocked to the bone as well, when he hears about it.

I drive to the police station. Like a few days ago, he is sitting on the bench in the same clothes. His hair has become grey, the unkempt beard is overgrown, while the untidy moustache gives him the appearance of a ramshackle beggar or a useless drunk.

Is he drinking more than he could take?

His weather-beaten thick, and dry skin seems to suggest that he is in desperate need of the comforts of home. I place my hands on his. 'Hey, this look doesn't suit you.'

He half smiles before returning his gaze to the ground. 'Today is the fifteenth day since Ovya has gone missing but the police don't have anything. Please tell me you've had better luck than them.' He starts to cry softly, the pearl-shaped tears rolling down his cheeks. There's a rawness to his cries—his pain is an open wound that festers every time he realizes his wife is missing. He stretches his hands to clasp on to something for support and his entire body shakes when he doesn't find it. He clamped his face with his hands and looked up, as if asking the heavens about the whereabouts of his wife.

I say, 'I have found something.'

He jumps on his seat. 'What is it? Please tell me. Have you found Ovya?'

I shake my head. 'No, I haven't found Ovya yet, but I have found out that she was in touch with Harsh. The two of them have been in touch since his wife passed away and they met each other the day she disappeared.'

He clenches his jaws. 'Do you even know what you are talking about? I thought you were Ovya's friend.'

I get up and face him. 'I know how difficult this must be for you to believe but this is the truth. I can explain.'

Aadit presses his lips together. 'Shut the fuck up. I should have never given you her private details. You are a disgrace.'

I say, 'You can call me whatever you like, but I want you to listen to me. Once. Then you form your own judgements.'

I could sense what Aadit was going through. It must feel like being stuck in a tunnel that curls away into the infinite dark, with no hope of light and no way out of the rough walls through a path that snakes away. He would have frozen in his tracks, his brain looking for the right way out. He wouldn't want to hear anything bad about Ovya, which is understandable, but he needs to find it in his gut to listen to the truth. I keep standing my ground, waiting for him to give me the signal that he's ready to give the truth a chance.

After standing in the same spot for a good fifteen minutes, I sit down beside him and say, 'Listening to what I have to say is the only chance for us to find her.'

He sighs and nods.

I explain everything to him. I tell him how I spoke to Harsh on the phone and forced him to meet me yesterday where he spilled the truth about how Ovya and he had been conversing ever since his wife died. How, all of a sudden, Ovya had not only started to respond to his messages but also initiated conversations with him. It was Ovya's way of getting back at Aadit for having lied to her about Saachi. She toyed with the idea of hurting Aadit by being friends with her ex. I told him they met on the morning of the day she disappeared and planned to meet again. Ovya had also mentioned to Harsh how she had been planning to visit Niagara Falls and that she would have loved to travel there with him.

Aadit speaks through clenched teeth. 'Where is that asshole? I want to meet him right now. I'll call that fucker and make sure he never visits any place ever again.'

I say, 'Let's not lose our heads over what Harsh said. We need to remain calm. Don't tell the police anything about it. He might get scared and go into hiding or run away to Canada.'

He clenches his fists and says, 'What do we do then?'

I say, 'For starters, let's get you back home. Clean up, have some food and we'll make a call to Harsh and invite him over to our house. On our turf, he'll be more vulnerable and we can take advantage of that.'

He says, 'Okay. Okay. I can't think straight. Let's go home and invite him to dinner.'

∽

The silence of the house made my blood as cold as ice. After I drank the entire night, I sank into the armchair. It was three o'clock in the morning. Om had messaged me that he would be late getting home from work. Most of our conversation happened on WhatsApp, and only on the days that he would be late from work. It had become customary for him to be late at work in the office. I crept outside the window in the slight hope that his car would arrive in our lane but it never did.

I drank in silence, every sip possessing a meditative quality. It soothed every pore of my skin. Every time my mind was hit by a vexing thought, I took a sip and made a note of it on the phone with my trembling hands. I put a reminder on my phone to go over these things the next day. I wished I could have wrapped my thoughts in stones and tied them in a piece of cloth and thrown them deep into the ocean. I drank and waited another hour for sleep and Om to arrive, but neither did. At last, when my miseries seeped into every corner, I picked myself up and moved my aching legs towards the bedroom. There, I rested, wrapped in the blanket and protected by the thick layer of absolute quiet.

The next day, when I opened my eyes I found Om having breakfast.

I said, 'When did you come?'

He said, 'Just an hour back. I have to rush to the office again.'

I eyed him dubiously. 'Aren't you spending a little too much time at the office these days.'

'We all are not blessed freelancers where we get to choose the clients and the hours of work.'

I didn't have the energy to engage in an argument with him. My head was spinning and I had a splitting headache. I got a Disprin and washed it down with cold water. 'When will you be back today?'

He finished his toast. 'Just don't wait for me.'

38

Aadit's shoulders are slumped as he sits in the car. His eyes are cast down in mourning. He never looks at me or the road ahead, or anything for that matter. His eyes are open but they are fixed on thoughts about Ovya. He's in there, but he has taken a huge leap back in life. I don't try to reach yet, because I know my words won't have any healing effect on him. With time, and with some clarity about what has transpired between Ovya and Harsh, he might have some closure. His insides are damp with cries that have never left him. The pain of betrayal is visible on his face.

The despair that engulfs Aadit is heady and black; there isn't any way forward. The notion of hope becomes as distant as the horizon. The more he tries to reach it, the more elusive it becomes. The bond that he shares with Ovya had kept his heart beating, but now it must feel like a terrible weight. To love is to care and help the other person grow. However, in this case, just like mine, it brings great discomfort. The lover makes the other person disposable, just like a piece of trash.

Aadit sighs. His resolve is leaving him. His face is like that of an old-fashioned kettle, which despite losing some of its steam, remains full.

He says, 'What do you think happens to people who betray?'

I am caught off guard by the question. I think about it

for a long time. 'I do not know what happens to them but I do know one thing. It is perhaps the greatest perversion of love.'

He nods. He becomes teary-eyed again. 'I just want to speak to Harsh once.'

Through the remainder of the way, none of us say anything to each other. I had no intention of bringing up Ovya in any way, and he only seemed to want to talk about her. I felt that the best way to avoid it was to not say anything to each other. Every now and then, he opened his mouth to say something, but he crumbled and nothing came out except for thin air.

At last, we were in the neighbourhood. Inspector Sarvin had told us that Aadit could go back to his home as all investigations had been concluded for the time being. The police could visit any time to collect more evidence and for interrogations.

I park the car outside my home. 'Hey, we're here.'

His stupor breaks. 'Yes, and it already feels like I shouldn't have come.'

I say, 'You could come to my place if you don't want to go to your house.'

He leans back. 'I was hoping you would say that.'

'Next time, don't hope. Just tell me whatever you want.'

I unlock the door, and for the first time I enter the house with someone of the opposite gender. The emotions rise all the way up to my face as he reclines on the couch. I had become adept at hiding my broken insides, but now, the storms I carry are a part of my surface again. The damage they still wreak fills me with fear. I need to find a calm core since Aadit won't be able to help me in any way. He is the one who needs all the support and care. I'll have to manage on my own. I have to become the support he needs and help him without any inhibition.

I bring him coffee and the brownies I had bought from the local café.

He takes a bite of the brownie. 'Do you think I have wronged Ovya in any way?'

I say, 'I don't know. Whatever we think she has done is an extreme reaction and there's no way anyone could have seen it coming. I don't think you should blame yourself.'

'But how could she meet that bastard?'

'It's all right. We'll find her soon and then you can confront her.'

'Did he say that Ovya killed Saachi?'

'What? No. He didn't say that and we don't know that.'

He leans forward. 'That is the only explanation, Ziva. She killed Saachi because she thought I was sleeping with her. Killing her wasn't enough, and now she wants to sleep with or has already slept with Harsh.'

I say, 'We are getting ahead of ourselves. Ovya isn't here to put her point across. Let's please not assume stuff.'

'Yes. We can't assume, but Ovya can assume and imagine me cheating on her. That's fair.'

Placing my cup on the table, I sit down beside him. 'We'll find her and then you can ask her all the questions you want to. For the time being, why don't you finish your coffee and freshen up? I'll make dinner. We have a guest joining us as well.'

'Harsh is coming?'

I nod. 'Yes.'

He says, 'You know, Ovya isn't the problem. Her imagination is. She has always imagined the worst outcome. Her pen didn't know how to write a cute, nice, boring story. Her paranoia always wrote horror scripts. It inked—ignoring all the wonderful times we had spent, always relying on the half-knowledge she had gathered. The rest she filled in according to how she felt in the moment.' He fills his glass. 'One time, Ovya and I went to a supermarket in Bangalore. As we reached the billing counter, we saw Saachi standing in the queue opposite us. She had recently got engaged. I met her and congratulated her, but Ovya stormed out of the store. She had the keys to the car and drove away. I didn't know what had happened to her. When I reached back home, she didn't talk to me for a couple of days. It was absurd, but that's how she was wired. She lost her sanity whenever she saw Saachi with me.'

He continues. 'I wish I had been more honest with her, but I also knew what it would do to her. Did you know someone had sent her notes that Saachi and I met secretly? Someone had also sent her CCTV footage from the one time I had taken Saachi to the dentist.'

I say, 'I don't know what to say. I wish I had the answers you are looking for. The only thing we can do right now is to wait for things to clear up.'

He says, 'Harsh will make things a lot less murky. I'll get ready.'

∽

I kept the mangoes of the garden in the bowl as I tiptoed my way through the plants in the garden. The splash of bright flowers was vibrant upon the grey fence. I picked up the soil and let it run through my fingers. I knew that the more I tried to hold on to something, the more it slipped away. The same thing was happening with Om. The more I tried to reach him, the more he shut himself off. The more I tried to be with him, the further he slipped away.

Sadness was just a layer beneath my made-up face, but my eyes always remained dry and my face expressionless. I knew if I let my guard down and allowed even a single tear to come out, it would be an invitation to a never-ending stream of tears. All I did, all day, was sit in the garden and admire the plants, flowers, fruits and trees. I hadn't taken on any new projects and had been on a sabbatical from work. Sasha kept asking me to return, but I wasn't ready to face the world and their questions. My baby had been taken from me. I was on the brink of losing my husband. Work was the last thing on my mind. The thing that I wanted to see was affection in Om's eyes.

Even though a new financial year had started, he was still spending more time than usual in the office. Whenever I asked him why he was always late from work, he would shrug. 'I need something to keep my mind off things and fortunately, there is plenty of work for that.'

His staying late at the office didn't trouble me as much as the fact that he found every opportunity to avoid me. Even on weekends he would stay away, saying that he was going to the office to check some documents. In the past, he would have done the work at home. I had a weird feeling that he was, in fact, not going to the office but somewhere else. Of course, it was just a hunch and I couldn't confront him about it. The only way to know what was going on was to find proof.

On Sunday, when my husband stepped out to go to work, I decided to follow him. Like always, he took his car and stopped at the corner shop to buy a pack of cigarettes. I booked a cab and told the driver to follow the black Mercedes in front of him. I felt a tad uneasy at the notion of following my own husband, but he had left me with no choice. Had he been open with his emotions, I could have worked on the things that discomforted him. He had left me in the lurch with nowhere to go. As the cab followed Om, I looked around and found that my apprehensions were in fact true.

He was headed somewhere else.

As we continued to trail him, he took a right turn off Chester Street. I knew where he was going, but I decided to give him the benefit of the doubt. He stopped his car near a pink building and told the guard who he was meeting before parking it underground. I got down from the cab and took the other elevator. My heart was thumping like a drum. A part of me wanted to just return home. However, I kept my resolve and pushed the button to get to the fourteenth floor. When it came to a stop, Om was already there, walking towards flat number 143. I hid behind the walls. As he continued his march, I tiptoed around the corner and slid towards flat 141 from where I could get a clear view of what was going to happen next. He pressed the doorbell and my heart skipped a beat. Sweat leaked from my face and underarms as I waited to confirm my doubts.

The door opened and there they were. Om and Osheen. They were soon locked in a tight embrace, which was broken by a passionate kiss.

39

I stare at Aadit for a while. He is sitting on the couch, whisky in hand, his back arched and his eyes fixed on the front door.

I say, 'There's still an hour to go before Harsh arrives.'

He murmurs, 'Yeah, I know.'

'Look at me, Aadit. It's fine. I know what you must be going through, but things can only get better from here.'

His expression suddenly changes. Switching from abandonment to hope, his eyes seem to radiate joy for the first time in a while, as if he has been promised a great gift. A hint of a smile makes its way to his face. He is excited and eager to meet Harsh, his last hope of finding his wife. He runs his hand through his hair. 'You know, Ovya always said that drinking whisky before an important meeting is like walking blindfolded on a cliff. You will fall.'

I say, 'Why are you drinking then?'

'Because tonight, I won't listen to her.'

He gets up, the impatience wrapping him in nervous energy. I can tell how he is feeling. A tingling sensation is spreading through his body, like sparks, as he finishes his drink, hoping that it will help him calm down. He pours himself another glass of whisky and positions himself on the window from where his house is visible.

'You get a terrific view of our house from here, don't you?'

I wasn't expecting such a question from him and it throws me off balance. For a moment, I freeze, and then I say, 'I wish I was watching your house when Saachi was killed. That way, I would have had a lot of answers.'

He says, 'Yeah. For once, being snooped on would have been good.'

I can't fight the approaching darkness of the night any more than I can fight the dread that rises inside me. Dread has always felt like a slowly approaching train; it doesn't matter where you run, you always end up on the same track. *Did Aadit know that I watched him and Ovya from my window?* The thought in itself is dangerous, but it is possible that Inspector Sarvin might have told him. It doesn't matter now. Our focus has to be on extracting as many answers from Harsh as possible. It is 7 p.m. and he could be here any moment.

Aadit's eyes hold the kind of concern Om once had for me. He never opens his mouth, but it's as if he is trying to convey that it's okay that I watched them fight on that fortuitous day. He lays his hand on my shoulder and I am soothed by it. He keeps his hands there. He whispers in such a soft voice that his way of speaking calms me more than his actual words. It feels as if I am cocooned in a blanket of care. I have to be careful about how I do things from now on since they affect us both.

The doorbell is shrill and it jangles my nerves. Harsh has arrived. There was a time, not too long ago, when the ring of the doorbell sounded cheerful to me, announcing the arrival of Ovya. Today, however, it announces the person at the centre of everything that has gone wrong for Ovya ever since she got in touch with him. I walk in short, quick steps and open the door.

It is Harsh with a bottle of wine.

He says, 'I thought it would have been rude had I come empty-handed.'

I take the bottle from him. 'You should have brought Ovya instead and we could all have had a drink together.'

Harsh comes inside and extends a hand towards Aadit. Aadit ignores his hand and gets up to bring three glasses, ice cubes and a bottle of whisky from the bar. He serves whisky on the rocks to everyone before settling back on the couch.

Aadit takes a sip. 'We have nothing or no one to raise a toast to. I guess we'll just have to drink without reason.' He finishes his drink in one go and refills his glass again. Harsh sits down on the sofa opposite Aadit. He keeps shifting in his seat. 'I know why you wanted to meet me, but I told Ziva everything I know when I met her last evening. I'm not too sure if I can offer any more help.'

Aadit gets up from the couch, circles around the sofa Harsh is sitting in and settles down on the sofa next to him. 'It was extremely kind of you to talk to Ziva and share whatever you know about Ovya. Now I'd like you to be honest and share whatever you held back.'

Harsh coughs and spills the drink on his shirt. 'I have told Ziva everything. I wish I had the answers you are looking for, man.'

Aadit shakes his head. 'You know what I wish for? Some fucking honesty from you. Now, spit the truth out.'

'Like I told Ziva, I met Ovya in the morning. We had planned to meet more often and revive our friendship, but that didn't happen. I called her multiple times, but every time, her phone was unreachable. Then I got a call from Ziva that Ovya has been missing for a few days. I don't know where she is. If it pacifies you, I'm happy to show you around my house.'

Aadit thinks for a moment and asks, 'What did she say about our marriage, the day she met you?'

'Nothing. She never discussed Saachi, you, or the marriage. All we ever talked about was my dead wife and how life is fleeting and that we should stay in touch.'

Aadit bangs his hand on the table and that makes Harsh jump. 'I want the full fucking truth. Not incomplete pieces that you sprinkle here and there.'

Harsh looks at me and places his hand on Aadit's shoulder. 'I can understand what you must be going through. I promise that I will get in touch with you if I hear from Ovya.'

∽

Om continued to stay away from home. He only returned for breakfast. I didn't confront him or Osheen about what I had witnessed the other day. A part of me thought that perhaps I deserved it. A part of me also thought that perhaps Osheen had orchestrated it all. What had she done to make my husband lean on her for sex and support? After all, she did say that she wished that Om had approached her instead of me. Her disastrous relationships were testament to the fact that she was yearning for a stable and balanced man. No one she knew was better than Om. She could have taken advantage of his withdrawn state after what happened to the baby. Of course, I couldn't be sure who approached who, but it was wicked on so many levels for them to go through with it. It was as if a knife had pierced my skin and I couldn't do anything except feel the pain.

Om's eyes, which were once filled with so much love and tenderness, now overflowed with bitterness and indifference. The only resemblance the present Om had to the person he was till a few months ago was his innate desire.

With me, he had stopped feeling anything.

I heard his voice even though he hardly spoke to me. I remembered all those moments where Om could transform into his goofy self and say the silliest things just to make me laugh. His ideas were fireworks and I never knew what he would do next. I used to feel like a princess being swept off my feet. He had promised, that no matter what happened, we'd be together and I had believed him. Over the years, he had become the bedrock of my personality. Then, one fine day, I figured that he had, in fact, pulled the support out from under my feet. He'd never said anything to me. My presence had started to suffocate him and had he told me that, I would have left him myself.

The girl Om met in that pub many years ago with big round eyes and a gentle heart had forgotten how to hate. However, that day, I was consumed by a hatred I never knew could blossom in my veins.

I was yesterday's news, while Osheen was as new as dawn. He had stabbed me with the knife of betrayal. I would respond with my vengeance.

40

It's been more than a week since Harsh visited my house, but Aadit and I are still nowhere close to finding Ovya. The police have gotten busy with the high-profile murder of a celebrity and Inspector Sarvin tells us that he will get back to us as soon as they find something. We both know that he isn't going to get back to us anytime in the near future. In a way, we know as much as we did on the night she disappeared from her home. We probably know less since neither of us knew what was brewing inside her head. Ovya getting in touch with Harsh and renewing their friendship has stupefied both of us, especially Aadit, and there's not a lot that we can do right now except wait for her to get in touch of her own accord.

Ever since Aadit started living in my house in the guest room, I haven't seen him sober. He does everything drunk, whether it is taking a bath, going out for a walk or talking on the phone with Ovya's friends who repeat the same story. He always carries a bottle of whisky with him. There are enough bottles in my bar, and yesterday, we got more from the market. He is on the brink of becoming an alcoholic. I'm not sure if he realizes that but I don't stop him from drinking either. He is smart enough to know that drying out would be a painful process now, and from his state of mind, I figure he is not inclined to change yet. He is determined to stay drunk until he becomes numb every day. He can't bear to sober up.

There are other ways to clear the mind, but I know

it from experience that drowning yourself in alcohol is by far the easiest. But to actually let the bad memories pass like it is a song that you'd like to skip is easier said than done. The good memories of Ovya come with the bad stuff, which colours what she has done. I wish Aadit would steady himself before the booze takes control.

I need to have patience and compassion because it will take him time to cross the bridge when it comes. I can extend my hand and stay by his side while his scars heal. The mess that has been created and the fear of the unknown is too grave for him to admit needing help. He closes, hides, and returns to his original state without revealing anything. There is no magic bullet for pain as deep as this. The only thing that Aadit can do right now is stay put and wait for things to unfold, and the only way I can support him is by allowing him to get to things in his own time.

Aadit's phone rings. He doesn't answer. 'It's from my office. I can't just go back to the office pretending things are normal. I need to know what has happened,' he says.

'You will. You just need to give it time. You're in it for the long haul.'

He shakes his head and takes a sip of his drink. 'It's been more than a month since I last spoke to my wife. We don't know where she is. Heck, we don't even know if she is alive. For all we know, she too was murdered, along with Saachi.'

I sit down beside him. 'That's not what happened. She is alive and hopefully well wherever she is. I have a strange feeling that we'll hear from her soon. Please have some faith.'

He sniffles. 'Having faith when all the doors slam

shut on your face is possibly the hardest thing to do.'

Aadit is a man with emotional warmth, unlike Om, who betrayed me at the first chance he got. Beneath his hardened skin lies a warm heart that shines through. The fact that he is willing to give Ovya the benefit of the doubt after her betrayal echoes what he thinks and feels about her. He still values his relationship with Ovya and has every intention of going back to her. Family and community are still the foundation his life is based upon.

He says, 'You know, we were planning to have a baby. I refuse to believe that she would leave me even when all the evidence suggests she backstabbed me.'

I sit beside him and rub his back. 'I know what you must be going through. I myself have gone through something similar in the past, and I know it hurts. It hurts to the point where dying seems easier than living, but you must endure. You must live on in the hope of a better future.'

All of a sudden, my phone beeps. Harsh has sent a few pictures on WhatsApp. I grab my phone and download them. I almost leap in the air as if a gun has been shot past my ear. I am wide-eyed, hand over my mouth. I open my mouth the next moment. However, words refuse to come out. I sit as still as grass. I unblinkingly stare ahead and shake my head in utter disbelief. The mind tries to make sense of what the eyes have seen but I fail to come up with an explanation.

On my phone are pictures of Ovya and Harsh. The time stamp says they are in Canada right now.

Ever since I lost the baby, Om had started resenting everything I did. I could tell from his oppressive silence or the disapproving look on his face. Recently, I discovered that he had added infidelity to his response. He had been sleeping with my so-called best friend, Osheen, for I didn't know how long. This marked the beginning of the end, but I wanted to hear the truth from him.

I waited for him to get back from Osheen's house in the morning. I sat on the porch, right at the front door, waiting for his car to pull around the corner. He came around 8 a.m. He parked the vehicle and got down. He was a tad surprised to see me sitting outside.

I gestured for him to sit down beside me. 'Is there anything you want to share?'

He said, 'Share what?'

I said, 'How about starting with where you are when you're not in the office?'

The expression on his face changed. He was flustered, his skin reddened as if he had been caught in his lies. 'When I'm not in the office, I'm at home.'

'Whose home, Om?'

'Well, yes, we can hardly call this place home.'

He got up and went to the bathroom for a bath and to change. Perhaps, he didn't want the scent of Osheen's skin to linger on him, but I knew what he had been up to last night—and plenty of nights before that. It made me mad to even think of the two of them cheating on me. It was unbearable and it hurt to the point of death, but I had to resist the temptation of giving up. I needed to carry on and confront him. I was aware that he would become silent and unresponsive as if he had not heard me.

The bottom line was that both Osheen and Om had betrayed me in such a lowly manner because of some deep rooted hatred. Despite doing everything I could to keep Om happy and keep the marriage going, I had been subjected to such shame. He had stopped smiling and had become silent and would never talk to me.

When he came out of the bathroom, I said, 'I think we need to talk.'

He sat down next to me. 'What do you want to talk about? You want to talk about the baby you killed with your carelessness or do you want to talk about how good it feels to get high? Let's not engage in conversations, but instead, let's sit here and drink and smoke until we waste ourselves.'

I wiped the tears from my eyes. 'No. Let's talk about adultery and you can tell me whose body you prefer more? Osheen's or mine?'

41

I get up and go to the kitchen and fetch a glass of water. Drinking cold water soothes me for a moment, but the pictures stare at me. I am pulled into a vortex of fear and dread. I cannot hide this from Aadit. He deserves to know and he will have to find the strength within to face it. Horror clutches me within its tight grip. It pushes against me like an invisible gust of wind, commanding me to get back to the kitchen. Dread has my entire body locked tight, and even making the slightest movement seems like a task. I, however, endure. I lift my feet and move towards the couch where Aadit is sitting—whisky in one hand and his mobile phone in the other. He is engrossed in studying something on the screen.

I tiptoe and sit down beside him. He doesn't look at me but keeps looking at his phone. After a couple of minutes, he hands his phone to me. Harsh had sent the pictures not only to me, but also to Aadit.

There it is, the date and time stamp of today evening.

He coughs and lights another cigarette. 'Is it possible that these pictures might be photoshopped? Would you be able to verify?'

'I can try. Give me ten minutes.'

I grab my Mac and open Photoshop, image editor and a few online tools to check for the veracity of the pictures. I run them through all the tools to check for discrepancies, patterns, shadows and other parameters that could give me a definite answer whether the pictures are real or morphed. The results don't surprise me one bit. I close my laptop and print the generated report and hand it to Aadit.

I say, 'All the tools I used suggest that these images are a hundred per cent real without any editing or fakery.'

He throws his glass to the floor and it breaks into tiny pieces and they scatter all over the floor. He shouts. I sense pain behind the shouting.

'Ovya!' he shouts. 'Ovya! Why would you do this to me?'

I look at Aadit and let him vent. He yells his lungs out and turns into a crass, vengeful and defeated person who has been crushed by his wife's adultery. Like a tangled knot and a ticking bomb, he explodes and I hope that this will destroy whatever love he still has for Ovya. The shouting strangles the life out of him and he collapses on the couch. He breathes slowly. He looks at his phone, at the pictures, but he doesn't utter a word.

He gets up and starts cleaning up the mess.

I get up too. 'That's not necessary. I will take care of it. You please sit.'

He doesn't listen to me but continues collecting the broken shards of glass. He brings the dustbin and deposits every last piece into it. 'I'm sorry for having broken your glass. I should have controlled my temper. The truth is out now, loud and clear, and there's nothing I can do to change it. It's time I start accepting that Ovya is gone for good.'

I console him. 'There will come a time when she will realize that leaving you was the biggest mistake of her life.'

'What I cannot understand is why would she kill Saachi? If she had decided to leave me, why kill an innocent person?'

I think about it for a while. 'Perhaps she didn't want you to go back to Saachi after she left you. She wanted you to suffer alone.'

'You think so?'

'That is the only possible explanation I can think of if we are assuming that Ovya killed Saachi.'

He nods. He has a hand over his mouth. With his other hand, he keeps zooming in on the picture sent by Harsh until it can't be zoomed in any further. He shuts his eyes tightly. The eyelids begin to twitch. Silent tears rise in his throat as his knuckles knock on the table. It is as if he is trying to find an explanation for what has happened. His body begins to shudder and he falls on the floor saying only one word.

'Why?'

I pick his crumpled body from the floor. I don't know what I can say to him that would assuage his pain. I don't want throw meaningless words at him. I have always been against using words like confetti—paper-thin, fragile and inconsequential. It is easy to just toss consolations in the air, let them free fall and land wherever they may wish. I want my words to make him feel safe. I want him to know that I am here to listen and allow him to vent without judgement or prejudice. I have been in exactly the same position and it's okay to break down and collapse and think that the world is unfair, because it is. It would be terrible for him to give up.

I say, 'I understand your triggers, your anxieties, your ghosts and the actions that drive you mad. I want to

tell you that I'll always be here right beside you. I know
trusting someone right now will be next to impossible
for you, but you'll have to start somewhere.'

He looks at me and embraces me tightly. 'Thank you,'
he finally says, 'but I need some time alone.'

He gets up, fetches his car keys and walks towards the
door. I don't know where he wishes to go, but I know
that he is inebriated and in no state to drive.

I block his way. 'Where are you going?'

'Going to the police station to tell Inspector Sarvin
about Ovya and her whereabouts. Perhaps he might have
found something with regard to Saachi's murder as well.'

I say, 'I'll come with you.'

He doesn't resist. In some way, I believe I have
managed to become Aadit's friend and ally. I like that.

∽

His facial expression didn't change. It was as if he had
expected this to happen all along. 'So you know?'

I grit my teeth as I said, 'You bet I do.'

He started shaking his head. 'You can't blame me for
this. It was all your doing and your failing.'

I got up and started pacing back and forth. 'Of course,
it is my fault. Everything is my fault.'

I was astonished by the absence of guilt and shame
in Om. In his head, his actions were not a betrayal of
the promises he made to me. Sleeping with the bitch,
my best friend, was normal, a routine thing for him. To
love is to heal. To love and then unlove is to destroy.
It wasn't enough for Om to leave me. It wasn't enough
for him to divorce me. It wasn't enough for him to cut

me with words. He wanted to destroy my mind and soul. That day, I decided that I would take away the person that mattered to him. Losing the baby was an accident, but the havoc that I would unleash would not be one.

I had lost my mother's instinct to love and nurture. Instead of becoming numb, I was bombarded by things that I could do to hurt him. A sly smile appeared on my face. Om must have seen it.

He said, 'What are you thinking about?'

I laughed. 'I was thinking that during our third marriage anniversary, when you said you wanted to take a break, whether you were fucking Osheen or someone else.'

He shook his head. 'You know exactly why we took the break. It wasn't my exclusive decision, Ziva. You agreed too.'

I said, 'I agreed because I couldn't bear our conversations about my failed attempts at leaving alcohol.'

'Yes, we all know how that went, considering what you did with the baby six months ago.'

I shouted. 'You are crossing the line.'

He said, 'I thought I crossed the line when I slept with your best friend for the first time.'

I laughed again. 'You are just a tool for her. She'll sleep with you for a few months, possibly a year if you're good in bed, and then she'll throw you out like garbage.'

He didn't say anything. I thought he knew that it wouldn't last long. Perhaps that was the reason he never divorced me. He would have thought that fooling around with Osheen would be the best way to get back at me. However, he had underestimated me. I could never go back to being with Om after all that had happened and his lack of guilt. I would need to move on, but not before annihilating him. I would discard the parts of me that were broken, like a ghost, a ghost that disappears into nothingness.

What would remain in the end would make me stronger, ready to take on the world with whatever it threw at me.

42

It has been almost twenty days since Aadit and I went to the police station and told them to stop looking for Ovya. Inspector Sarvin was astonished to hear about Ovya being in Canada with Harsh. He was pretty sure that she had murdered Saachi, but he couldn't do anything about it now. He wasn't going to pursue an extradition order. It would mean spending a lot of money and resources for the murder of someone who hardly mattered in the public eye. Aadit understood that justice is a fallible notion; he didn't push the police.

Loss is on the other side of love. You are never warned of it. I learned it the hard way myself. Aadit too has his share now. The realization buries your soul too. There is no coming back and the world becomes obscure and eclipsed with shadows. Each breath comes out with difficulty and you feel hollow in the chest. You start resenting people who reach out to help you. You just want to be alone and remain hidden and unknown.

What he once treasured is now a nightmare in the form of memory. Like a shadow persisting in every corner of his mind, it didn't matter what he tried to do, all thoughts gravitated back to Ovya. It's a bitter thing to lose something you once had and cherished. Just how your innocence keeps slipping away, you grow up never realizing you lose one of the most pleasant qualities. In a similar way, Aadit kept losing Ovya without him ever registering it. She just decided to leave without warning him. The little space that separated them has now expanded and neither of them will be able to cover this distance. The bottom line is that she has left him and he is alone.

Aadit had moved back to his house right after we met the police. Even though I wanted and suggested that he stay a bit longer in my house, especially until he started getting used to life without Ovya, he didn't stay. He wanted to return to his place and I couldn't force him.

I visited Aadit last week. He was sitting outside on the porch and smoking. He was staring at the horizon and twisting a copper wire around his fingers. In the radiant summer sunlight that shone with a fierce vivacity, beads of sweat had formed on his face. I stood in front of him. He glanced at me and gave me a half-smile that revealed his sadness in ways more than his words could ever express. He kept twirling the copper wire, like how a python controls and grips its prey. He kept wrapping the wires around each finger until the skin was concealed. His face remained passive and it started to unnerve me. Blood dripped from his hand while I stood motionless, not knowing what to do.

He said, 'I wish I could have held her like I can hold this wire in my hand.'

I said, 'Come on. You're hurting yourself. Let go.'

He looked at his hand. 'That's what she did. She let go.'

I haven't gone back to his house since then. I am afraid. Moreover, I don't know what to say. The few occasions when I have said 'good morning' from my

house, he rebuts by saying 'good mourning'. He doesn't
step out of the house often. He prefers to stay inside,
cocooning himself with thoughts of the past and times
gone by. I fear that in his aloofness, he might take a
drastic step. He is perfectly capable of that.

It is hard to stop loving someone all of a sudden,
especially when you have loved the person for more than a
few years. Ovya has cut him and his heart into a thousand
pieces, and yet, she crawls back into his thoughts. He
still calls for her, holds out his hands and lets his face
become wet with tears. But she doesn't return his love.
His world has become empty in her absence, and the
loneliness is crippling him. With Ovya his heart was strong
and tenacious, but now it is simply lost and broken.

I watch him through the window of my living room
and more often than not, I find him looking at photo
albums, the television or the mobile. He doesn't cook but
has been ordering food online. I asked him if he could
drop by at my place or if I could visit and bring him his
meals, but he declined. He believes that it would trouble
me. On the contrary, I would be happy to become his
support system and help him get back to his former self.
I'm certain that with time, he will look at things with a
more open mind and allow me back into his life, and
that he will start accepting that his wife is gone for good.

Today, as I look through the window, I find him
sitting on the couch with his laptop. I can't tell what
he is looking at but I guess it is pictures of Ovya and
him on his MacBook. His eyes become teary as he gets
down on the floor. He starts hitting his hand on the floor
before getting up and opening a new bottle of whisky
and drinking directly from it. My heart skips a beat when

he twists the lid off a bottle of pills. I can't quite make out what it is, but I think of the worst. *Are those sleeping pills?* I know that whisky and sleeping pills make for a lethal combination and they can have disastrous results. I leave my binoculars and grab my cell phone. I call Aadit's number, but he doesn't answer. I run outside towards the house. I ring the bell like a maniac. I hear a crashing sound and my breath becomes quick and shallow. I get knots in my stomach as my hands and legs tremble with fear. As the pulse pounds in my temples, Aadit opens the door.

I embrace him in a tight hug and squeeze his back.

'Did you take those pills?'

He shakes his head. 'No.'

I heave a sigh of relief. 'I wouldn't have forgiven myself had you taken them. Please promise me that you'll never think of suicide ever again. Please. I need to hear it from you.'

His shoulders shake with grief as tears start streaming down again. It takes him a moment to open his mouth. He whispers, 'I promise.'

I pull him closer to me and kiss him softly. He doesn't push me away, but kisses me back and before we know it, we are kissing each other with the same passion and intensity as the last time we kissed our respective spouses.

∽

Om had left the house and had started staying with Osheen. This was a revelation and a sort of announcement to the world that things had fallen apart between us. Osheen hadn't dared to get in touch with me ever since she had started fucking my husband. In hindsight, it seemed that Osheen meeting me that day for drinks was a ploy. She must have wanted to get under my skin and force me to do something that would have a catastrophic impact on the baby and our marriage. After all, I had informed her about how difficult it was for me to conceive and that even the slightest mistake on my part could lead to me losing the baby. I was a fool to fall prey to her viciousness.

As I looked back on things, it became more and more apparent that Osheen had always liked Om. Her accepting the fact that she wished he would have approached her instead of me, the way she ogled him every time the three of us met and her telling me every time as to how lucky I was to have found someone like Om, that she wanted someone like him. I always knew that Osheen could go to any extent to get what she wanted, but I could never imagine that she would backstab her best friend to get her husband.

I was devastated and, in my devastation, I opened a bottle of wine to drown myself in a whirlpool of my stupidity and sorrow. I should have been careful and not let her instigation and my own craving for doob get in the way of my child. The child that was living inside me after plenty of struggles and sacrifices; it was too precious. I let Om down and I let myself down. Blaming Om for cheating on me with Osheen wouldn't do any good, but I needed to confront Osheen the way I had Om.

I knew if I called Osheen and asked her to meet me, she wouldn't agree. I had to visit her unannounced when Om would be at work. The next day, I woke up at 6 a.m., got ready, kept my gun in my purse and drove towards Osheen's residence. When I reached her society, I parked my car around the corner so that neither Om nor Osheen could see it. I waited for Om to leave. Even though I was going to face Osheen after the longest time, I didn't feel anxious or nervous. In fact, I was unfazed and quite determined to show Osheen her place.

After sitting tight for more than an hour, I saw Om drive away in his car. The next moment, I got out of the car and walked towards Osheen's house. I hoped that I wouldn't explode and let my hatred get the better of me. I was just there to talk to her and call her out. I hoped that she would let me vent and not react in any way to inflame me.

I pressed the doorbell. It didn't take Osheen long to open the door. In fact, it was as if she was expecting someone.

She held out a white handkerchief with a big smile on her face. 'How many times will you forget...?'

Her smile disappeared the moment she realized it wasn't Om. Her face turned white and blank as she stood fixed on the ground.

I smiled. 'When you can fuck Om and forget that he is my husband, doesn't forgetting handkerchiefs seem like a trivial matter?'

43

I close my eyes and become thoughtless. Aadit strokes my hair absent-mindedly and takes me to his bedroom. It is freezing. I wonder if he has switched the air conditioner off even once since he moved back to the house. We slide into the bed and the cool and soft white sheets give us goosebumps. The lights are off and the curtains are drawn. He is shy, a touch unsure about what we are doing.

I run my finger from his forehead to his lips. 'You don't have to worry about a thing now.'

I place on his mouth a fragile kiss. His body undergoes a series of sensations but he doesn't say anything. Everything he might be thinking of is irrelevant. Ovya is gone. I'm here waiting for him to devour my body. Tender, like the touch of a feather, Aadit caresses my hair. We both feel powerless and start kissing again.

I knew Aadit had been missing making love to a woman. I had been missing making love as well. It's a strange sensation to have yearned for something so long and to get it. You lie there and wait for that euphoric moment, but instead, the many moments that lead up to the climax make it worthwhile. Our slow and soft kisses metamorphosed into a fast and frantic exchange. I bring my hand to his face and find his skin to be smooth. The beard is gone, and along with it the scratch he had gotten the other day. He puts his face against mine and sweeps it with his tongue.

He reaches for my breast. A quick gasp of air and a deep noise escapes me as my body twitches when he licks my nipples. I can't believe that this is happening. I wonder if Aadit is over Ovya or if I'm just a diversion. I, for the moment, am enjoying what is happening. Aadit moves towards my belly and tastes my skin. His tongue flutters like a butterfly, covering the entire length of my abdomen before he finds refuge on my legs. There is an incredible strangeness. He is mimicking the moves Om made and I can't tell if it is Aadit or Om. He pulls my pants off as I lift my hips. He tosses them aside and removes his jeans and pushes them under the bed. For the first time in ages, a fire runs through my body as I feel the excitement and pleasure of his body against mine. He spreads himself out over me, skin over skin. He curls his finger between my legs and slips it in. My body trembles. It seems as if an earthquake is happening inside of me; it is breaking down all the walls and defence systems I had built up.

He whispers, 'It's all right. It's fine.'

He moves his finger inside me with increased fervour and intensity before removing it altogether.

An intricate silence follows and it seems as if our bodies are imprisoned in the room. As I think it's over, he thrusts himself inside me and starts pushing against my body. I lie stupefied for a moment, unable to move my body. As he increases the momentum, jarring convulsions, growling jubilations and flooding sensations hit me. Every time he hits my vagina, a strong electric shock flashes through my body.

As more time passes and his thrusting comes to a

halt, fleeting visuals of Om and Ovya appear. It's as if I have entered a dreamlike state where truth and fiction blend together.

I place my hands on his chest. 'How do you feel?'

He says, 'It's probably the best I have felt ever since that night. You?'

I nod. 'It's the best I have felt in a long time. Do you think we can live like this for the rest of our lives?'

'I would like to believe so,' he says.

He smiles and lights a cigarette. 'You know, Ovya and I were married for eight long years and only recently had we felt the need to have a baby. The two of us were sufficient for each other all this while. Of course, it would have taken us some time to plan everything so that we could give the child the best life possible. Now when I look back, I am glad we didn't have one.'

I caress his hair. 'I think the best way to look at the past would be to remember the good times spent. You spent eight years married and possibly a couple of years before the wedding. That's an entire decade. You can't just wake up one day and start hating the person. The feelings will simmer down. Just give it time.'

Having someone so close to me after all this time brings a sense of peace and curiosity. All logic and reasoning leave me as I still feel his touch on my skin. All my past demons and future worries melt away. The only thing that matters now is my complete union with Aadit. My heart rate accelerates just at the thought of it. I look away, at the window, as if the world outside can hold my attention. A small smile covers my face and I get goosebumps all over my body. I know that the higher the high, the lower the low, my emotions are extreme. The truth is that I haven't felt such a high in a long time.

∽

Osheen didn't say anything back to me. She put the handkerchief away on the table and looked at me as if she didn't recognize me. I knew her heart was in her mouth when she first saw me. I knew she must have tried to make sense of how I could land up at her house after all that had happened. I was sure that she would have thought that I would never want to face her and just end up deriding her in my thoughts. To her utter shock, I was there standing in her apartment, about to ask some onerous questions.

I sat on the couch while she stood in front of me, waiting for me to get on with whatever I had to say. I looked around and found Om had bought new shirts for himself that were lying on the chair. Along with that, he had also bought a new pair of shoes and they were tucked under the centre table. Her living room was a mess and it reminded me of the times when Om and I weren't married but living together. There was so much freedom then. We got to live in an unrestrained environment. It was a mess and we both loved it. Today he was enjoying the same mess with Osheen. It burned me and brought down whatever little warmth and friendship I had felt for her.

She says, 'Why are you here? Om would not like it.'

I say, 'Oh, you are already becoming the perfect wife. Putting so much thought into Om's likes and dislikes.'

She laughs. 'Yes, you couldn't do it. Someone had to.'

I smashed the vase next to me on the ground. 'You

lured me into going out and smoking that weed. It was you. You always had your dirty eyes on Om. The only mistake that I made was underestimating how low you could stoop to have what you want. That's my only mistake.'

She sat down opposite me. 'You listen to me. It was your fault that you couldn't stop yourself from getting high that night. You could have stopped at one drag, but you chose not to. Not only that, you also drank as if you hadn't tasted alcohol in a lifetime. Did I force you to do any of that? You never cared about the baby in the first place, or about Om for that matter. All you cared about was your own happiness.'

I was fuming. My face was flushed and my hands began to tremble a little. 'I wonder how a person like you could ever become my best friend. I would have been so needy to be friends with you for all these years. You are a whore. I'm sure you know that. You must have slept with more men than the days I have spent with Om. But somehow, you wanted him too inside you. When will your hunger for dicks end?'

She thought for a moment. 'I think it has ended now. Om really is a beast in bed. I will settle down with him. He will divorce you, in fact, he has gone to meet his lawyer and I will be the mother to his babies. You can't be a mother any more, can you?'

I lost it when she said that.

Fires of fury and sheer hatred smouldered in my eyes as I weighed what I was about to do. The next moment, I jumped on her like an enraged panther. I grabbed a shard of glass from the shattered vase and pierced it deep inside in her heart. The pointed edge was like a bayonet as it met the soft and pudgy flesh. It made a squishy sound before the room reverberated with Osheen's screams. I twisted the glass in my hands and it sank deeper and deeper. Her skin tore to shreds as I rotated this thing as sharp as a knife. Her veins and nerves were torn with every passing moment. In one striking movement, I pushed the shard of glass all the way, until it disappeared inside her.

I clutched another piece of glass and stabbed her tattered skin. She cried with excruciating pain. The brilliant sound was mixed with growling chokes and agonizing screams. I had a smirk on my face as I took another shard of glass and shoved it into her stomach. Her screeching didn't stop. By the time she hit the floor, she had grown white. She convulsed and quivered like jelly. She was a mangled mess with blood gushing out of her wounds.

As life cascaded out of her body in all directions, I didn't show any mercy. I sat there looking at her while she tried to cry for help. Her bloodstained hands were on my feet and her eyes begged me.

I pushed her away, and in a moment of finality, I crushed her face with my shoes until she could no longer cry.

44

Rays of sunlight fall on the trees and fill the leaves with abundant warmth. The rays tumble down to the flowers and the grass gleams with morning dew. The dark edges of dawn are being washed away as the sky ripens, like a fresh orange. Thread-like wisps of white clouds remain stagnant. The world around me looks like a new photograph, every colour is new and bright. The clock reads 7 a.m. The time that I spent with Aadit last evening intoxicated my senses and I don't remember when I fell asleep.

As I get up from the bed, I feel quite well, after ages. The high that I felt yesterday has subsided now but the low I usually feel isn't there. Instead, it's a warm feeling, the kind you get after a nice spa session. It's as if I'm on a smooth road that doesn't have any speed breakers and sharp turns. I can go on driving forever. The constant emotional storm and turmoil I was in has subsided. The next step will be to find a place of peace and tranquillity in my inner world; apart from emotional wellness this includes cutting off the people who bring hurricanes into your life. Now that Aadit is close to me, Om won't be able to affect me. I will be able to focus all my efforts into making meaningful and quality contributions to Aadit's life. With all the chains of the past broken now, I will be able to make amends to my life as well.

All this time, the lights had been turned off and

my soul had lingered in the darkness. Despite all the gloom, there is a flame in my heart that has waited a long time to be set ablaze. I close my eyes and the morning light falls on my skin and leaves a sense of positivity. An everlasting fire begins to run through my body, and I am ready to be with Aadit for the rest of our lives. I'm certain he wouldn't have it any other way.

I get my phone and start reading the chats I had had with Ovya. They were mostly on trivial topics, like my garden, the recipes that we wanted to try and make together, the places that we had planned on visiting in Delhi and how we both couldn't wait to start working again and possibly in the same company. She never used WhatsApp to talk about her marriage troubles. She would either call or come over to discuss and take advice on it. Thinking about it, I get sucked into the past as our conversations have a vice-like grip over my mind. Its twisted reality begins to distort mine now. I'm aware that my prosaic existence will overlap with Ovya's every now and then, considering that Aadit is unlikely to be able to get over her any time soon. Even though he might not say it out loud, I will know that he has been transported to the past and is reliving the times he spent with her. I don't blame him. To this date, I think about Om and miss him.

I look through the window of my house. Aadit is sitting on the couch and working on his laptop, as usual. I guess he has started working from home. After all, he needs to return to work. Going out and commuting to the office back and forth will make the healing journey easier. If this time he stumbles and falters, I will be right behind him to catch him and prevent him from falling.

I have always believed that it is imperative to burn the bridges with the past and surge ahead with confidence. For that to happen, the crimes of the person who has wronged us either need to be forgiven or dealt with. I will deal with both, Aadit's and mine. This will allow us to be the people we truly are around each other, without any masks, filters and expectations, or help us arrive at such acceptance. Now, just the inner healing must be done. It will happen on its own. In the life that will follow, all my paper drawings of the man I dreamed of and held in my mind so closely will be with me. There's no use of them now. I bring a lighter and start burning the drawings. The glowing embers leap and twirl as if it's a coordinated dance. Twinkling like stars in the hot air, they cascade on the ground, falling like drops of rain. I bring the notes I had received about Aadit. They had stopped coming ever since Ovya went to Canada.

I open them one by one and start reading them aloud. It makes me laugh. The vile intentions in them hadn't affected me in the least and had not led to me forming a negative opinion of Aadit. I had seen the authenticity and genuineness the first time I had seen him with Ovya when she had moved to our locality. I could see through him; my nerves had tingled at the thought of being together with him. I knew I could trust him and like always, with trust came love. I light the matchstick to burn them. However, I am startled when Aadit calls my name.

He is inside my house. 'Why aren't you answering the doorbell? I had to use the duplicate key to enter. What are you doing?'

I hadn't told him about these notes for the simple

reason that he might feel hurt upon knowing that Ovya had sent them to me. His pain would come cycling back and hit him with the same fervour all over again. 'You know, just burning a few old papers.'

He comes and sits down next to me. 'These old papers must be special enough to have caught all your attention that you didn't hear the bell ring.'

I smile and look at him. 'Is the doorbell working?'

'Oh, it is in pristine condition. I checked it myself. Now, I want to see these old papers.'

I hesitate and put the notes back in the bag. 'I really don't think you should.'

He looks at me. 'Do you trust me?' I nod. 'Then there is no reason for you to not show them to me.'

I take out the notes from the bag and hand them to him. He goes through each note, studies them and looks at me. 'Have you shown these to the police?'

'Of course, I did. Like everything else, they couldn't determine who sent these. At the time, it perturbed me and I had no idea as to who was sending these to me. I even confronted Saachi about it, but she denied it. But now, I know who would have sent these.'

He asks, 'Who?'

'Ovya. Who else? She wanted to pit me against you. I think she wanted me by her side in case things escalated out of control between the two of you.'

He looks at the notes again. 'No, Ovya didn't write these. She despised this font. She always had a habit of using margins. Moreover, this is not how she writes. I know how my wife used to write. You tell me who sent you these notes.'

I say, 'Oh, don't be stupid, Aadit. You thought you

knew your wife but she is in Canada with Harsh basking in the sunshine, leaving you here in despair.'

He becomes silent for a moment. 'We don't know that for sure. We haven't even spoken to each other since that day. She could be in danger for all we know.'

I raise my voice. 'Listen to yourself, Aadit. Harsh sent us pictures of him and Ovya from Canada, which I verified and found to be real. Do you remember?'

He shakes his head. 'I know that these notes aren't written by Ovya and it wouldn't do any harm to speak to her.'

I grab Aadit and kiss him. He doesn't kiss me back and pushes me away and walks out of the house.

∽

My breath was caught in my lungs before I could finally exhale. The tension in my body gushed out in a quick stroke. A one-way mirror now separated Osheen and me—she was on the other side and would never be able to touch and impact my life. Despite that, going back and reuniting with Om wasn't an option. It was time for me to move on.

A hint of satisfaction arose in my body upon seeing Osheen's dead face. She had used her pretty face to destroy the lives of men she had dated, but she had gone a little too far when she tried to mess with me. We had a great friendship and despite all her faults, I loved her; she loved me despite my shortcomings. We shared an unshakeable bond, but like all good things, it had to end. If only it could have happened earlier without irreparable harm to either of us.

I was certain that when Om returned home he would have plenty of questions about Osheen. I decided to stay back and wait for him. He would be back the moment he realized that he had forgotten his handkerchief. Osheen was right on that account. Throughout our marriage, Om always forgot to carry it and then he would come back to take it. It wasn't long before the doorbell rang. I saw though the peephole and opened the door gently. It was him.

As soon as he stepped inside, I pointed the gun to the back of his head. 'Sit. Don't make any noise unless you want your head to be blown to pieces.'

He sat on the couch, tears rolling down from his eyes. He didn't shout or scream, and like I had thought, he complied without making much of a fuss.

I tapped his head. 'Good boy.'

45

I run after him but he is already in his house. He has locked it and unlike my house, it can't be opened from the outside. I do the only thing I can do—I knock and call his name. However, he doesn't relent and open the door. I keep sitting outside on the porch, at the same spot where he sat when he had that fight with Ovya. I wonder what has gone wrong. How is it that all of a sudden the love for Ovya has returned with the same fervour? Did I overlook something? I knock on the door again but the result is the same. Aadit keeps himself locked. With all the windows shut, I can't even peep inside and see what is happening. I hope he doesn't take any drastic steps.

My mind is a perplexed mess. Aadit's words and actions are contradictory, pulling in opposite directions. Yesterday he said that he loved me and that Ovya is buried in the past. Today he won't even speak to me because of the notes I said were sent by Ovya. Just because she despised the font, the margins were missing and it didn't sound like her, he had pushed me aside and locked himself in his house. I play the incident again in my head and still am not able to come to terms with what he just did. If he feels the notes weren't sent by Ovya, we could have had a discussion, but no, for some odd reason not talking to me seems like a better option.

I gasp in excitement as I remember how Aadit made love to me. He is in no position to distrust me. Perhaps, it's just one of those episodes when he needs time alone because accepting reality is hard. I'm sure he loves me and perhaps also resents me a little. All my life I have tried to figure out the motive behind people's deeds. I believed those days were over at last and I had the freedom to come out and show my heart and soul to Aadit. But no, there will always be something that restrains me. At times, I think I'm in a cage. I am always held back by my inhibitions or the fear of others. Aadit always takes my breath away, for I am of the opinion he is the only one who can heal me. The converse also holds true. I do believe that I am the only one who can heal him. Sitting here outside somehow breaks me. It's as if he has forbidden me from coming closer and that hurts like hell. I sit here outside in love that brings sorrow while he keeps himself locked, not allowing his heart to stray towards me. My mind fails to make sense of the situation because it has permitted my heart to roam and reach out. Aadit reciprocated too but has held back again. I wonder what he is up to.

After waiting for more than an hour and feeling miserable, I get up again and knock on the door. However, as expected, he doesn't answer, but I do hear his voice. He might be speaking to someone over the phone. Who could it be? I am taken aback as I hear him raising his voice. He starts cursing in sheer rage. I don't know what the conversation is about, but from the taut tone of his voice, I can make out that he is not exchanging pleasantries with whoever is on the other side. His venomous speech slashes through the locked door that separates us. He goes on like that for the next half an hour, and just like how it started, his voice

fizzles out. There is complete silence and it tells me that
something is very wrong.

I make up my mind and decide to wait for another
ten minutes outside Aadit's house. Finally, Aadit opens
the door, slowly. He stands inside, looks at me and then
takes a step out. He frisks and searches me to check if I
am carrying anything. It seems strange for him to check
me like that, as if I am waiting to harm him. He then
grabs me and pulls me inside and closes the door. He
gestures for me to sit on the couch and brings me a
glass of wine. He sits opposite me with a glass of whisky.

He raises a toast and clinks the glass with mine. 'To
our love that ended before it could take off.'

He empties the glass while I don't take a sip. 'What
is that supposed to mean, Aadit?'

'Masks are off. You can, for once, be the real and
authentic you. You can be honest with me. Come on,
your game is over.'

I say, 'I don't understand, Aadit. What are you trying
to imply here?'

He says, 'As you must have figured out, I was speaking
to someone on the phone. In fact, I made two calls. Can
you guess whom I spoke to?'

I think for a moment and slur, 'Ovya?'

He shakes his head. His breath is laboured as he
struggles to open his mouth. 'No. You made sure that I
won't be able to speak to her ever in this life.'

'What are you saying? I don't understand.'

He pours another glass of whisky. 'I spoke to Harsh
and I demanded to speak to Ovya. I threatened him
that if he doesn't get my wife on the phone, I will call
my friend in Canada who's with the police department

and get him arrested for killing his wife. Yes, you are not the only one who has friends in Canada who can look through a person's life to the minutest detail.'

I can't move. I want to say a hundred different things but none of them come out of my mouth. I know he has misinterpreted my deeds and my words. It is as if I have been speaking a foreign language all this time. This is the moment I realize nothing I do will bring back whatever little trust we had built up between us. My heart breaks, and this time, I know there will be no healing. There will be disaster and destruction.

He continues. 'It's okay. Harsh told me how you coerced him to lie to me about Ovya. Why would you do that, Ziva?'

'Because you were miserable and I wanted you to move on with your life. I couldn't see you the way you were. I'm certain you would have killed yourself with alcohol and I couldn't let that happen.'

'Why?'

I caress his face with my right hand. 'Because I love you, Aadit. I love you.'

He almost kisses my hand but jerks it away. 'No. You only love yourself. In fact, you don't know what love is, because if you knew you wouldn't have killed Ovya and Saachi.'

'What? What did you just say?'

'Evidence suggests that you killed both of them and I was a fucking fool to not have seen it. I always thought that you had Ovya and my best interests in mind, but, boy, I was such an idiot. Ovya loved you. She had begun trusting you more than she trusted me, but you betrayed her friendship. You bloody killed her.'

I plead. 'Will you sit down?'

'Why, so you can kill me off as well? It's over, Ziva.'

'I beg of you to please listen to me.' I try to calm him down, but he pushes me away and takes out the knife from his pocket.

I let out a laugh. 'A knife? You want to punish me?'

'Just stay away from me.'

Letting go of Om was difficult. Letting go of Aadit with whom I thought I had found the right connection would be even more arduous. When you let go of someone, you let go of a part of you with them. I want to be a part of Aadit's journey to recovery but he believes I am the source of all damage instead. That is the thing about perspective. When it comes from a lens of fear, everything feels wrong. He has the knife not because he wants to attack me, but to protect himself from me.

Just like Om, he doesn't understand. His lack of faith in Ovya, and now in me, is what has cracked his house, which was otherwise built with love. Om took all the love I had for him as if it was his birthright and in return he gave me deception and rejection. The only thing I have ever wanted is unconditional love. Now, Aadit is waging a war against me when I just want him to look at things from my lens.

I remain silent. There's no point in saying anything. The opinion he has formed in his head about me is hard-wired. There's nothing that I can say or do to change that. Moreover, he isn't wrong. I did kill Saachi and Ovya. But that was for his own good. Neither of them deserved him. If they did, Saachi would have married him and Ovya would have never doubted him, despite all the provocations. He needs someone like me, someone who'll stick by his side at all times. He won't understand it now. Perhaps in the future.

The doorbell rings. It is Inspector Sarvin.

Aadit says, 'That was my second phone call.'

∽

Om had gone numb the moment he had seen me. However, when his clammy eyes fell on Osheen's dead and mutilated body, his eyes grew wide and the hair on the nape of his neck became as erect as barbed wire. Even though the air conditioner was on, his forehead glistened with sweat. He closed his eyes, as if waiting for me to end him. He was trapped in his fear. He never made an attempt to get up and run.

He glanced at the body again and his eyes watered. I'm certain he had never seen something of this kind, not even in his worst nightmares. He must have hoped that his new life would be permanent in his mind for as long as he lived. The adrenaline rushed through his veins like a ship sailing through the water, and yet, he didn't move a single muscle, not even to scream. The absolute horror incapacitated him and with every passing moment, he understood that he wasn't leaving the room any time soon. I had never seen him this scared in life, and little did he realize that it was just the beginning.

I crouched in front of him and raised his face with the gun. 'Did you feel this scared when you cheated on me?'

He whimpered, 'I promise I will not tell anyone about what has happened here and we can go back to living the way we used to.'

I took a walk around him. 'I think we are a little

late for that. I only have one question, Om. Would you answer that for me?'

He nodded. 'Of course.'

'That day, when Osheen and I went out, were you aware that she was going to try and dupe me into smoking up? Did you use the death of our baby as an excuse to get rid of me?'

He cried. 'No, and you know that. I wanted that baby as badly as you did. I sacrificed everything along with you. I was there every step of the way, supporting you and making sure that we do it right.'

I said, 'Support me every step of the way, except one.'

'I do not understand, Ziva. Please let me go.'

'You didn't support me when things went wrong. You didn't support me when we lost the baby. You chose Osheen when it happened and that, in my opinion, is a betrayal of the highest order. Only despicable individuals like yourself are capable of that.'

Om dropped on the floor and grabbed my legs. 'I'm so sorry, Ziva. I had no idea how much it would hurt you. I wish I could go back in the past and instead of blaming you, be there with you because you were in pain. I see it now. I'm sorry.'

I picked him up and kissed him one final time. I pushed him to the couch and sat down beside him. I clocked the trigger and shot him in the right side of his head. The bullet pierced through his head and got stuck in the red refrigerator. Then his eyes were fixed and empty. He was gone and with him, any semblance of love and sympathy I had for people who degraded human relationships by choosing to cheat. Closing his eyes, I picked myself up, my hands cold, pale and lifeless. More than my hands, I felt life escaping me, as if condemning me to perpetual desolation.

I placed the gun in Om's hand to make it seem like he committed suicide after killing Osheen and oh boy, wasn't I right?

Epilogue

I am not interviewed immediately. Instead, I sit in a room with walls as thick as steel. The windows let no light pass through. Apart from the lone bulb that flickers in the corner, there's not a speck of light in the gloomy room. The wooden door is closed, as I expected it to be. The ceiling fan rotates unwillingly and I find myself swamped in sweat. If I had to sit in the same spot for another ten minutes, I would in all probability faint on account of dehydration.

The next moment, Inspector Sarvin walks in with a bottle of cold water and a bar of chocolate. He hands both to me and I gulp down the entire bottle in one go. He makes a call and asks the person on the other side to get another bottle of water. He waits for a few minutes allowing me to settle down. The moment he feels that I'm composed, he begins to speak. 'Ziva, I always had a hunch about you. You can call it an inspector's sixth sense, but I could never put the pieces together.'

I smile. 'You still won't be able to put them together unless I confess to the crimes.'

He says, 'That might be true, but at least now I have something to work with. I can smoke out your past and connect the dots of your present to ensure that you spend your future behind the four walls of a gloomy prison cell.'

I consider his statement for a moment. He must have asked his team to look into my past to see if I have wronged people or the system in any way. I'm sure he is smart enough to find out that all the people related to me are now dead. He will soon figure it out that this cannot be a coincidence. I know I am on a tightrope here and all the doors seem to be closing.

He asks, 'What are you thinking?'

I say, 'Can we talk off the record?'

Inspector Sarvin lets silence do the talking first, then he fixes his gaze on me as though trying to size me up. He seems to be going through a mental list of dos and don'ts, but eventually gives in to curiosity. He turns off the tape recorder and gestures for me to continue.

I take a deep breath. 'Ovya didn't deserve Aadit and that is the reason she had to go. If she could have doubts about someone as good as Aadit, she didn't deserve to be his wife.'

He leans forward. 'You made sure that those doubts crept into her mind?'

I nod. 'The moment I saw Aadit for the first time, I was awestruck by his charm. The day I spoke to him, I realized how good a person he is. I started following him and one day I saw him give a lift to a woman. Saachi. I clicked pictures of them in the car and sent them to Ovya. I knew Ovya didn't like Saachi. She had spoken about the strain Saachi brought into her marriage with Aadit and I knew I could use the information to my benefit.'

'What happened after that?'

'Ovya told me how she had received those pictures and asked my opinion on them. I told her to stay put and keep a watchful eye on Saachi and Aadit. One day, I had gone to my regular dentist. I knew Saachi and Aadit would visit the same clinic. Saachi had problems with her gums and Aadit, as a good friend, was trying to find the best doctor in the city. Long story short, the day they visited, I paid the security guy ten thousand bucks and asked for a copy of the CCTV recording, which he gave me gleefully. I sent the recording to Ovya, which, as I expected, was the breaking point.

'She couldn't take it any more and confronted Aadit about Saachi on multiple occasions, but she never told him anything about the pictures or the CCTV recording. It was just the perfect set-up for their falling apart. I faked being on her side by deciding to meet up with Saachi and ask her about why she still tends to meet Aadit despite Ovya's reservations.'

He says, 'Go on. This is intriguing stuff.'

'That day, Ovya came to my house in the morning seeking advice about what she should do. I told her to look Aadit in the eye, show him all the pictures and the CCTV footage and ask him about his present-day situation with Saachi. I also told her to tell him that she couldn't go on any longer with him sneaking behind her back and secretly meeting Saachi because, one way or another, the truth comes out. As expected, things went out of control and Aadit left the house.

'I had met Saachi the same day and invited her over by telling her that Ovya and Aadit would be present in my house and would want to resolve this peacefully. She agreed. You are smart enough to figure out what happened next with her.'

He says, 'I still don't understand how you managed to kill Ovya while Saachi was at your place.'

I smile. 'When I killed Saachi, Ovya had been present in the house all along, however, she was asleep. The moment Saachi and I entered her house, I secretly injected her with Propofol which caused her to sleep almost instantly. Saachi started frantically trying to wake her up which gave me enough opportunity to attack her. The moment my business with Saachi was over, I brought Ovya to my house. You remember the day when you had visited my house for interrogation?'

He nods.

'Well, Ovya was alive and sleeping like a log in my basement. It is only after you left that I took care of her and got rid of her body.'

My garden has since then become more splendid.

He gets up and takes a walk around the room. 'There's one thing that doesn't quite make sense to me. I know you liked Aadit and wanted to be with him and that's why getting rid of Ovya makes sense, but why kill Saachi?'

I circle my fingers on the table. 'Because I couldn't take a chance. If I had just killed Ovya then Aadit could have gone back to Saachi, but when I killed both of them, I was the only one who offered him the love and security he had been deprived of.'

'Makes sense. You are truly a genius. I'm impressed.'

I roll my eyes. 'But I'm not. An inspector half as smart as me would have figured it out.'

He laughs. 'What good did any of it do? You are alone again. You killed a good friend. You killed someone whom you only met once, and in the process, you ruined multiple lives, including your own. I am not sure whether I would call that smart. In any case, I can promise you that I will personally make sure that you hang for your crimes. Why did you fake that Osheen was alive?'

I say, 'Ovya would often ask me about my past, the

friends I had, how my married life ended, and other questions fuelled by her untiring curiosity. The day I had gone to her house for dinner, we had spoken at length about that. Of course, I never told them that both are gone for good. But I did say that Osheen is still my best friend and it'd be hard for me to survive without her.'

He says, 'One last question. Were you behind all those notes about Aadit?'

I nod.

'Why?'

I say, 'Because I wanted to portray that Ovya is behind those notes.'

He smiles and shakes his head. I wait for him to ask further questions and when he doesn't, I get up from the seat and take a round of the room.

'What are you thinking, Inspector?' I ask.

'Oh, nothing in particular. Just drawing a plan in my head on how to put you behind prison bars."

'Good luck! I will wait to hear from you,' I say.

He shakes my hand, 'I'll see you soon.'

Acknowledgements

Cold Blooded Love happened because of my love for psychological thrillers. Firstly, I'd like to thank every author who continues to blow my mind with what they write in this genre.

The next person to thank would be Harshil Gurha who was the first one to read the manuscript and assure me that it has been written brilliantly. One needs that kind of encouragement, especially when one has spent a good one and a half years on something.

I always rely on Ushnav Shroff to proofread everything before I start sending out book proposals. He has been instrumental in instilling confidence in me about my work, thus motivating me to write the way I want.

Next, I would like to acknowledge Kapish Mehra and Dibakar Ghosh from Rupa Publications for believing in this book and helping me in every step of the way.

The book would not be in the shape that it is today without my editor Pallavi Ghosh who has done a remarkable job. From highlighting plot holes to removing unnecessary words and phrases to making the writing compact and powerful, she has instilled depth in the story.

I am indebted to Tarun Matlani, my designer-in-chief, and Nigameash Harihar for his ocean of knowledge in marketing. They have always been by my side, guiding me in every step of the way.

I owe a debt of special thanks to my family and all my close friends who have always encouraged me to go after my dreams.